Praise for *Enzan: The Far M[...]*

Multi-layered and satisfying, a welcome and well-developed addition to an accomplished martial arts series.
—*Kirkus Reviews*

A Zen master, a princess, and a martial artist burst out of their archetypes to reveal deep and likable characters.
—*ForeWord Reviews*

North Korean thugs, the Japanese family, an Hispanic gangster, a retired cop, a nymphomaniac girl, and a Zen monastery. Mix all these with a variety of agendas and you have an incredible basis for a "can't put it down" novel. We rated this novel our max 5-heart rating.
—*Heartland Reviews*

Read *Enzan* and you'll sense sharp swords somewhere in proximity. Read it, and you're involved in the multi-layered, pulsating life that can only be found in a book about Connor Burke.
—*Michael DeMarco, founder of* Journal of Asian Martial Arts

What makes this book worth the review, and worth your reading time is ... Donohue's wise, asides ... regarding martial arts, Japanese culture, and Zen influences. [They] lend *Enzan* its true promise—namely to render traditional martial arts practice as a way of living relevant to the warp and woof of the modern world. Doing so lifts John Donohue's work into the mainstream of crime/adventure fiction.
—*Arthur Rosenfeld for Huffington Post*

A classic Japanese structured myth of a questing warrior... set in our modern thriller struggles. Authentic and exciting!
—*James Grady, author of* Six Days of the Condor

When it comes to martial arts action and suspense, John Donohue is the grandmaster. I'm a big Connor Burke fan!

—*David J. Montgomery, mystery and thriller critic for Mystery Ink*

It's great to see Burke and Yamashita back in another martial arts action adventure. Told by a hard-hitting writer and martial arts expert, John Donohue is at the top of his game.

—*Loren Christensen, (ret) police officer, Portland P.D., martial artists, author of* Dukkha *(series)*

Donohue equals Eisler and Van Lustbader as a fiction writer who deftly mixes a crackling plot, martial arts action, and vivid characters, for an unforgettable thrill ride.

—*Brian R. Sheridan, martial artist, author of* American Life in the 1930's

In this installment, Donohue skillfully weaves parallel narratives wherein the secrets of the past have powerful consequences for the present, and even the most jaded readers will be caught by surprise by the secrets that are exposed.

—*Meron Langsner, award-winning playwright*

A meaty story that can be read as a darn good thriller, or as a study in human nature, or as a commentary on the traditions and inner workings of the martial art. Pick it up on Friday night when you don't have to be at work Saturday morning. If you're like me, you'll be up half the night reading—just one more chapter.

—*Dr. Susan Lynn Peterson, author of* Western Herbs for Martial Artists *and* Contact Athletes

ENZAN
THE FAR MOUNTAIN

Also by John Donohue

Sensei
Deshi
Tengu
Kage

JOHN DONOHUE

ENZAN
THE FAR MOUNTAIN

YMAA Publication Center, Inc.
Wolfeboro, NH USA

YMAA Publication Center, Inc.
Main Office
PO Box 480
Wolfeboro, NH 03894
800-669-8892 • www.ymaa.com • info@ymaa.com

ISBN Paperback	**ISBN Ebook**
9781594392818	9781594392825

Enzan: The Far Mountain was edited by Leslie Takao, and its cover was designed by Axie Breen. This book has been typeset in Adobe Garamond Pro and printed on 55 LBS FSC-Env100 Ant EDI Creme paper.

10 9 8 7 6 5 4 3 2 1

Publisher's Cataloging in Publication

Donohue, John J., 1956-

Enzan : the far mountain / John Donohue. -- Wolfeboro, NH : YMAA Publication Center, Inc., c2014.

p. ; cm.
ISBN: 978-1-59439-281-8 (pbk.) ; 978-1-59439-282-5 (ebook)
"A Connor Burke martial arts thriller"--Cover.
Summary: Chie Miyazaki is wild and spoiled-- the pampered child of a cadet line of the Imperial House of Japan. When she disappears in the US accompanied by a slick Korean boyfriend, the Japanese seek out Connor Burke, student of renowned sensei Yamashita, for a quiet solution. Burke is swept along in a covert search and rescue operation that turns into a deadly confrontation with a North Korean sleeper cell. He experiences the power of his sensei's decades old connections, and the secret that drove Yamashita from Japan now pulls him back into the service of the Imperial family.--Publisher.

1. Burke, Connor (Fictitious character) 2. Martial artists--Fiction. 3. Missing persons--Investigation--Fiction. 4. Princesses--Japan--Fiction. 5. Royal houses--Japan--Fiction. 6. Espionage, North Korean--Fiction. 7. Martial arts fiction. 8. Suspense fiction. 9. Mystery fiction. I. Title.

PS3604.O565 E59 2014   2014939377
813/.6--dc23   1407

Printed in Canada.

To Aidan James Brough
As you take your first steps in life's journey
(you can read this later)

PROLOGUE

Life is a path: a thing of direction and purpose. Yamashita taught me that we forge ourselves in the *Do*, the Way, that we pursue. My relationship with my teacher is deep and complicated and reverent. Yet there are doubts ghosting around in my bones. On good days I hope we were formed for a purpose, but there is also a deep throbbing, a grim Celtic warning that life can be either full or futile. And there is no sense to how that will be revealed; we graft meaning on our lives as best we can.

My teacher has led me on a disciplined quest to find that meaning, although I didn't know that for a long time. I was focused instead on the surface aspects of his art. We worked together on technique, perception, and reaction time. It was a craft that insisted on minute attention to the vivid present. There was little room for doubts or distractions. And if you're fully immersed in the here and now, how could you be wondering about anything else? It was a mystery. In fact, Yamashita, my teacher, was a contradiction himself: a master of the moment who lived with memory swirling around him like some bitter fog. Maybe he hoped his blade would ultimately cut through it. Despite all his activity, his mastery, the rock-solid self-confidence he projected in the martial arts training hall called a dojo, I've come to learn that in the quiet times even he had doubts.

But I never doubted him. Not really. The secret manuscript his old friend Mori left to us, the tale it told, helped me understand Yamashita better. And appreciate him more fully.

He never spoke to me of the life he had lived in his early years. Mori filled in the gaps—an old story that reached me long after the author himself was dead. But the strands it revealed were alive enough; they uncoiled into the present, the skein rolled out, unraveling but still intact. In the end, it ensnared both my teacher and me. Looking back, I'm not sure I would have wanted it any other way. For in some strange sense, our lives had become joined; no longer two strands, but one.

A splicing of two skeins that continue to unwind.

CHAPTER 1

He arrived at the dojo as the training session was ending. We were all soaked with sweat and the heavy blue quilted tops we wore were pressing on our shoulders like the weight of Judgment Day. The visitor carefully slipped off his shoes, placed them neatly to one side, and bowed. It was a good bow, the kind you see from someone who's been in a dojo before. He moved like a martial artist too: smooth motion that hinted at years of labor in the precise economy of violent action. He stood at the rear of the room as the training session came to a close. He was still and watchful. Only his brown eyes glittered under the high lights of the training hall.

They're so self-contained, the Japanese. You think after all these years I'd be used to it. But at that moment, I just wanted to reach across the room and smash his face in. I didn't, of course. Partly because my teacher Yamashita has trained me better, but mostly because it was what my visitor wanted, and why give him the satisfaction?

I called to the class to line up and they flowed into a long row with the unthinking ease of repeated practice. In the Japanese martial tradition, every training session begins and ends with a ceremony. It's a reminder of who we are and what we are doing. That sounds like a simple thing, but my experience is that we're all hardwired for distraction and delusion. The Buddha pointed that out. So, for that matter, did Jesus. I hate to have to admit the nuns who tortured me all those years in Catholic school were right about anything. Yet it's true, and the

3

need to focus on purpose and identity is a real one. So martial arts students in the dojo line up at the end of every class. They stand in rank order and face their *sensei*, their teacher.

That's me.

I knelt in the formal position, carefully setting the white oak training sword down at my left side. I nodded and the students sank down as well.

The dojo captain, the most senior student present, called out *"Mokuso!"* the barked command to meditate. It's just one of the more interesting contradictions of the art I practice. It was a command to be like empty vessels, bereft of ambition or aggression, an order to clear the mind and become one with all things. But, of course, every one of us in that room had spent the last two hours achieving, learning the finer points of killing someone with a sword.

There's a lot written about the martial arts: all these complicated ideas about transcending the self, a dense thicket of words and description. It's cool and calming, the promise of an experience of measured beauty, like water flowing. Alluring, but not completely accurate. Just so much clutter. Step out with me onto the hard floor of a practice session. No incense here, just the smell of heated bodies; no chanting, simply the grunt of effort and the thwack when a blow hits home.

And losing the self? Please. There's sublimation, for sure. Training is a heavy yoke. But look around at us. The reasons we train are varied, but in the end they are deeply and depressingly similar. Skill gives us control and the illusion of a manageable universe. Achievement brings approval. Effort is penance. Safety. Love. Forgiveness. We chase what everyone else is chasing. We've just figured out a really complicated and dangerous way of doing so.

But it's what I know. So that day when the lesson ended and I sank down into *seiza*, the seated posture for meditation, I tried not to think about the visitor. The feel of the hardwood floor, the warmth of my folded legs, the ebb and flow of controlled breathing, were all experiences that had been part of my life for so long that the sensations were old friends. I can move into seiza in any dojo in the world and feel I am home. OK, add belonging to the list of things we seek.

But I couldn't give myself over completely to the experience. He was there. My Japanese visitor with the good bow and knowing eyes.

Visitors are rarely good news. Yamashita's school is one with a daunting reputation. Martial artists train for years just to get a crack at being considered for admission. Visitors seeking to join us are eager and polite, but a pain anyway: there's all that testing to put them through to see if they have what it takes. It's necessary, but it interrupts the training process. And we're all about training.

The uninvited guests are even worse. They show up at odd intervals like young gunslingers, swaggering into town, looking to make a name for themselves. They're eager too, but not as polite.

And I get to deal with them.

Which creates another break in training. And I take my teaching seriously. I used to feel a certain apprehension when challengers sauntered in, asking for a "lesson." These people are usually dangerous in a commonplace kind of way, and I've learned you should never underestimate their potential. It only takes one slip, one millisecond of distraction, to fall. So over time I've learned to leave all the worry behind and just get on with it, channeling my irritation into action. It's not pretty, but

5

at least it's over quickly.

Like the cage fighter who came by one day, shaven head and square jaw, sleeve tats snaking up both arms. He had slabs of muscle covering him like warm armor. He wore the baggy fighting shorts of a Thai kickboxer.

"We don't have to do this," I told him.

He had a mean smile: "Sure we do," he told me.

He shrugged his shoulders and rolled his head, snapped some tight punches out into the air and took a few test round-house kicks. Then he got ready to square off.

I came toward him, the oak sword in my hand. He gestured at it. "What gives?"

I shrugged at him. "We use swords here."

His eyes narrowed and his mean face got even meaner. "Come on, man!" I could tell he thought I wasn't playing fair, but that was not my problem. The dojo is an orderly place, and the austere lines of traditional Japanese architecture make it seem like things should be placid there. Another great illusion. It's a box like any other, although it's filled with dangerous things. He was a fighter used to being in a cage, but even in that place there are rules. In Yamashita's dojo there are rules of a type but only one really important one: real fighting has no rules.

The *bokken* I carried is a hardwood replica of the sword used by the old warriors of Japan. The oak shaft is a symbolic sword and a real bludgeon-like weapon. You can kill someone with one of these things. I should know.

The cage fighter circled me warily, protesting. "No one said anything about weapons." His taped hands were held out in front of him like paws, and even as he protested he shrugged into his stance. Anyone else would have thought he was having second thoughts. In reality, he was looking to create a distraction, an opening where he could close with me and drive me to the floor.

But I ignored his words. Thoughts of any type just slow reaction time and draw events out. I've learned that over the years. Better to ride the storm and get it over with quick.

He would want to close the distance between us and get inside the sword's arc, wrap me up, slam me to the floor, and pound me into submission. He'd batter my weapon away, lunge forward, and grab my legs. He'd launch at me like an ugly, calculating animal.

It was an explosion of feints, blocks, angles worked, and weaknesses exploited. The usual sweaty blur. In the end, I broke his arm, both collarbones, and dumped him on the floor. Then I went back to training.

So you can see why our latest visitor made my stomach clench and my scalp tingle.

I'd seen people like him enter our little world before. He was dressed in the dark blue suit, white shirt, and red tie these people wore like a uniform. The way he moved, the way he looked, made me uneasy. And somewhere deep inside my brain a voice hissed: *Be careful, Burke.*

It sounded like Yamashita's voice. I know what you're thinking: hearing voices? This sort of psychic event had started happening to me a few years ago. At first, I couldn't be sure what I was experiencing. But with time, the voice in my head grew in strength and authority. Now, whenever it came, it rang with a bell-like quality. And it seemed to me, as Yamashita's physical powers had waned as he aged, his spiritual force had only gained in strength. I can't really explain it, but there is a link between the two of us. And in times of confusion or danger, his voice comes to me, unbidden, but welcome nonetheless.

I study something called the Yamashita-ha Itto Ryu. It's probably not like anything you've ever seen. Most people are familiar with modern martial systems like judo or karate. What I do is both more complicated and more elemental than these modern styles. For two decades I've worked to master a body of knowledge that has as its end the achievement of a type of aesthetic violence. I can drop someone with a sword or staff. I know joint locks that make your skin feel like it's been set afire, and nerve strikes that will make the body convulse and the universe shrink down to a bright, white-hot nova of pain. It's a system of refined force and channeled aggression. At least that's what Sarah Klein, the woman who left me, thought. But I don't think she got the entire picture. It's not simply about danger and violence, but also about the ways in which we acknowledge the chaos in life, deal with it, and come out the other side. So if the tradition has left me with a butcher's knowledge of human anatomy, it also strives to provide me with a monk's insight into the frailty and transcendence inherent in human nature.

The dojo I was in that day was simply a large, high-ceilinged room with a polished wooden floor. There were racks for weapons along one wall, and one long scroll of calligraphy near the wooden shrine. It's an admonition from an old archery sensei that Yamashita liked very much: *Be in the dojo wherever you are. Live like a sage or exist like a fool.* Not many people could read it, but that wasn't a problem. Yamashita and I send the same message in every practice session we teach.

We bowed out at the end of class and I turned my attention to the visitor. He came across the dojo's broad expanse of floor toward me. He moved well: good balance, with the momentum coming from his hips. These kinds of guys are usually pretty well trained in judo or karate: fifth-degree black belt or higher.

He wasn't close enough for me to guess. If his ears were banged up, I'd bet judo. If his hands were banged up, I'd go with karate. Fifteen or twenty years ago I'd have been impressed, but not anymore. Yamashita operates on a whole other level.

The man bowed politely. "Please excuse me, Dr. Burke, for disturbing the end of your lesson." He held out a business card, a *meishi*, holding it with two hands, very formal, very polite.

"*Choudai-itashimasu, Ito-san,*" I began. I'd glossed his name from the kanji on the card. In Japan, business cards like this have one side in Japanese characters and the other in English. Technically, Ito was correct in presenting the Japanese side first, but I couldn't be sure if he was paying me a compliment by assuming I'd be able to read it or hoping I'd have to turn it over to read the English translation and thereby lose face. This is part of the fun of hanging out with the Japanese. If you get invited to lunch, you can't be sure whether you're there to eat or be eaten.

Then the ritual began. I welcomed him to the dojo and apologized that I had not been able to prepare for a visitor. He said the fault was his and he was honored to be welcomed to such a renowned school. I invited him upstairs for tea, suggesting we would be more comfortable. He declined. I insisted. He declined again. I asked him to reconsider, but he demurred. Only then could we get down to business.

The conversation was formal and it proceeded along predictable lines, but my mind was racing during the entire exchange. I had read more than his name on the business card. What I saw there alarmed me. I tried to mask it, even as I searched Ito's face for some hint of the danger he was bringing into my world.

"We are, of course, honored to have you as a visitor, Ito-san,"

I said. "It's a shame you did not come earlier. Perhaps the training would have interested you."

Ito smiled tightly at that and his eyes widened in agreement. It was the first glimpse of honest emotion he'd let me see. "I agree. Perhaps you would do me the honor at some other time?"

I bowed slightly. "Of course." Now that we were close to each other, I could see he had the thick hands of a man who had spent his formative years pounding things. It marks you in all sorts of ways. The prospect of a good fight of any kind probably made his nervous system hum like a shark's when it senses chum in the water. Was it my imagination, or did Ito's nostrils flare slightly?

It was a fleeting twitch, however, and he got himself under control quickly. "The dojo's reputation is impeccable," he said politely.

"Yamashita Sensei is a true master," I told him. "It is unfortunate he is away and unable to welcome you in person." My teacher was spending a few weeks at a small *zendo*, a monastery in upstate New York. He went there for the solitude and the spiritual discipline—*not everything revolves around the sword, Burke*—but I also suspected he liked the hot baths as well. It's something I can sympathize with. I haven't been at this as long as my teacher, but even so there are days when my joints moan and I yearn for release.

"Yes," Ito said. "We had been informed Yamashita-san was away." He gazed around the room at the last of the students, racking weapons and preparing to leave. "A pity. I would have enjoyed seeing him after all I have heard …" Then he focused on me.

I expected some condescension. Some sign that I wasn't

quite living up to the standards set by my absent master. As the years have passed and I have assumed more and more teaching responsibilities in the dojo, it was a common experience for me to be judged a disappointment by others. The old-time Japanese sensei are skeptical that a round-eye can ever even approach a level of serious competence. They'd have preferred it if Yamashita had chosen someone else to be his heir. And even the American students who come our way seem disappointed. You think they'd know better. But deep down they yearn for the inscrutable East. For the magic of the exotic. For Master Yoda.

What they get is me. The thick forearms of a swordsman. A shock of dense, dark hair. Eyes the greyish blue of the shingle by the shore of a cold sea. Dressed up in the dark blue garments worn by warriors from another place and another time.

But there was no disappointment in Ito's expression. He was carefully studying me, a man sipping at some invisible nectar in the air. The hair on my arms and the back of my neck stood up and I tingled from the faint current that was passing through me.

I knew what I was feeling—*haragei*. It's the weird sixth sense the Japanese believe is a hallmark of the advanced martial artist. They say with *haragei*, you can sense the skill of an opponent just by being in close proximity to him. I realized Ito had this skill. Some people think I have it too. I'm not so sure about that, but Yamashita's a master of *haragei* and I've felt his force washing over me enough to know I was being "read" by Ito.

Ito's eyes shifted as if he were coming to some new realization about me. "Yes, a pity, Dr. Burke. It would be most instructive …" his voice tapered off for a moment. "But please excuse me. I am sent to inquire as to whether you would do me the honor of meeting my superiors."

"I'm sorry, Ito-san," I told him, "but Yamashita Sensei is not available and will not be returning for several weeks."

This was always how it started. The quietly contained men in the dark suits. The invitation to a meeting. Yamashita's past was largely a mystery to me, but it seemed as if these people had a hold on him. I wasn't sure why, but it was something that could not be denied.

But my teacher is aging now. I feared another summons would be more than he could stand. I wanted to protect him from that, like a man shielding an ember, fearful it will burn itself out without protection. I was ready to dig in my heels on this one. But Ito took me off guard.

"Just so," he answered, smiling. His teeth were even and very white. "But excuse me, perhaps I have been unclear. My principals," and here he nodded significantly at the business card in my hand, "wish to speak with *you*."

I looked at the card without saying anything, trying to regain my mental balance.

Ito took a step closer, lowering his voice to a confidential tone. "With the greatest respect, Dr. Burke, this is a matter of some urgency. We wonder if you would be willing to come with me. Now."

He was trying to flatter me. And I was curious. But mostly, I thought I should go simply to ensure that they wouldn't come back at a later date for Yamashita. Because if they did, he'd go with them, no matter what crazy plot they were hatching. That was the kind of hold they had on him. I knew he didn't need that. I also knew it was my job to protect him.

These people were dangerous. I'd seen them in action before. They operate in a world of obligation and honor, where it is assumed that some people command and some people serve.

And all who serve are expendable. It's dressed up in mythology and ritual that's thousands of years old. And no matter what they say, it exerts a powerful hold on the Japanese, even today.

But not me. I was going into this with my eyes wide open. Or so I thought. I looked at Ito's *meishi* and the embossed golden chrysanthemum on the card. He was a messenger from the Imperial House of Japan, the longest line of serving monarchs in the world and the descendants of the sun goddess herself. He didn't impress me.

But I went anyway.

CHAPTER 2

We rode in a limousine. I always feel uncomfortable lounging in the back of one of those cars. My formative years had been spent ranged along the bench-like seats of a series of overloaded station wagons with my brothers and sisters. Those vehicles rocked and swayed on shock absorbers that were almost as exhausted as my parents. The cars were white or green or blue, depending on the year, filthy and mottled with rust. They all burned oil in the same way and were the type of lumbering gas-guzzlers preferred by the Burke clan.

Ito's limo was night black and shone from meticulous attendance. I leaned back in the leather seats and watched the traffic. It was cold on the streets; my breath fogged the window for a brief second until the cabin heater wiped it away with luxurious efficiency. We were hermetically sealed, protected from the winter cold. The tinted windows prevented the riffraff from looking in at us. The ride was quiet and smooth and distinctly unreal. Ito stretched out in an opposite corner of the car, comfortable in this environment, and watched me.

I looked over and nodded at his thick hands. "Kyokushinkai?" It's a karate school renowned for its devotion to breaking techniques.

He smiled and corrected me. "Shotokan." His voice had a self-satisfied tone, as if the idea that he'd study the Kyokushinkai style was beneath him. It figured. Shotokan was a much more mainstream karate style, and Kyokushinkai's founder had, after all, been a Korean. They're big for pedigree in the service of the Imperial House, even down to the details of work out partners. Shotokan was the right choice for someone like Ito. And someone like Ito had probably made the right step every day of his life—going to the right school, developing the right connections. He was cultivated for a life of service in the vast governmental bureaucracy of Japan. If I had thought about it, I would have realized there was no way he was going to spoil his prospects by studying with a renegade group of Kyokushinkai board breakers, no matter how much he might have wished he could. It wasn't particularly surprising. Duty trumps desire almost every time in Japan.

I wondered whether someone like Ito even felt any struggle between duty and desire anymore. Think of a bonsai tree, bound into a shape not of its own choosing. Does the tree dream of another, wilder form? Probably not. The gardener dreams. The tree simply bends to his will.

I sometimes yearn for that type of surrender, the placid numbness of unquestioning obedience. But it's just not in me. One of the great ironies of my life is that I'm always trying to avoid being controlled, and yet I have yoked myself to studying an art that demands total surrender. I like to think it's my choice and I can break free whenever I wish. But I'm not so sure anymore. After all, there I was. I had no real interest in getting involved with these people. I'd dealt with them before, and they always seemed to get what they wanted and then faded back into the shadows while the rest of us were left to clean up the pieces and nurse our wounds. This wasn't going to end well. But even as it chafed, the yoke compelled me. I had a duty of sorts to perform. I needed to protect Yamashita. From them.

That two-word conversation about karate styles was it for Ito and me. We were both comfortable with silence and it's not a long trip from Red Hook to Gotham anyway. I sniffed the leather upholstery appreciatively, listened to the tires hum along the road surface, and watched as we popped up out of the Battery Tunnel and arrived in Manhattan. I tried not to speculate too much about what was going to happen. It's a waste of energy. But deep down, I must have been anticipating certain things and so I felt a spurt of surprise when we slipped past 299 Park Avenue. I hadn't been consciously aware of it, but I suppose I had thought Ito was taking me to the Japanese Consulate. Instead, we continued down Park Ave. and across East Forty-Ninth to the Waldorf Astoria hotel. I nodded to myself in appreciation. Conveniently close. Yet nicely separate. *They think of everything.*

We took an elevator and, in the foyer of an elegant hotel suite, another flat-eyed, fit young man in a dark suit frisked me before letting me in. I wondered if the Japanese were simply cloning them. "Tell him I left my throwing stars at home," I said. Ito smiled in apology, but the pat down proceeded. It struck me then: *They think I'm dangerous.* This was not something I usually gave a great deal of thought to. I do what I do, and the rarefied little world Yamashita has created has grown familiar and unexceptional to me. But looking at it from the outside, my teacher and I must have seemed like strange beasts. And with that realization, another thought came to me: *Dangerous? Well, I suppose I am.*

The suite had a conference area: a highly polished wooden table and well-padded chairs. A credenza along one wall featured a silver coffee service and some fruit. An old man, his face blotchy with age spots, was in a wheelchair to my left at the far end of a table. He had a narrow, pointed jaw and a broad forehead. Sparse strands of iron grey hair were plastered over his pate. The pronounced skin of his epicanthic fold made his eyes appear sleepy, but a closer look showed me an old reptile, alert and ready for a meal. The long fingers of his hands were gnarled with arthritis—they rested on the polished wood of the table like old claws.

A second Japanese man sat at the long side of the table. He was middle aged and growing stout, a compact man with flat cheekbones and short salt and pepper hair. He rose from his seat as I approached, came around the table, and extended a hand.

"Dr. Burke, thank you for coming. I am Miyazaki Tokio." He bowed in the direction of the man in the wheelchair. "This is my father." The old lizard remained motionless.

Miyazaki ushered me to a seat across from him at the table. I could sense Ito and the other guard watching from a discrete distance while my host fussed with the coffee service. "You prefer your coffee black, *neh?* As do I." There were manila file folders arrayed before his place at the table, but they were ignored for a time as he served us and we both made a show of sipping the coffee with polite appreciation. Miyazaki inquired about my trip. The health of my master. He was obviously tense, but etiquette is etiquette, and he did a good job of playing the host. His father said nothing. I could hear the faint phlegmy rattle of his breathing, but other than that, he seemed to play no part in the meeting and showed no overt interest.

Finally, I decided this had gone on long enough. One of the nice things about being a *gaijin*, a foreigner, is that the Japanese don't expect good manners from you. If I had known these people or wanted to somehow impress them, I might have played along. But I didn't. I set my cup down on its translucent saucer and leaned back in the chair.

"Excellent coffee, Miyazaki-san." I thought it interesting that he seemed to know how I liked my coffee. That he knew when Yamashita was going to be away. They were facts I'd ponder later. "But you haven't gone to all this trouble just to invite me over for a drink." I looked directly at the father and arched my eyebrows quizzically. It was very un-Japanese of me. You never make a direct inquiry like that, especially to the senior person present. The whole reason the old man sat at the far end of the table was so he could watch me but I could not watch him. At least that's the theory. I was expected to talk to the younger Miyazaki, sitting across from me, but all the real power was really in the clawlike hands of the old thing sitting to my left. So I decided to refuse to play along and rattle them with my lack of couth.

But the younger Miyazaki merely blinked and smiled, unruffled. He looked at me mildly, as if studying an exotic animal in the zoo. He nodded. "Indeed, Dr. Burke. Please excuse me. I understand your desire to get to the point." He smiled again, as if the use of the colloquialism was a way to show off his language skill. But the Japanese nod and smile for many reasons. Sometimes they are agreeing with you. Other times they are simply indicating they have heard what you have said. Sometimes, it's because they are deeply uneasy. I wondered which reason made Miyazaki smile.

I gestured at the files. "The point, I suppose, is in there?"

Again the smile. But it was tight and fleeting, more a grimace than anything else. Miyazaki took a breath, as if bracing himself. One hand pressed on the pile of folders, an unconscious expression of a wish to keep them forever closed. But he couldn't.

I sensed movement on the periphery of the room and Ito

appeared at the table. He silently asked for permission to join us and, for once, Miyazaki's facade cracked and he nodded wearily in acquiescence. Ito sat next to me on the right and reached over for the files.

"Dr. Burke," Ito began, "what we are discussing here is highly confidential. The Miyazaki family would ask for your utmost discretion." I just nodded. Across from me Miyazaki raised a hesitant finger. The younger man paused for a fraction of a second, then slid a piece of typescript in front of me. "With respect, Miyazaki-san asks you to sign this nondisclosure agreement." Ito's voice was distant and formal, a sign of just how uncomfortable he was with the request.

I pushed it away, back toward Miyazaki. "Don't be ridiculous. You asked me to come here. If you want to talk with me, talk, otherwise I'm leaving." I stood up.

The old man croaked something: a name perhaps, or a command. I didn't catch it, but the man who had frisked me at the door appeared by my side and put a restraining hand on my shoulder. It wasn't a light touch, and I felt my core tightening and the anticipation of a fight spiraling up within me. It's a familiar feeling. I wonder sometimes whether I like it too much. I leaned in toward Miyazaki.

"Tell him to get his hand off me, Miyazaki. I'm only going to say it once. If you can't trust me, you wouldn't have invited me up here. Don't insult me with a piece of paper."

He sighed, closed his eyes, opened them, and nodded at the goon at my side. The hand came off my shoulder. But I didn't sit down.

"Please, Dr. Burke," Miyazaki said, and his voice was small and tight, like a man being choked. "We need your help."

I looked at Ito. He was standing as well, and watching me

with tremendous interest, his eyes lit up with anticipation. Part of him wanted me to sit down; it was his duty to make that happen. But part of him would have liked to see me tussle with the man standing by my shoulder. He was the only honest person in the room. I don't know whether I liked him for it, but at least I understood him.

"Please," Miyazaki begged, gesturing to my chair. And there was something familiar in the tilt of his head, in the cast of his eyes. So I sat down, if only to try to figure out what was creating that sense of familiarity.

Ito sat down, too, and arranged the files in front of him. He took out some color photos of a striking young Japanese woman. Wide eyes, long black hair that shimmered with highlights that seemed almost blue. She had a playful smile that almost made you feel she was mocking the camera. But it was subtle and it could have been my imagination. "Miyazaki-san's daughter Chie," Ito told me.

"How old?"

"Twenty-three," he said. "After graduating from Tokyo Daigaku, she came last year to New York for graduate work." I nodded. Tokyo University is Japan's most prestigious school. A child of someone like Miyazaki would have gone there. But there's an allure to study in the United States, and it's not unusual for people to come west for grad school. I looked across at Miyazaki, his face once more impassive. I wondered how he'd felt about his daughter slipping her chain and getting loose among the barbarians. Probably like most fathers, I realized. Then Ito passed me another picture.

In this one, the mocking smile was more fully in place. The eyes seemed narrower and her long hair had been cut shorter in a choppy style and was streaked with pink and green. It wasn't a formal posed shot. It was taken outside and the blurry background of building and people made me wonder if it was a surveillance photo taken with a long lens.

"Nice nose ring," I said to Ito, then regretted it as soon as the words popped out. I was getting the picture: child of privilege running amok. Miyazaki didn't wince at my comment, but it must have been hard for him. *Sorry, Dad.*

"She has taken to her new environment," Ito ventured an understatement. The old man at the end of the table snorted.

"We have," Miyazaki began, then cleared his throat, "I have deep concerns about my daughter and the people she is associating with, Dr. Burke."

I sighed inwardly. The daughter-gone-wild-in-grad-school story is as common as it is sad. Kids breaking free. Parents holding on. Lots of room for hurt feelings. But the sheer grind of life imposes a type of conformist gravity. Most people eventually fall out of orbit. It takes a lot of sex, drugs, and rock and roll to hit escape velocity. The probability was that she'd be OK. But I'm not a parent; maybe probable isn't good enough to let you sleep at night.

How was I supposed to change this for him? "I don't see any role I can play in this problem, Miyazaki-san. Have you spoken with her?"

He looked down at the polished surface of the table. "Numerous times. And each conversation is worse than the last."

"She has stopped attending classes," Ito added. "She hasn't been in her apartment for weeks."

I looked from one to the other. "If she's been out of contact, you can file a missing-person report." The old man snorted again.

Miyazaki was shaking his head. "She is in sporadic contact with us, Dr. Burke. But we do not know exactly where she is." He was clearly uncomfortable but didn't seem eager to explain.

I shrugged. "Cut off the money. That usually brings them back." Miyazaki's shoulders slumped. He looked at his father, whose eyes gleamed with anger. *This is a conversation they've had before.*

"I am afraid it is more complicated and delicate a situation than that," Ito interjected. He paused and looked toward the two other men at the table. "It is a matter of the greatest delicacy and involves the family honor." And now he seemed reluctant to continue. Miyazaki was silent. His face was stone.

"Honor," the old man snapped. His Japanese was guttural and harsh, but the word *makoto*, honor, rang out in the room. "Look at him!" A claw waved in my direction. "What does this one know of honor?" He probably thought a barbarian like me wouldn't understand him when he spoke Japanese.

I turned my head and stared at him. "*Saya wa naku tomo mi wa hikaru,*" I spat back at him. He looked shocked. *Though the scabbard is lacking, the blade gleams.* It's an old samurai chestnut, and even now I'm amazed I was able to locate it in the dingy, cluttered storage space of my memory, but it seemed to stupefy them all. I was relieved I had come up with a somewhat elegant rejoinder. My original impulse had been to tell him to shove it.

Ito suppressed a wry smile. The old man seemed incensed: probably offended that I had the nerve to speak his language. His mottled face flushed and his lips grew wet with spittle as he spun himself up for a tantrum. Miyazaki rose in alarm. "Ito," he said, "my father is not well." He reached the old man and began to wheel him away. "Please continue with our guest," he commanded over his shoulder as he pushed the old lizard out of the room.

Ito stood watching until the door shut firmly behind them. He sighed. "Perhaps it is just as well." He moved to the table and sat down, his hands resting on the folders before him. "The rest of the story is not so pleasant. As a father, it would be distressing for Miyazaki-san to share these things about his daughter."

I raised my eyebrows and sat down. Now at least I was getting somewhere. There was no reason I could see why a highly placed Japanese family would need my help in corralling a wayward daughter. I've got a degree in history, not social work. I give lots of advice in the dojo, but most of it is highly specialized: I don't care about how you feel about your relationship with your father. I am concerned with proper hip placement and correcting that really bad grip you're using on the sword.

But they knew that. They knew about me: my background, my likes and dislikes. My skills. So there had to be something more to the situation. Something that made them reluctant to go to the authorities.

"So," I offered. "Let me guess. Drugs?"

Ito nodded solemnly. "In part. What you call party drugs. Ecstasy. Crystal meth."

"Some party."

"Yes," he sighed. "And there is more." He fished around in his files and spread out a series of black and white surveillance shots: Chie with an Asian man in wraparound sunglasses and spiky hair. Another picture of the same man without the shades, lighting a cigarette outside a bar. "Lim Ki-whan," Ito said. "Her boyfriend." He tried to be dispassionate, but I could hear the note of disdain creeping into his voice. The name was Korean, and even today there is a deep chauvinism among some Japanese regarding the Koreans. For a family like the Miyazaki, it would have been bad enough to have a daughter wander off the reservation in America. To do it with a Korean would be beyond the pale.

"He's her drug connection as well, I suppose?" Ito nodded in response. "Love is a wonderful thing," I told him.

He didn't think I was funny. He was probably right.

"There is more, Dr. Burke. Chie has a troubled psychological profile … issues with behavior. Issues with authority." *Don't we all.* He rustled through some papers, dense with text. "And sex." He paused for a moment, clearly uncomfortable.

This was curious. Japanese attitudes regarding sexual matters are considerably different than traditional Western ones. The same culture that has elevated tea making to an art form is also the largest producer of pornographic comics in the world. So I waited for Ito to say more. He sat there, arranging and rearranging the order of the folders in front of him. Finally, he simply slipped one folder across the table in front of me. He shrugged. "There. Please take a look."

There were a great many photos of Miyazaki Chie with a variety of men. The pictures seemed to have been carefully posed to be both sexually graphic and to ensure she could be clearly identified. Many times, she was looking right at the camera, her eyes slightly unfocused, and I assumed that was from the drugs. But you clearly got the sense that she knew she was being photographed. That she knew someone was going to be looking at her in these photos. And that she liked it. I shuffled through the collection quickly and wondered once more at the human capacity for making something potentially good so deeply creepy.

Ito watched me, waiting for a comment.

"I see she's gotten some tattoos as well," I offered.

"She is a nymphomaniac," he said curtly. "And a drug user." His voice took on heat and speed as he continued. "She is the daughter of one of the most respected families in Japan and she is being exploited by this Korean thug."

There are lots of ways you could exploit someone, so I pressed for more information. "Has he turned her out?" I said.

Ito cocked his head, taking a moment to make a mental translation of the phrase. "Ah, has he made her a prostitute? No, Dr. Burke." He reached over and took possession of the photos, sliding the folder beneath the others.

I nodded. "At least there's that." But Ito didn't seem comforted.

"She is with him, we believe. But we do not know where. We want her back, Dr. Burke."

"I can understand that, Ito-san, but I don't see why you need me to help."

Ito rubbed his hands together as if he were thinking about using them to mangle Chie's boyfriend. It seemed to calm him. He peered up at me. "You have resources that could help us find him."

"True." My brother had been a cop for twenty years before he retired to set up a security consulting firm. He's widely connected, deeply cranky, and very busy. But he could probably find Chie in about twenty-four hours if I asked for his help. "But there are many people in New York who could help you do this," I told him.

Ito nodded. "Just so. But as we have stated, there are complicating factors. The drugs. The prominence of the family. We would insist on the utmost discretion."

I thought of the pictures I had just seen. "That would be refreshing."

"We know of your past service to the Kunaicho," he told me. The Kunaicho, the Imperial Household Agency, was deeply involved in matters relating to the Japanese royal family. At one time, in another life, Yamashita had been instrumental in training its security personnel. It was a complicated history, filled with good things and bad. Some of them had almost gotten us both killed.

I didn't respond to his comment and Ito took a sipping breath. "We would be honored if you would help us, Dr. Burke."

"I think," I said as I stood up, "that you are not telling me everything, Ito-san. I think you're looking for someone who can find her, sure, but you also know she's not going to want to come home, and whoever finds her is going to have to knock some heads together." He started to respond but I held up a hand to silence him. "And it wouldn't look good to have some Japanese government agents involved in what would essentially be a kidnapping. So you figured I could do the scut work for you and take the heat. You know, for old times' sake. Am I right?"

His eyes never wavered. "We will pay you generously."

"Great. I can buy extra cigarettes in prison," I told him. I headed toward the door.

"Wait," Ito called. His partner, who had remained in the background during our discussion, moved to block my way out of the suite.

"Get out of my way," I told him. But he didn't move.

"Please, Dr. Burke," Ito continued. "It is an extremely delicate situation. And extremely complicated."

I turned my head back toward Ito. "Not half as complicated as your friend's life is going to be if he doesn't get out of my way." I felt the early tremble of an adrenalin dump start to work its way through my muscles. Ito must have sensed it as well. He made a quick motion and the man by the door stood aside.

"Did I tell you how we got those pictures?" Ito called as I headed out into the hall. I kept moving, but his voice followed me.

"Chie sends them to her father."

CHAPTER 3

The training hall is called a dojo—a place of the Way. The name has all the exotic allure of the Mystic East: the promise of hidden wisdom and esoteric powers. But step inside a training hall and stay awhile. Venture out onto the floor with us. There are no wizened sages popping out cryptic advice. Instead there is the bark of commands and the hard, relentless gaze of your sensei. There is sweat in the eyes, the burn of muscle, and the constant presence of fear, surprise, pain, and frustration. Yet occasionally, as your hand slides in to grip the hard wooden shaft of the training sword, in the steamy pause between bouts when your heart is hammering in your ears and your breath scrapes in and out, something wells up inside you. It touches you like a phantom hand: the sense of connection, of potential, and the overwhelmingly clear beauty of the moment. Then it's gone.

So if there's a way we pursue in the dojo, it's a way back to that sensation, as intense and fleeting as a flash of light at midnight. It's as simple and as complicated as that.

I've been chasing the spark for almost thirty years. I've spent close to twenty of them with Yamashita, practicing the brutally elegant system he teaches. It encompasses sword and staff arts, unarmed combat, and more. If modern systems like judo or karate specialize on one segment of the fighting spectrum, the Yamashita-ha Itto Ryu blends as many of these segments as possible into an integrated whole. My teacher uses sword and staff as the main vehicles for his teaching, but insists they are merely means to an end. He trains warriors, and uses whatever is on hand to do so.

He once showed us a *tanto*, a short knife. Yamashita held it comfortably in his thick hand, moving the blade so the light played dully along its surface. "This," he said, "is a sharp piece of metal. Nothing more. In one man's hand it is good for cutting carrots. In another …" he held it up for the assembled class to take another look. He smiled. Then his face went totally blank. The sudden movement of his arm was fluid and almost too fast to see. The *tanto* shot across the room and buried its point into one of the wooden pillars along the dojo's perimeter. You could almost hear the metal hum as it struck home.

"In another," Yamashita concluded, "it is something very different. So …" He smiled at us. "In swordsmanship there is *ki, ken, tai*." Spirit, sword, body. "Without spirit, without the force of the warrior, there is no sword." He shrugged. "It is a spike, perhaps, or a cleaver. Just metal." His eyes narrowed. "*You* make it dangerous. You *create* the sword."

And then the lesson continued. He left the knife buried in the wood of that pillar as a reminder to us all.

I carry on that tradition, but without the elegance of my master. All of the pupils he accepts for training are required to have black belts in more than one martial art. Many of them have trained with bokken, the oak sword that forms the centerpiece of Yamashita's training, but they have rarely plumbed its depths. As a result, new students often focus on the sword too intently, momentarily forgetting the other valuable lessons they have learned.

So I have to remind them. I like to think of it as an awareness exercise. But as some of my students limped off the floor after one session, I heard them ruefully calling it "hammer time."

I'm not a cruel man, you understand. Yamashita used to chide me for sometimes being too gentle with the students. And over time, I've learned ours is an austere discipline, set against a hard world. Compassion is only possible when it follows mastery. But even in the rigors of training, I remind myself what is taking place is not mere battery, but a pounding more akin to the blows of a swordsmith as he forges metal into a blade of terrible beauty.

That day on the dojo floor we were working on different counters for attacks at distant and close intervals. Most sword work takes place in *issoku itto no ma*, the distance where you cross swords with an opponent and one small step will bring your weapon into striking distance. Some of the students had spent time studying kendo, the modern version of Japanese swordsmanship, so the concept was second nature to them. And the others quickly got the hang of it. They all had the body awareness of fighters.

The members of the class were paired off, a long line of swordsmen in the midnight blue of the traditional uniform, gripping the white oak bokken. I worked their wrist and forearm muscles in the quick jerking parries that are designed to deflect a strike and, with luck, expose an opening for a counterattack. We moved on to the sliding deflection of the *suriage* technique, then the move known as *kaeshi*, and finally to *uchiotoshi*. By that time, I could see the fabric of their heavy training jackets growing limp with sweat. In the pauses when we would rotate partners, people wiped their hands on their uniforms to keep their swords from slipping out of their hands. The constant repetition of the training session, the ceaseless back and forth of attack and counterattack, was taking its toll on them. They were straining to maintain focus, working hard at their swordsmanship. It was, as they say, a teachable moment.

I called the class to a halt and asked for a volunteer. A guy named Rick stood up. He had been training with me for almost a year, a diligent student who was skilled enough to be a good demo partner. We paired off and the others dropped to one knee to watch, grateful for the break. "So," I began as I squared off with Rick. The tips of our bokken crossed. We were in *issoku itto no ma*. "From this interval, a number of attacks are possible. And a number of parries." I nodded at him and we began, running in sequence through the techniques we had been practicing. As the senior member of the duo, I would attack, giving my junior a chance to respond. He did. Then we squared off once more and I came at him with a different technique. Again, the smooth response. I held up a hand to pause as we squared off one more time. "But now, what happens if something changes?"

Up to this point, I had been moving in what I call training speed. It was fast enough to be dangerous, but not so fast that a student like Rick didn't have the opportunity to counter my attack. There was no point going at him full speed. I would have struck him every time and he would have simply grown frustrated. That would have been battering, not forging. And a good sensei must teach, not simply humiliate.

But now, I came at him for real. I shot toward him so fast that I got inside the striking radius of his sword. For a moment, Rick froze. I shot diagonally to the left across his front my right hand let go of the bokken, and my free arm curled up and across his neck. I saw the realization of what was happening come into his eyes, but by then it was too late. I was facing his rear, our hips on the same line. I extended forward and down, driving him into the floor. It wasn't a hard throw, and I didn't put all my energy into it, but coming down like that onto a hard wooden floor is bound to ring some bells in your head. I kicked his sword away and it skittered across the wooden floor.

Rick looked slightly cross-eyed for a moment, and then he shook it off. Even half stunned, he began to roll to his feet. I nodded in approval. Training is designed to help your body respond even before the conscious mind orders it to. But I must have dumped him harder than I had intended. His movements seemed slower than usual. Yet he doggedly began the long slog to his feet. I liked him for that, and felt the urge to help him up. But I didn't. In the end, what we teach is not victory, but the capacity to endure. He deserved the small dignity of the struggle to stand upright once again.

Rick took a breath and set himself for the next attack. His sword was gone, so he set his hands in front of him in the unarmed *tegatana* posture, and waited. I nodded in approval, then backed away, showing him there would be no further attack.

"*Irimi nage,*" I told the class. "You've probably all seen it at one time or another, right?" Rick nodded ruefully and some other heads nodded as well. "So what happened?" I gestured to him, someone handed him his bokken, and we slowly went through the motions of what I had just done.

"We're working on sword techniques and you're getting tired. So you're trying to compensate and you're trying really hard. But your brain is sticking, focusing on the idea of using the sword." I looked at Rick. "Here I come."

I replicated my move and got in close. "For Rick to strike me, he needs to take a step back and swing the sword up, right?

But that'll be too late. So …" I smiled at them, "here's Burke's secret technique for the day." I gestured at Rick. "You come in at me and do the same thing I did." Rick glided in and across my front. He was now inside my strike radius to my right and my arms were extended in front of me, holding the bokken in the classic two-handed grip. "Now the sword is useless, yes?" I could hear Yamashita's vocal cadence sneaking into my own. "But look!" I let go of the bokken with my left hand and raised the weapon horizontally and mimed hammering the butt of the sword into the side of Rick's head. Well, maybe I gave him a poke in the nerve point under the ear where the jaw hinges. I pivoted around and placed my left hand against the back of the sword, slicing it down in a deep, vicious arc across the triceps of the arm that should have been snaking across my neck to throw me.

Rick nodded. I ran through the sequence again, letting him try the technique. We bowed to each other.

"The sword is a great weapon," I told them. "But don't get locked into thinking about it one way. It's a spear. It's a cleaver. A hammer. And sometimes it's just an impediment. In fighting, there's only one way to use a sword," I told the class. "The way that gets the job done." I swept my arm up and they reformed the line.

"*Hajime*," I said. Begin.

Some people won't take no for an answer.

Ito unfurled the small tube of paper, carefully smoothing it down on the coffee table between us. Below the loft apartment, the dojo was silent and empty. I could hear the refrigerator's compressor cycle on in the kitchen and the distant hum of street traffic. Before me, the old paper crinkled.

It was a sheet of calligraphy in a vaguely familiar hand. The two large characters at the head of the paper were clear enough: *seiyaku*, a written vow.

"Can you read this?" Ito asked. He wasn't being arrogant: the grass writing of personal calligraphy is cursive and often more suggestive than precise. But the characters were simple enough. It was addressed simply to a woman named Chika-hime.

I glanced at Ito. "*Hime?* An honorific of some sort?"

He nodded. "Princess."

I scanned the lines, striving to get an English translation that mirrored the elegance on the page. "Each snow an ... echo of this warrior's promise ... heart and sword."

"*Kokoro ken to*," Ito repeated—heart and sword—pleased with my rendering. "You see the signature below, Dr. Burke?"

I said nothing, staring at the calligraphy. It was the product of a younger brush, but the underlying stylistic structure was there. There was no denying I knew the handwriting: it was the same thick sprawl of ink that marked my training certificates as authentic, the signature of Yamashita Rinsuke. My sensei.

I didn't know what to think or what to say. Yamashita's past was largely a mystery to me. This note offered a glimpse into his secret life. It was as if a heavy curtain had shifted in a breeze and a shaft of light had briefly flickered across a dark room. I was intrigued, yet felt vaguely guilty. A pledge from the heart. Surely it was meant for only one pair of eyes other than his, and they weren't mine. Yet the impulse to question Ito was real and irresistible. I gave in, but only a little. "It's not dated," I said.

"No, it isn't," Ito admitted. "If we were to ask Yamashita Sensei, however, he would surely remember the date."

I squinted at the man sitting across from me. "Why would I ask him that?"

Ito shrugged. "You wish to know the date."

"No, I don't. Not enough to bother him." But the protest sounded feeble and untrue, even to my ears.

Ito smiled tightly, then sat back and watched me calmly for a time. He leaned forward and carefully rolled the note up and placed it in the narrow bamboo tube. "It was written in the winter of 1962. Your master was twenty, Dr. Burke."

"And the woman?"

Ito's eyes widened. "It does seem a heartfelt note, does it not? Terribly sincere. Terribly young."

"Terribly sad, I think," I told him.

Ito nodded in agreement. "Oh, very much so. It was the last … well, the only note between them, Dr. Burke."

"But someone went to great pains to preserve it," I noted.

"Just so," Ito agreed. "It must have seemed important. And a pledge is something to honor." The implication was unmistakable. It had occurred to me even as I read the note. But Ito didn't know me very well; he wouldn't suspect that I'd be sensitive to issues of honor. The Japanese tend to believe they have a monopoly on this quality. When he looked at me, despite his polish, Ito looked with Japanese eyes and saw just another gaijin, a foreigner with little or no subtlety.

"I'd like to meet this woman," I said. "For Yamashita Sensei to write this … She must be a remarkable person. I assume you know her, Ito-san? After all, she gave you this very personal note." I was needling him a little, letting him know I was wondering how he got hold of something that wasn't meant for anyone but her.

Ito let out a sigh. "Miyazaki Chika was a remarkable woman, Dr. Burke. A precious child of a cadet line of the royal house. A princess, truly." He smiled. "It sounds comic to speak of a princess, does it not? But even today, they exist." He gathered his thoughts. "And even were she not related to the Imperial House, she would have been remarkable. Beautiful. Gifted. But so sad—a woman who knew well the fleeting nature of happiness."

The mention of the Miyazaki name piqued my interest and got me wondering all sorts of things. But I held myself back and covered the emotion with a tangential comment instead. "*Mono no aware*," I said. The Japanese aesthetic of frail and transient beauty that makes life so bitter and so sweet.

Ito's face brightened in pleasant surprise. "Yes! Exactly. She was a remarkable woman."

"Was?"

He nodded. "Chika-hime was the mother of my principal, Miyazaki Tokio."

"And the old man?"

"Her husband, Dr. Burke."

"He gave you this note? The old man?"

He shook his head. "Oh, no, Dr. Burke. Had he known of it, this note would never have survived. Chika-hime passed it to her son on her deathbed. In time of need, he was to seek out your master for help."

"Why," I demanded. "Why, after all these years?"

"It seems a pointless question, does it not, Dr. Burke? There is need. More importantly, there is a pledge. There is honor. These things do not fade with time."

"My sensei," I began. But Ito reached out as if he were going to touch me.

"Is not well," he finished for me. "I understand. Time and old wounds have taken their toll. But surely he would wish his pledge to be honored." He left the last sentence dangling.

Maybe I was wrong. Maybe he thought more of me than I had supposed.

I stood, feeling agitated. The trap was swinging shut. I glanced around the room. The clean architectural lines of a traditional Japanese room provided no shadows within which to hide. The space was quiet, but the air was charged with expectation. Yamashita's favorite *sumi-e* painting of birds perched on a bamboo stalk was so delicately rendered that the leaves seemed to tremble as I looked at it. When I glanced away, my eyes fell on a table in the place of honor, and the black slash of lacquered scabbards where the swords of my master's art slumbered. The blades had been polished through a life spent pursuing mastery. And honor.

The thing about training in a dojo is that there is no escape and nowhere to hide. You are there precisely because of that reason. You place yourself there to be hammered into something better. It's not easy. It's not pleasant. But it teaches you the importance of even small things and small details. Because, in the Way, all things are important, even a pledge given in the first blush of manhood so many years ago.

I sighed, and turned to Ito.

"OK. I'm in."

CHAPTER 4

An elegant cocktail lounge, humming with activity. It was the season between Thanksgiving and Christmas, and suburbanites were in Manhattan to see the tree in Rockefeller Center, to stroll down Fifth Avenue, and do a little shopping. It was cold outside and it was the holidays, so we weren't the only people in the hotel lounge having an afternoon cocktail. Deep down, I knew we were being boozers. But we were being stylish boozers.

The waitress brought us our drinks, setting them down on napkins with great care. A glass of Jameson's is, after all, a beautiful thing and worthy of a certain reverence. Art, however, was having a martini. He saw my questioning look and shrugged.

"I'm expanding my horizons," he said. He was big and pleasant looking, and above the serious cop mustache his eyes crinkled easily with amusement. They were bright eyes: blue and clear. But if you looked closely, you saw these eyes never stopped moving. He had been a cop for twenty years and, even in retirement, he never lost the habit of watching.

My brother Mickey sipped his drink, taking care not to spill any on his suit. He and Art had been, and still were, partners. Mickey was thinner, darker, and, if I were to be honest, sourer than Art. He, too, had the same cop mustache and the same cop eyes. After leaving the NYPD, the two of them had started their own security firm. In post–9-11 New York, it was wildly successful in a way that left both men mildly astonished. They shouldn't have been. They made a perfect team. Where one was all heat, the other was calm. They could play good cop/ bad cop like nobody else. They were tenacious, and so deeply experienced in the ways of people that nothing surprised them anymore. Except me.

I explained about the visit from Ito, the Miyazaki and their wayward daughter, her sleazy boyfriend, and the family's need to save her. An old pledge that had to be honored.

"Well," Art began, "it's not the dumbest thing you've ever done."

"But that's only because you are the king of moronic adventures," my brother cracked.

He should know. Both he and Art had been in some dark, wild places with me. Mickey, my older brother, felt that I was congenitally predisposed to getting in way over my head, and that he had an obligation to pull me out. In my defense, it wasn't always my fault. But that didn't change anything. Mickey was a man who walked through life deeply convinced of his own competence and wildly suspicious of the ability of almost everyone else. Especially me.

"Hey, come on," I told them. "I'm not here to get dumped on."

"You're here to drink some fine liquor on our expense account," my brother pointed out.

"You invited me," I said. Mickey opened his mouth to say something else, and then thought better of it. He looked across the booth to Art, who was draped along the padded seat like a man on his living room sofa. Art was smiling slightly, listening to us talk, but watching the people come and go.

"What?" Mickey prodded.

Art jerked a chin. "See the woman in the black parka who just came in?"

Mickey took a peek. "Fur-lined hood, red boots?"

Art nodded. "We've seen her before, but I can't place her."

Mickey squinted in thought. They had seen a lot of people in their time. Some were crooks. Some were just familiar. "She a pro?" he asked, meaning a prostitute.

Art closed one eye and tilted his head. "I don't get that vibe …" he said. He sighed. "Well, not my problem, I suppose." He turned to look at me. "You, on the other hand …"

"You idiot," my brother added.

I rested my drink on the napkin and looked down at it as I slid the glass in small circles on the wooden table. "Look, I'm not crazy about the deal, either. But it's something I've gotta do for Yamashita."

"Ooh, we've been to this movie before, eh Mick?" Art smiled, but the smile didn't reach his eyes.

Mickey leaned forward, brushing his tie down with the flat of his hand. He had spent most of his adult life in crumpled sport jackets bought off the rack at Sears, and now success had made him curiously fastidious, as if the absolute chaos of the world he worked in could be somehow kept at bay through good grooming.

"Jesus," he muttered, and took a sip of his drink. The two of them were deeply skeptical of the Miyazaki and their request. I had been there myself, but since I had agreed to help, I had the disorienting experience of repeating the same conversation with Ito all over again, only now I was arguing the exact opposite point of view.

"They just want this guy's daughter found," I explained. "She's a wreck. They want her home."

Mickey took a breath, but Art held up a calming hand. "Let's walk through this step by step, Connor, OK?" I nodded in agreement.

Art came out of his slouch and sat forward. "They would like her found, yes?"

"Yes," I said.

Art nodded. "Fair enough. But why come to you? There are any number of people who do this professionally." He placed a big freckled hand on my arm. "And I don't like to hurt your feelings, Connor, but they can probably do this better than you can." Across the table, Mickey snorted in agreement.

"Look," I said, "I pointed that out to them. But it's a Japanese thing. It has to do with family reputation. They don't want some stranger involved."

"You *are* a stranger, you idiot," my brother pointed out.

"No, I'm not. I'm Yamashita's senior student and he's got some connection with them. He owes them."

"How? Why?" Mickey was skeptical.

"I'm not entirely sure," I said.

"OK, leave that for a minute," Art continued. "It might be useful to know more, but you know what you know. Let's get to the heart of things here." He leaned forward and took a sip of his martini. "Mmm. Shaken, not stirred."

Mickey looked suddenly alert, and I knew we were about to take a detour into the odd version of Trivial Pursuit they had developed over years of stakeouts. "You mean, 'shaken *and* not stirred,'" he said, eyes gleaming.

Art appeared affronted. "Surely you jest. The movie *Goldfinger*, my man—1964. Check it out."

Mickey smiled wickedly. "And yet, when we go to the source, Ian Fleming himself wrote the phrase 'shaken and not stirred.' First uttered in the book *Dr. No* in 1958. They left the word 'and' out in the movies."

Art was not impressed. "Like you've ever read a book, Mick."

The two of them had an almost inexhaustible interest in pop culture trivia, especially when it came to action flicks. I let the bickering go on for a while, and then interrupted them.

"You know my favorite line by James Bond about martinis?" They stopped arguing and looked at me with the disapproval you give to people who let themselves in on a conversation without being invited. "*Casino Royale*, 2006," I continued. "Someone asks Bond if he wants his drink shaken or stirred. Know what he says?"

Art smiled, his eyes crinkling almost shut. "Sure. He says, 'Do I look like I give a damn?'"

"Exactly," I said, pausing for effect before I continued. "Let me just say he speaks for many of us."

Art looked at Mickey. "It seems not everyone shares our interests."

"Go figure," Mickey said. "Too busy getting tangled up in half-assed schemes, probably."

"Well, it appears that I digress," Art commented, and took another swallow of his drink. "Where was I? Oh, yeah. What do these guys really want?"

"They want her found," I answered.

Art smiled. "Oh, my boy. So easily misled. Yes, they want her found, but that's just the prelude. Once you find her, what then?"

"They want her to come home."

Mickey leaned in. "But they've had this conversation with her, haven't they? And she's not home, is she?"

"She's messed up, Mick," I told him.

"Doesn't matter," Art said, shaking his head. "She's not a minor. She's not being held under duress that we know of. She's free to be as messed up as she wants."

"Which means," Mickey put in, "what they want you to do is not just find her. They want you to take her. Against her will. And deliver her to them." He looked at Art. "Now why would they want someone to do that for them, Art?" His voice was dripping with sarcasm.

"Hmm, good question, Mick." Art rested his chin in his hand, miming deep thought. "Perhaps because, hmmm, let me see, perhaps because, oh, I don't know ..."

"Because it's kidnapping, you asshole," Mickey hissed at me. "A federal offense. They want it done, but they don't want to get their hands dirty doing it. They won't hire someone to do it because they can't trust them not to roll over if they get pinched."

"I would," Art said.

Mickey looked at me. His eyes are grey and can be terribly cold. "So they sell you a line about honor and favors owed by Yamashita and figure you'll get it done for them."

"Why would they ask me to do it, if I'm such an amateur?"

Art smiled. "Now, Connor. Don't be sullen. You're very capable in your own special way." He paused to scan the room once more. "I also imagine these people are very well informed about your skills. Your persistence."

"Your incredible knack for generating shit storms," Mickey added.

"An unpleasant point, but true," Art concluded. "And they are connected to the Kunaicho, which means they have a good line to various intelligence agencies."

"Which means they know about us," Mickey said. "We do enough work with the NYPD's intelligence bureau to be known. They figure you can use us as an asset to locate the girl.

Then you swoop in and get her. There may be some heads need knocking. Which, I have to admit, you can do." The admission that I had any sort of competence seemed to pain him. "Once that happens, they can have her loaded on a private jet and out of the country well before anyone raises a stink."

Art held up a finger. "Although a stink will be raised." He nodded somberly at me.

"And you, you moron, will be left holding the bag," my brother concluded.

I said nothing. I knew deep down they were right. But I also knew they didn't get the whole picture.

"Walk away, buddy boy," my brother urged.

"I agree, Connor," Art said quietly. "We're gonna pass on this one. You should too." Nobody said much after that. Art looked down at his glass. It was empty. So was mine.

Even in a crowded room, Osorio seemed alone. It wasn't just the minders who watched, unblinking, from the corners of the room. It wasn't the regal solitude of the man as he sat at the best table in the house, savoring the bouquet that swirled from a brandy snifter. There was a space around Osorio at all times, a zone filled with threat and innuendo and the memories of old violence.

"Dr. Burke," he said, smiling. His face was lined like old leather, his teeth square and strong looking. He swirled the brandy around the crystal glass, watching the languid wash of the liquid with deep appreciation. I stood a pace away from him, hands held at rest by my sides. I waited.

You don't get too close to Don Osorio without an invitation. He's a legend in Brooklyn's criminal underworld. And the stories of his rise to his current undisputed prominence as a Latino crime boss made Macbeth seem squeamish. You can say his crazy days were long behind him. And looking at him, dapper and placid, an old lion at rest, you might almost have believed it. But don't be fooled. Yamashita had once confided to me that Osorio was the second deadliest person he knew.

"Who's the first?" I had asked Yamashita.

He had almost smirked. "I am, Burke."

We had done Osorio a favor once and he had reciprocated. He understood deals. He even might have understood honor, if the cost were not too high. I thought he might be willing to help me with the Miyazaki, so I arrived unannounced at his dinner table. He might have been surprised—it was hard to tell—but the old gangster was certainly amused. And that and only that explained why I had gotten this far at all. I saw the subtle dismissive wave he gave his bodyguard. The man sat back, coiling down into stillness, but not into rest. His eyes never blinked. In contrast, Osorio's eyes crinkled in expectation.

I needed help finding Chie Miyazaki and her low-life boyfriend. There are two types of people who have the information that can help with problems like this. You can go to the good guys—people like my brother. Or you can go the other way—to people like Osorio.

I apologized to Osorio for my intrusion. "I've come seeking help, Don Osorio." I could tell that he liked that, the way I called him "Don," the archaic title of respect. Osorio knew nine-tenths of successful intimidation is reputation alone. He worked hard at cultivating his aura of Old World menace, and pleasing him was always a good strategy for any supplicant. Osorio didn't smile at the flattery, yet he waved a hand in invitation and I sat down.

And waited. The crisp table linen, the image of the old man

caressing a brandy snifter, the hum of the conversation of the other diners could almost lull you into relaxing and speaking your mind. But that wasn't the way the game would be played. It wasn't exactly Japanese in approach, but it was close enough so I understood the dynamics.

"And how is my sister's son?" the old man inquired.

Some time ago, Yamashita had agreed to train Osorio's nephew, an aspiring young martial artist. It went against most of my teacher's standards for admission to the dojo, but at the time it seemed a small price to pay for the help we needed. Osorio had delivered the requested service, and his nephew picked up the sword with us. Surprisingly, young Ricardo had endured.

"Fine," I said evasively. I remembered my recent class demonstration and what I had done to Rick, but kept it to myself.

"And Yamashita Sensei?"

"Aging gracefully."

Osorio smiled tightly. "Grace … a welcome companion in old age, Dr. Burke. But do not be fooled. Old tigers are often the most dangerous." His eyes were brown and knowing.

"Indeed they are, Don Osorio."

A waiter arrived, seemingly unbidden, and set a second brandy snifter down in front of me.

"*Salud*," the old gangster said, extending his glass.

"Salud," I answered. I sipped carefully, letting the fumes engulf my face. A drop of brandy pooled on my tongue. Warmth. The scent of oak and vanilla. A fine drink, shared with a vicious felon. But you take the good things in life where you can find them.

"You mentioned help?" Osorio said. He set the brandy

down on the table and was very still.

"A minor thing," I shrugged, "some information. Nothing more."

Osorio's head tilted to one side as he watched me. "There is information and there is information."

"This matter has nothing to do with your immediate …" I paused to think of a good euphemism, "… concerns."

His lips tightened in displeasure. "My concerns are many, Dr. Burke. I doubt you are intimately familiar with them."

I held up a placating hand. "I meant no disrespect. As far as I know, the information would not directly impact upon you. Nor would it be used that way."

Something flickered behind his eyes. He sat forward slightly. "We shall see."

So I explained about Chie Miyazaki and her boyfriend Lim, and how I needed to find them for her father.

"A father's concerns are to be respected," Osorio said, nodding. "But why come to me?"

I didn't fidget, although I felt the need. "This Lim, the boyfriend," I ventured. "He's a conduit for drugs."

"And you thought?" Osorio left the question dangling.

"I thought someone with your … wide range of acquaintances might be able to find some hint as to his whereabouts."

Osorio smiled then, big square teeth. "A wide range of acquaintances. I like that, Dr. Burke." He sipped his brandy and his eyes narrowed. "And in return?"

I sensed the whisper of warning swirling up inside my head. "As you know, Don Osorio, I am a man of limited resources and poor skills." He smirked at that, but he let me continue. "I can offer my goodwill, my services as a teacher …"

Osorio was not impressed. "I left the schoolroom many

years ago, Dr. Burke." I started to speak, but he held up a hand.

"Please. Let us simply say I may call upon you in the future for a discussion if I have the need for you?" He gave it the intonation of a question, but there was nothing interrogative about the statement. The message was clear. I was in his debt.

I took a deep breath, sure I had made a terrible mistake. "Thank you."

Osorio shook his head. "Please. Who is to say my own 'limited resources' will be of any use? Let us simply say it is my pleasure to offer this gesture to *un maestro de la espada*."

I stood up and nodded my thanks. But our eyes locked and we both knew what had just happened. I owed him now. And he never forgot a debt and never failed to collect payment.

I left the murmur of the restaurant and headed out into the cold. As I pulled my collar up around me, I shivered.

I remembered seeing a film once about someone who raised wolves. When the interviewer saw how the wolves appeared tame in their owner's hands, he asked whether the animals were capable of affection, whether they loved him.

The trainer ruffled the thick neck of one of the animals. Its eyes were clear and wide and totally unfathomable. "Love me?" he asked. "They tolerate me because I feed them."

I thought of Osorio then: similar eyes, similar appetites.

CHAPTER 5

The second man who stood guard with Ito was named Goro. He never said much, simply waited in the background. He was deeply contained in much the same way a bear trap is: stretched to stillness and ready to snap. Ito must have been similar when he was younger, but time and discipline had polished him. It wasn't that he was any less dangerous, simply that he had grown more comfortable with waiting. He sat easily across from me in a Midtown bar, nodding as I described my activity to date.

"Perhaps your contact can find something we could not," he admitted. "Lim's known associates are terribly difficult to locate." Goro sat at the bar, a few steps away from our table. He glared at me.

"Goro doesn't seem very happy today," I commented.

Ito's eyes tightened in amusement. "Goro's emotional state is of no concern of mine, Dr. Burke. He serves the Miyazaki family. To the extent that he does that well, he should be content."

"And you?"

Ito sipped at his scotch carefully. "I serve my government. The Miyazaki family is an important one. The son has a significant position in the diplomatic corps …

"And you take care of your own?"

Ito cocked his head, considering an answer. "Let us just say in this instance, the concerns of Miyazaki-san regarding his daughter are shared by my superiors."

I sat forward. "And why is that, I wonder."

Ito took another careful sip of Johnny Walker Blue. Then he set the glass down, perfectly centered on the cocktail napkin. His face was totally empty of expression. "With all due respect, Dr. Burke, the details are no concern of yours."

He was wrong, of course. The details are everything. Somewhere in that thicket, the devil lurks. But he was also in a business where even he probably never got the full story; someone simply winds him up and off he goes. The sense of honor that comes with unquestioning service is bred deep in Japanese of a certain type. The days of the samurai may seem long past, but the tradition endures.

I tried a different angle. "When we met in the hotel … the elder Miyazaki …" I let the sentence trail off unfinished, fishing for a response.

Ito smiled slightly and shook his head. "That old demon. He is vastly wealthy, Dr. Burke. And deeply connected. But I am not sure how much he shares his own son's concerns for Chie."

"She's his granddaughter."

"Familial relations with the Miyazaki are," he paused, seeking the right word, "complex. I believe Chie's father is truly worried about his daughter's well-being. Among other things." I tried to keep my expression blank when Ito said that. It was the tiniest end of a thread I might be able to pull on.

"But the old man?"

"The elder Miyazaki considers her an embarrassment and something of a lost cause."

"So why not simply cut off the money and let her drift?"

Ito was scanning the room, his eyes moving across the crowd with practiced efficiency. His body language told me there was nothing really to worry about. It was probably force of habit on his part. Or a stalling tactic used while he decided what to say to me.

"The old man would like to see her ... go away." He was feeling his way along in the conversation, no longer as comfortable as he had been at the beginning. His cadence had changed and the words came out more slowly, as if he were screening each utterance.

I lifted my eyebrows. "That has a sinister ring to it."

He looked at me. "Indeed? The old man comes from another time, when different methods were perhaps more acceptable." He moved his head to indicate Goro. "He surrounds himself with people who yearn for a return to a more," he paused yet again, and then smiled, "a more brutal simplicity."

"Goro's a headbreaker," I said. "I know the type. He likes it."

"He is useful. Nothing more. In this situation my government is concerned that Miyazaki Chie is recovered and reunited safely with her father. He is an important man and needs to regain focus on some critical issues. I will control the grandfather. And Goro."

Ito slid a large manila envelope across the table. "Funds as agreed upon. I have provided you with copies of the material we have collected on Lim. Background and contacts for Chie." He paused. "I have also included a USB drive with the electronic files of the correspondence and photos that have been sent to Miyazaki-san by his daughter." He looked down at his drink. "The fewer hard copies the better."

"What about the originals?"

"They were all sent electronically, Dr. Burke."

"That may give us a way to trace them."

"It may give *you* a way to trace them, Dr. Burke. I have been instructed to keep my distance from this operation." There was something in the tone of his voice that suggested irritation. But it was a faint note, subtly pitched, and it faded and was gone, swallowed in the hum of cocktail hour. I wondered about that hint of annoyance.

"And Goro," I smiled. "Will he keep a distance?"

Ito didn't smile back. "It would be very dangerous for us all if he did not."

I sat there, stone-faced. Two could play at this game. Finally Ito sighed. He took out a business card and a gold pen, and carefully inked out a phone number. "Your contact numbers are provided in the envelope, Dr. Burke. But in critical moments it might be best to go through different channels, agreed? My personal cell phone."

I didn't pick up the card. "Ito, what's the deal here? I'm not a complete idiot, you know. This all seems so convoluted. You people could pull some strings, get her tracked down and picked up. But you won't. Instead you want me to do it. At least some of you want me to. What the old man really wants is anybody's guess. And you. What's really your role here? What are you doing?"

He stood up. "I am doing what I can, Dr. Burke." He gestured and Goro moved away from the bar and headed toward the door. Ito watched him go. "*Kekki no yu wo imashimuru koto*," he said and looked at me. "Are you familiar with it?

"Guard against impetuous courage and refrain from violent behavior," I translated. It was part of the pledge recited at the end of every training session in Shotokan Karate.

"Indeed. Goro says the words, but I am not sure he truly accepts them."

"Like I said, he's a headbreaker," I added, shrugging.

Ito nodded. "Don't judge him too harshly, Dr. Burke. And don't underestimate him either." He moved away from the table but turned for one last comment. "Besides, were we so different when we were young?" He flashed a quick smile.

"You again," she said. She was as pale as ever, but sporting a new look: long, limp hair, dyed black with neon blue streaks. She still had the nose stud and I wondered whether it bubbled and leaked mucous when she had a cold. Fortunately, the question would remain a mystery. She seemed healthy enough at the moment, although undernourished. Librarians are often less than robust.

The university's map collection was state of the art and the special section where she worked was state of the art as well: good light, clusters of computer work stations with flat screens, and a smattering of well-stuffed modular furniture. The room was empty except for a student sprawled in a loveseat in a far corner of the room, his eyes closed and mouth sagging open. The quest for knowledge is exhausting.

"Hello, Ann." I used my winning smile, but she somehow resisted my charm. She had helped me out with a puzzle some time ago, working with me as I placed GPS coordinates on a map of the Southwest border territory. I'd been grateful for the help, but I hadn't seen her since. Standing in front of the blond wood of the reference desk, I realized this had been a mistake. She was now a dark wraith nursing a grudge.

I noticed there was a strand of fake evergreen garland arranged along the desk's edge and a small plastic candy cane scotch-taped to it in the very middle of the strand. I gestured at it. "I like what you've done with the place."

Her eyes betrayed a number of emotions, none of them

positive. I didn't remember what color they had been the last time I saw her, but now they were a striking blue. Probably contacts selected to match the highlights in her hair. This was the only hint of color in her gypsy-punk outfit. The little Christmas display seemed out of character for her, but perhaps there were hidden depths to Ann. The decorations were minimalist, but carefully placed. I shouldn't have been surprised at the symmetry of the desk ornament: she was, at heart, a librarian.

She eyed me skeptically, thinking of some response. "Christmas," she finally said, "is a crock."

Ann seemed definitive on that point, and I wasn't interested in debating it, so I explained to her that I needed some research done on the Miyazaki family. I gave her the general outline of the issues.

"Seems like a hairball," she said. "I mean, why get in the middle of a family thing?"

"The girl sounds screwed up."

Ann rolled her eyes. "Uh, yeah."

"The family's got some connection with Yamashita, my sensei. There's a debt of some kind owed."

"Like what?"

I shrugged. "They were vague."

Ann made a frown and touched the jeweled stud in her nose with the tip of a finger. Her nails were painted navy blue. She thought for a minute. "Why not ask your sensei about it?"

There was the real problem, I explained: if the story of the debt were true and I told Yamashita, he'd insist on helping. And he wasn't up to that. A lifetime of injuries sustained in and out of the dojo had taken their toll. He was too proud to admit it. And I cared for him too much to have him confronted with that fact.

"You're doing this just to satisfy a debt of honor?" Ann said, and her tone rang with the conviction that I was a fool and the concept of honor itself was obsolete.

"I'm doing it to protect Yamashita …"

"I hear an 'and' coming," she told me.

"I dunno," I said. "They seem so screwed up. The family. Maybe I can do something and help them out."

"Uh huh." Ann did not sound convinced. "Help out. The last little thing you went off on? In Arizona?"

"Yes?"

She crossed her arms and hugged herself. "It work out OK?"

I frowned. "I'm not really allowed to say." I suppose it had worked out: I was still standing. It's not much of a standard to judge things by, but at least it's concrete.

"Huh," she said, more a rush of air than a vocal expression. It might have been my imagination, but I could swear her nose stud whistled slightly.

"Come on, Ann."

"Why should I help?"

I looked around the sleepy room, my eyes wide. "Yeah. Easy to see why you wouldn't want a break from all the excitement."

"Funny." She was still skeptical.

"Look," I said and touched her lightly on the arm. "I don't have many people I can depend on." I let the statement hang in the air. Gave her my earnest look. Eventually, she gave me a small, grudging smile.

"OK," she said.

"Wait," I said, "there's more!" I used my TV pitchman voice and her reluctant smile got a little bigger.

I explained that I had an expense account courtesy of a mystery client, and this time, I could afford to pay her for her assistance. At that, the neon blue of her eyes seemed to glow with greater wattage.

"Still don't believe in Santa, little girl?" I teased.

Ann looked down at the information I had written out for her.

"Ho ho ho," she said.

It was growing dark outside, the air bluing into dusk. Artificial lights grew brighter, and yet details were hard to see. But I felt it. Not a tingle or a chill. Perhaps feeling isn't even the right word.

There had been something that registered on a subconscious level. It may have been the flash of a face in a crowd, something familiar, or something out of place. Eyes that should have washed over me but instead were looking intently. I don't know what it was. But I had learned to pay attention to these feelings.

In the days when I still thought I would eventually be some sort of college professor, Yamashita had frequently chided me for living too much in my head. He would sit in front of me after training, an implacable god in swordsman blue, critiquing my latest string of errors.

"Think less," he often told me. "*Be* more."

I sighed. I sighed often back then, especially when Yamashita went into his Master Yoda mode. It was particularly annoying because my teacher was always right.

If I've learned anything from him, it's that conscious thought is not the only way of knowing that is open to us. The mind can sometimes be an obstacle to seeing things clearly. In swordsmanship, we say too much thought makes you "stick": it slows down reaction time and interferes with accurate perception. A brain in overdrive can drown out the signals your other senses are trying to send to you.

And as he has aged, Yamashita has become acutely focused on developing in me the intuitive awareness of *haragei*. I work at the arcane exercises he has set for me, but I frequently despair of the effort. Still sometimes, in the slash and stomp of the dojo, time seems to slow down and I see the opponent before me with new eyes. It is as if the light has changed, and I am possessed of a strange acuity and ease of motion. There is no longer any sense of effort, no real awareness of self. Just the flow of breath and the arc of the sword's blade. At moments like that, I can't even feel the sensation of gripping the weapon. There are no hands, no arms, no Burke. Just the flow of the sword.

Then, of course, the sensation is gone and I'm left breathless with disappointment. And from across the dojo, my sensei's eyes bore into me, alive with knowing, aware of what I just experienced. *This is what we seek, Burke.*

Haragei: there was someone following me.

And that was a puzzle. If the initial efforts by the Japanese to find Chie Miyazaki had jangled Lim's nerves, he'd have people watching. It's possible someone tailed Ito and Goro to our rendezvous, but my experience was that the people from the Kunaicho were more competent than that. Ito hadn't picked anything up at the bar. And even if someone had tailed him there, it was highly unlikely there was more than one person and that the tail would abandon him in favor of me.

So here was a puzzle that needed solving. It meant I needed to take some time in my travels home to find out for certain if I was being followed. It was annoying, because I'm a pretty straight-line kind of person: when I go home, I simply go home. I like to think of it in terms of a Zen-like directness. My brother Mickey claims it's because I am, at heart, an uptight nerd. But now I needed to make things complicated: start and stop, wander uncertainly, window shop. With a tail, you try to string them out a bit, make them unsure of what you're up to. They get nervous when you change the distance between you and them. Slow down, and they do too. It makes them stand out in the New York crowd, chugging relentlessly along the cold sidewalks. Speed up and the tail has to break cover to hurry and catch up. Either way—busted.

The library was too thinly populated for a tail to risk coming in, so they must have lingered about at the entrance, waiting to pick me up. I hadn't registered anything consciously on the way in to see Ann, but now I was sure. As I threaded my way down the avenue, I could sense the focus of someone following me.

If the tail knew me, they would expect me to head home for Brooklyn, to go from Washington Square to the Eighth Street subway station. It was, in fact, my plan. But now that plan had changed. So I chugged uptown, an erratic pedestrian bobbing along the thickening crowds of rush hour. West on Fourteenth Street. North on Seventh Avenue. I was a real pain and more than one impatient person bumped me slightly in their haste. I spent a good ten blocks going at a steady if somewhat sedate pace. No window shopping or pausing now: a man on a mission. It would set up an expectation on the part of whoever was tailing me. They'd grow more comfortable with my predictable behavior.

The chestnut roasters were out at the entrance to Penn Station. It was a smell I always associated with the city in winter. I dove through the doors and threaded my way through the crowd at top speed. The floor was slippery, but I kept it up, heading for the lower concourse and the Long Island Railroad. A bend in the hallway would have put me briefly out of sight of my pursuer. I went faster, using the staircase instead of the elevators, and then jagged left toward track 18. The green panels were flickering and announcing the Babylon Express. People were flowing to the track entrance, a thick river of commuters overheating in their coats as they rushed to make the train. I stood to one side and looked to my right. A figure came pounding down the stairs toward the concourse. He stood out because he wasn't focused on a destination. Everyone else in that place was moving like a guided missile toward a target. But the man rushing down the stairs was looking all over the place, frantic to catch sight of me.

But I'd already seen what I needed to and I flowed along with the crowd, down to the train platform. I kept walking to the other end of the station, pushing my way up against the flow of homebound commuters. I left Penn on Eighth Avenue and walked across to Herald Square.

I caught the N back to Brooklyn.

If you ride the trains enough, the jolt and sway lulls you into a type of trance. The announcements come; the doors open and close. You hear the whine of the electric motor and the distant screech of the wheels as they take a curve in the tracks. People read, or nap, or stare off into the distance. Eye contact is frowned upon. It's almost soothing. Or it would be if the molded plastic seats were actually sized for an adult human being.

I thought about the situation. People follow you because you are doing something they want to know about. Ito was going to get a report on what I was doing. It made no sense for him to have someone follow me. Someone might also wish to tail me simply because they didn't trust me. But again, if Ito didn't trust me, why contact me in the first place?

The final option: Someone was keeping tabs on me so they would know what I was doing before Ito did. This meant things were a little more complex than they seemed.

The subway rattled through Brooklyn. I got off at Fifty-Ninth Street just for a change of pace. The Chinese would get off at the Eighth Avenue stop. The sights and sounds of the neighborhood were familiar and my feeling of being followed was gone. I had lost my tail back in Penn Station. I thought about the man on the stairs at Penn, frantically scanning the crowd in the train station. I smiled.

Goro, you impetuous devil.

CHAPTER 6

Burke. The voice was clear. Insistent. The sound rang in my head, tolling with strange clarity. A summons unbidden, jerking my eyes open and making my heart pound.

Darkness. I lay for a moment in bed, wondering. The voice comes to me, but I am never sure whose it is. It could be Yamashita's, or that of an old love. Perhaps it is a simple stirring of my conscience. But it comes in the tail end of the night, when the stars fade and the sleeping world begins to hum awake.

I rolled out of bed, the wood floor cold on my feet. I left the kitchen light off, working by feel as I set up the coffee. I like to be in the dark and sense the dawn slowly wash over me. The dining room is high ceilinged and I had emptied it of furniture a long time ago. There is a sword rack along the wall and two windows that open toward the sea. Across the tar-papered roof-tops of Brooklyn and the cement arc of the Gowanus Express-way, the lights on the top of Verrazano Bridge were still bright.

The day begins with discipline. Then coffee. I sank to the floor and stretched, warming my way through old injuries, loosening up muscles and a frozen shoulder joint. There was an early training session at the dojo, and I needed to be ready.

When I was done stretching, I held the coffee mug to my face; the steam played across my skin. I wondered about the voice that had awoken me. I wondered at my involvement with the Miyazaki family. Was it simple foolishness? Was I rational-izing by alleging I was trying to protect Yamashita? Before she left me, my old girlfriend Sarah Klein said there was a part of me that craved violence, and, no matter how hard I protested, I unconsciously put myself in dangerous situations. To prove something. Why I felt the need to do this and to whom I was proving it were probably questions for a good shrink, Sarah felt.

I wonder sometimes whether she was right. I'd been laboring for years at my art and it had gradually displaced almost everything else in my life. I like to think it has been worth it: it's brought me new skills and new insights about myself. But if it has made my vision clearer, what I see has not always been what I expected. And the discipline is relentless, the training never ending. I slog along, and on good days I am sure I can glimpse something wonderful in the distance. On bad days, I wonder about myself. I remember my brother Mickey's dismissive comment: "You're a grown man who spends his time dancing around in pajamas for Chrissake!"

I wondered whether I had drunk too much of the martial arts Kool-Aid. Who was I to think I could help someone like Chie Miyazaki? I'm a specialist in exotic etiquette and archaic weapons. The Miyazaki family seemed to me to have a number of needs, but I don't think martial arts training was one of them.

But I had said I'd help them. In the end, it was as simple as that. Motivation is a murky thing. I've come to prefer the clarity of action. I finished my coffee. Outside my windows, the world shrugged off darkness. I decided I would too.

He came for me later that morning. "I am Alejandro. From Don Osorio." Alejandro wore a grey overcoat and a silk scarf. His shoes were shined and his hair was recently cut. He was thin, and his ears stuck out, making him appear almost boyish.

But he moved with an efficient self-confidence that hinted at a life of experience. You had to wonder about that, but I couldn't dwell on it. I had asked for help and didn't get to choose the form it would take.

I'm not a trained investigator, but I know the basics. You start at the beginning. You check the scene. You go over the backgrounds of suspects. Some of the information had already been provided to me. But not enough. I had, for instance, asked Ito whether I could see Chie's apartment. But he had been dismissive. It was not necessary, he explained, since members of his staff had already done so and found little that was helpful. Or unexpected. No concrete clues about her whereabouts. Just the detritus of a messy life. Perhaps, I speculated, an extensive lingerie collection.

Maybe Ito's refusal to let me see the apartment was part of the Miyazaki doing some damage control on public awareness of their wild child. But I didn't get it. I had already been let in on their little secret. Life is filled with rocks, however, and I've learned some can be moved, while some are simply things to flow around. I was beginning to feel the Miyazaki were trying to steer me. I didn't know why. But I've made wandering off in unexpected directions a life's work. No reason to change now. *Flow*.

Alejandro and I drove from the dojo in Red Hook, across the bridge into Manhattan. "This man, Lim," he began. "He's got a number of places he stays, which is not surprising. It's always wise to have several places to crash or hide out." Alejandro sounded like someone speaking from personal experience. "But he keeps one place, an apartment, just for himself. He never takes his crew there. He never even brings his girlfriend there. I think this is really interesting." Alejandro turned his head to look at me, his brown eyes liquid. "I had the opportunity to ask some of his associates about this. Many claimed not to know the apartment existed."

"How did you find it, then?"

A hint of a smile. "I am a persistent questioner, Dr. Burke. It is why Don Osorio employs me."

We eventually pulled up in front of an apartment building on the Lower East Side. My guide double-parked and we went to see the building superintendent.

The man opened the door, looking at us with a face that was grey from exhaustion. Alejandro had a brief, quiet conversation in Spanish. The man looked at me with suspicion, then nodded at Alejandro in resignation. He shrugged his way into a worn canvas work jacket and grabbed a huge ring of keys.

We walked up one flight and down a hall. There was the faint sound of a distant TV playing somewhere, but the hallway was empty and the place was quiet. The walls were freshly painted and the industrial carpet muffled our steps. The super sifted his key collection, selected one, and unlocked a door. He nodded once at Alejandro, ignored me, and shambled back downstairs.

"Here you are," Alejandro said, and pushed the door open.

I nodded. "Yes. But where exactly is here?"

"Lim's apartment," he answered.

"How'd you get the super to let us in?"

He shrugged. "Don Osorio requested his cooperation."

"Just like that?"

He smiled a full smile this time. Alejandro had very white and very even teeth. "*Sí.*" Suddenly he had a small automatic pistol in his hand. He motioned for me to wait, slipped into the apartment, then came out. "It's empty. I'll wait by the car. Take your time. But hurry up, if you know what I mean."

The apartment was not what I expected. It was a one-bedroom place with modern furniture and understated decorations. I had a hard time reconciling it with the punk drug dealer who had been portrayed to me. In the photos I had seen, he had been smoking. But there was no odor of tobacco in the apartment.

A tiny foyer opened on to the living/dining room. There was a coffee table with some ski magazines. A side table was piled with copies of the *Times* and *Wall Street Journal* from a few weeks back. One wall was lined with books, most of them involved with politics, economics, and history. I saw Karl Marx, but Immanuel Wallerstein was there as well. So was Braudel. And the three volumes of the life of *Theodore Roosevelt* by Edmund Morris. Lim appeared to be an eclectic, if serious reader. And he was disturbingly neat for a lowlife. The place was clean: no crack pipes or ashtrays filled with roaches. There was a galley kitchen. No dishes in the sink. The fridge was stocked with real food. At the end of the hall leading off the foyer was the bathroom. To the right was the bedroom.

I was at a loss as to what to look for. My preference would have been a note lying around that was entitled "Places I will take Chie Miyazaki." No go. I peeked around and rifled through the drawers. Nothing. There were men's clothes hanging in the bedroom closet. There was a duffle bag on the floor. I opened it up: a clean martial arts uniform with the black piping of a taekwondo enthusiast.

So. He cleans. He reads. He doesn't smoke at home. He works out. Lim's public persona wasn't fitting with his private one. And that was interesting.

A laptop computer sat on top of a desk in the bedroom,

neatly placed in the center of the work surface. It was already open and when I hit the "Enter" key, the computer woke up. The screen showed four different camera shots of the apartment. In one of them, you could see my back as I peered into the screen. *Shit.* I was blown. I folded the computer screen down, and headed out of the bedroom. Right into the arms of an angry stranger.

I never heard the apartment door open. He was that good. Probably the only reason he didn't try to kill me right off was that the narrow hallway we were standing in constricted his range of motion.

Not that he didn't try to kill me, of course. He tried hard. A sudden attack at this level of lethality is often paralyzing: the force of the blows, the sudden shock as the body's nerve endings shriek danger and the system is flooded with adrenalin. All these elements work to stun the mind and freeze the untrained into momentary stillness. Which is when you are finished off.

But Yamashita has changed me. In times like this, I don't rely on the mind; it's all body think instead. It's the only way you have a chance of surviving. Thought is too slow. You need something faster because you're back in the jungle now, in a place where it's all heat and hate and the mad scramble for survival.

Jesus.

It wasn't Lim. I didn't recognize the man, but that fact was fleeting and irrelevant, an idea that flashed and was gone. I had bigger concerns. He came at me like a pile driver, a fist driving for the plexus to stop my breathing and a knife-hand blow chopping at my clavicle. It's an easy bone to break, and it renders your arm effectively useless if the attack truly hits home. I got my hands up to take the first shock of the attack, and worked at deflecting the succession of strikes that followed. I pivoted, ramming my back against the wall and letting his momentum carry him through the attack zone. But he was good and didn't overcommit. His head turned precisely and he drove an elbow strike at my face. *Move!* You've got to keep shifting with someone like this, altering the target profile and changing angles and distance.

I slammed my knee into the side of his thigh, but I was dodging left to get away from the elbow strike as I did it, and the blow wasn't solid. I gave him a short left to the ribs, then tried to get my right fist into play. But the narrowness of the hall was constraining us both. We hammered and grunted around. We were wearing winter coats and they absorbed some of the force. It meant I had to work on attacking his head instead of the body, but that was like beating at a bowling ball. I slapped a palm into his ear and saw him wince in pain, but I don't think I broke his eardrum. He pivoted around on me and I got my first good look at him: square face and slit eyed, black shaggy hair. One of Lim's people. Young. Strong. Well trained.

I hate them like that.

He took a shuffling half step forward and then unleashed a wicked snap kick. I jerked back just out of range, but staggered a little.

He was on me then. I saw his eyes light up like some cyborg acquiring target lock. He thought he was closing in for the kill while I was off balance.

But it's an old trick. I've seen Yamashita use it many times to suck in the unwary. He'd done it to me. More than once. And now I'm older and craftier. Meaner. I've learned my lessons. And I was about to teach this guy some of them.

I wasn't as off-balance as I seemed. I just wanted to bring

him close to me. I'd been lucky to have dodged his first few attacks, but I could tell this guy was a hitter. There's a distinctive quality to the strikes of someone who's really proficient: tight solidity, wild speed. This guy had it. In a few short seconds he'd pummeled me good. I knew something had to give soon. If I gave him the opportunity, he'd put my lights out.

As he closed the distance between us, I reached out for his coat lapels, and slid down and under his forward momentum. I got my foot up into his stomach and executed what I thought was a pretty good *tomoe-nage*, all things considered, landing on my back and propelling him over me and down the hall. If you use your arms just right, you can put a little English on the fall, accelerating the impact. So I did, and when he hit the floor, a few pictures rattled right off the wall.

But it wasn't enough. The fall hadn't stunned him. I scrambled upright but he had already gotten to his feet, shaking his thick head to clear it. In about a second, he was going to come at me again. I would have run, but he was between me and the door.

There was a blur of motion behind him. Over his shoulder, I saw Alejandro slip in and, with a short, precise motion, slam a lead-weighted cosh down on the attacker's head. The guy's eyes rolled up and he collapsed in a heap.

We stood for a moment, looking at the body. "I coulda taken him," I protested. It would have sounded more convincing if my breath weren't so raspy.

"*Claro*," Alejandro said, and bent down to rifle through my attacker's pockets. He came up with a small cell phone, a wallet, and a passport. He emptied the wallet of its money, shoved the bills into his pocket, and handed me the passport and phone.

The man on the floor moaned.

"At least he's not dead," I said.

Alejandro looked at me with a hurt look. "Of course he's not dead. Give me some credit. I didn't mean to kill him."

"I think we should go," I said. I looked around, waiting for my breath to slow and my brain to come back on line. It reminded me of something. "But wait. Let me get Lim's computer."

"Hurry up," he said. "When this guy comes to, he's going to be angry."

I rubbed my arms: I could feel the bruises rising from where the man on the floor had slammed me. "Alejandro," I said, "that would be way too much excitement for one day."

The passport we had taken was blue with gilt lettering: the blocky rows of Hangul characters and the legend "The Democratic People's Republic of Korea." There was some complicated seal on the front with a shining star radiating something. Maybe it was meant to symbolize the affection of the Young Leader bathing his subjects in fatherly warmth. Then again, maybe it was just a plutonium leak.

No matter. The North Koreans. *Not good*.

"ISTG, Collins," the voice on the phone said. The tone was all business.

I stood outside on the corner of Fifty-Ninth and Tenth Avenue. "Owen? It's Connor Burke. Let me in, will you?"

John Jay College is awash with students coming in and out, but I knew I'd need an escort to get into the Institute for the Study of Terrorist Groups. Owen Collins was going to be my ticket in.

A few minutes later he bounded out the door, big and broad

and smiling. He was one of the better of a crop of young kendo students I had worked with at a seminar some time ago. Thick neck, square head with deep copper-colored hair. He had hands like catcher's mitts. When you sparred with him and he did the head strike known as the *men-uchi* cut, it felt like he was driving a nail into your brain.

I gave him a quick rundown of what I needed. I avoided mentioning my recent breaking-and-entering activities with Alejandro. Owen's a good guy, and he's working on a doctorate in criminal justice. He might feel somehow compelled to protest if I implicated him in a crime. But he pretty much saw right through me.

"So," he said. "You're working on a missing persons case and this laptop might have some clues?" I nodded. But his eyes were suspicious. "I don't suppose I need to ask how you got hold of it?"

I shrugged. "It's her boyfriend's."

"You take it from him?"

"No." *Not exactly.*

He could hear the evasion in my voice. "Is she in danger?" he asked.

"I think so," I said. At least that was honest.

Owen looked around. "You know, there's something called the affirmative defense of necessity …" I looked blankly at him, and he sighed. "It means sometimes you might do a bad thing to prevent something worse."

"Does it work? As a defense, I mean."

Owen smiled. "Depends on the jury. If things get that far." He turned back toward the building. He'd gotten even bigger and broader since the last time I'd seen him. Any larger and he'd start to blot out the sun. "Come on," he said. "I've got an 'in' with the computer forensics people."

For a big man, Owen's movements were precise, and he approached the examination of Lim's computer with fastidious professionalism. We sat in a small office ringed with computer screens and wires and various types of gear. Small diode lights glowed green or red. He set the laptop down in the center of the desk. He didn't open it. He didn't touch it any more than he needed to. He quietly asked me what I knew about it. I told him about the screen shots that appeared to indicate it was running a surveillance program.

Owen nodded and slipped a piece of chewing gum into his mouth. He stood up and flicked a few switches, then ran a USB cable from a wall unit toward Lim's computer. He took a breath.

"OK," he told me, "let's see what's up with this puppy." He was moving quickly at this point. He connected Lim's laptop to the cable and typed some commands on a keyboard unit connected to a grey box. A display popped up on a flat screen.

"What's that?"

"Solo-4 Forensic Capture Unit," he said. But he didn't stop working. Owen lifted the laptop's screen upright and the sleeping computer blinked on. Owen grunted, removed the gum from his mouth, and stuck it over something along the screen edge. "Built-in camera here," he grunted. "Now the machine is blind."

There was whirring. Owen watched his own computer's screen and the displays from the Solo-4. His eyes shifted to Lim's laptop, noting that the drive unit light was flickering. "Come on," he whispered, his eyes tracking back and forth from one screen to another.

"What's happening?"

He held up a hand. "Shhh."

I heard the CD drive start spinning on the laptop. Owen's eyes were locked on the progress bar on his flat screen monitor. "Yes!" he breathed. He severed the USB cord connection. Lim's computer was growling with activity.

"What did you do to it?" I asked.

"Nothing." He swiveled his chair over to the laptop, tapped some keys, and grunted. "Slick," he said. "Someone's logged on remotely. They're wiping the memory on the laptop." He saw the look on my face. "Don't worry. I mirrored the drive." He gestured toward the flat screen display. "We've got an exact replica. And now …" Owen slid over to his computer and began tapping. A rapid succession of windows opened and closed. Lines of text scrolled down the screen. It went on for some time, and I began to lose interest. Finally, he shoved himself back from the keyboard, a satisfied grin on his face.

"OK. I've disabled the security measures. They had a few nice touches: an open-source antitheft client named Adeona. A remote webcam security application …"

"That's what I saw?"

He nodded. "Something called Yoics. It's a bit complicated to install, but it can stream images from a webcam to a remote location and store the images on the home computer drive. Whoever set this one up did a nice job. They had a motion sensor feature installed, and when it's triggered, it sends an email notification along with the image."

I thought of how the attacker at Lim's apartment had appeared so unexpectedly. "Can you find out where it was sent?"

Owen nodded thoughtfully. "Sure. There's a logs and auditing function on the data capture unit. May take some time, but

I can do it."

"That might be important," I told him. Then I had another thought. "Could the messages have been sent to more than one location?"

"Sure," he said, shrugging. "But it's going to take more time to figure out than we have right now. The forensics guys aren't crazy about people playing with their toys."

"But you can do it, right?"

Again the shrug. "Sure. Whattaya have in mind?"

At that moment, I had ideas rushing around so fast that they felt like they were polishing the inside of my skull. It was a wild flock of hints and suppositions and questions. But I could sense that the swirling was beginning to take on a pattern.

I looked at Owen and smiled. "You and I are going to have dinner with a map librarian."

CHAPTER 7

Voices again. Distant chanting like the murmur of disgruntled ghosts. I sat in the stillness of the Zen master's office, awaiting his arrival. I looked out the window at a line of pines along the hilltop, a dark smudge amid the grey-blue of hardwood trees that stood, cold and empty-armed, in the winter afternoon. I shivered.

Another dawn and the internal call had come to me again. The bell-like chime of warning. It wasn't simply the effect of the information I had gleaned or the suspicions that were developing. The summons·was too clear for me to deny it any further. I hurried through the day's teaching, turned the dojo over to a senior student for the evening class, and began the trip north out of the city just ahead of rush hour.

I had to see Yamashita.

The *roshi*, the master of the monastery, arrived in a bustle of robes and a flurry of apologies. I could feel the cold streaming off his clothing. He had been outside, brushing the latest dusting of snow from the slate steps leading to a garden.

James Seki Roshi was somewhere in his sixties, a tall man with broad shoulders, bushy eyebrows, a shaved head, and a long face that got longer when he smiled. He smiled often.

"Connor," he said, beaming and reaching out to hug me. The roshi was notoriously exuberant and was famous for his laughing question: "How can we embrace dharma if we are afraid to embrace each other?" Over the years, as Yamashita has spent more and more time at the monastery, the roshi and I had nurtured a friendship based on our mutual concern for my sensei. Now, he settled me in a chair and plugged in an electric kettle to brew tea.

"No coffee, I'm afraid," he apologized. He usually teased me about this when I came for a visit.

I waived the inconvenience away. "I had a cup on the road," I said, "but it must be hard on Yamashita."

The roshi cocked his head. "It's funny, sometimes, how it's the little attachments that are hardest to give up. I, for instance, crave pretzels."

"So the origin of suffering is … pretzels?" I joked. The second truth of Buddhism is that attachment leads to suffering. But the roshi knew himself well enough not to take offense.

"The human gift for creating attachment is both a blessing and a curse, as you know, Connor." His expression was still pleasant, but his eyes were serious. He was watching me.

How do they do it? How do they get inside you like that? Is it intuition? Perception? Luck? I wasn't sure, but I felt my face flush with the implications of the roshi's seemingly offhand comment. It was as if he had some knowledge of what I was involved in.

"How is he?" I asked.

A slow nod. "At peace, I think. You'd think it would be otherwise."

I gave him a questioning look.

"For someone like your teacher, age is often not welcomed. And, truth be told, he continues to insist on sword practice. It's hard on him, because he knows his skills are going …"

I thought about the familiar feel of a practice sword in my hands, the comforting warmth of used muscles. What would it be like when your hands grow stiff and your body forgets? "It's a big part of our life," I acknowledged.

"Yes. But if your sensei is not willing to totally give it up…" he paused to correct himself, to find the right words and smiled as he found them. "If he is not mellowing, he is nonetheless seeking wisdom in new ways." The kettle's bell rang and the roshi poured water into a ceramic teapot. He looked up at me from under those bushy eyebrows. "A life of such discipline has its benefits, after all. He is a fierce student of the dharma."

I smiled at the mental image the roshi had conjured up of a swordsman in the meditation hall. Yamashita would be fierce, no matter what he was doing.

The priest settled into his own chair and waited in silence, seemingly content to let the tea steep. His lips were closed in a small half-smile. But his eyes never left me. After a time, I stirred.

"Can I see him?"

The roshi reached out and poured carefully, the pale liquid gurgling into small, handleless cups. "Unfortunately," he began, "your teacher has entered a period of meditative seclusion. A *seigan*."

Seigan—vow training. I knew the concept. It meant Yamashita had committed himself to a retreat that could not be interrupted except under the direst circumstances. I sagged back into my chair, and a long breath seeped out of me in frustration.

"I really need to see him," I said. I felt like a kid wheedling at a parent.

He nodded. "I am sure. And you will see him. At the end of the *seigan* in three days' time." The roshi regarded me for a moment, noting my disappointment. "You know, Connor, part of what I do sometimes is to set uncomfortable boundaries for people. But it's for a good reason."

I still wanted to see Yamashita. But the roshi had said no. I looked at him, sitting there, calm, certain, unwavering. I wondered what effort and what pain must have filled his life to bring him to this point. I wondered if I'd ever have the courage to replicate that effort. And then I buckled under the sheer force of the man, knowing he was right and I was wrong.

We sat for a time in the quiet of his study. I sipped at my cup of tea, but it had grown cold and bitter.

Finally, he spoke. "You understand?"

"I do." It sounded like a sigh.

"Good. It's more than I can say for yesterday's visitor."

He caught me off guard with that comment. "What do you mean?"

His eyes crinkled. "It's been a busy week here. Two men, arriving one after the other, both wanting to see the same broken down old martial arts sensei."

I set the cup down on the table between us, sitting forward. "Someone else came?"

The roshi nodded. "He was a young Japanese man. He said his name was Makiyama. He claimed to be from the Japanese consulate. But I'm not really sure I believed him."

"What did he want?"

"To see Yamashita Sensei. He claimed he had important information for him." The roshi stood up, arranging his robes. He walked over to the window and stared out at the darkening woods. "I told him your sensei was unavailable." He grimaced at the memory. "He was very upset with me." A shrug. "It is not unusual for someone like that. The anger." He turned to face me. "I thought at one point he might actually hit me, Connor."

He said this with fascination, not fear, like a man examining a new, curious thing.

"What happened?"

"Oh," he said, "the impetuous are often as easily pacified as they are excited. I managed to calm him down. Assured him I would deliver whatever message he brought. But it would have to wait until the *seigan* had ended." The roshi walked over to a bookcase and slipped a slim package from between some books. "It is here. He made me promise to deliver it as soon as possible."

The word impetuous clinched it for me. I described Goro, the Miyazaki henchman, to the roshi. "Could that have been the man?"

He nodded. "You describe him well, Connor. You have a knack for observation."

I shrugged. "I know the type."

"And is he a representative from the consulate?"

"Not exactly," I began.

The roshi's eyebrows came up in interest. He gestured back to the chairs. "Ha! I knew it." He smiled in triumph. "But how interesting. Perhaps you'd like to tell me more?"

So I did.

By the time I was done, night had blanketed the distant hills and the roshi moved around the room, switching on lights as he thought through the details of my story. The lights came on in slow succession, shedding a soft, warm glow that was a welcome counter to the cold rattle of the wind outside. "You are going to find this woman for them?" he asked. He sounded surprised.

"I am," I said. But he caught the reservation in my voice and smiled.

"You have something up your sleeve, don't you, Connor?"

I shrugged. "Why not? I get the sense they're not playing fair with me. Besides, she sounds like she needs some help."

"Yes. And I'm not sure her family sounds like a good place to get it."

"True. But there have to be some other options. You've got to admit she's screwed up. The drugs. The nymphomania …"

He leaned forward. "In my previous life I was a therapist. Did you know that?"

I shook my head. "What happened?"

The roshi smiled, the long jaw dropping and the eyes crinkling. "I don't know. I suppose I found out that looking for explanations was not the same thing as looking for meaning." He stood up and began to pace the room, his fingers working on a string of *mala*, the prayer beads Buddhists use to keep track of the repetition of sutras. The beads clicked rhythmically as he fingered them.

"They don't usually refer to it as nymphomania anymore, you know," he began. "Now I think it's called 'hypersexuality' in the professional literature."

"Does it make a difference?"

He looked up. "Not to the people afflicted." He slowed down and closed his eyes. "It's a compulsive disorder. An obsession."

"Attachment again," I ventured.

He nodded, eyes still closed. "Indeed. The possible causes are many: chemical imbalances in the brain, hormonal, or neural issues. It's commonly associated with a history of drug problems as well as abuse."

"Physical? Sexual?"

The roshi sighed. "Either. Both. Sometimes the history of

abuse can create a dynamic where the distinction between sex and affection becomes blurred. In those cases, the sufferer conceives of sex as the only way to create and sustain relationships. It's not about pleasure anymore. It becomes a compulsion, since it's the only way you know of to relate to people in an intimate way."

I had a distant memory of things I'd read by Freud. "In some ways, it's like a case of arrested development."

He nodded. "In some ways, yes. The complex range of emotional relationships available to a normal adult is not available to someone like this."

"But the physical capacity is."

"Precisely. A fully adult body. And the sex act is used as a way to ensure affection. Acceptance."

I considered what I knew of Chie's history. "I always thought of promiscuity as a type of rebellion."

The roshi opened his eyes. "Perhaps yes. Perhaps no. Perhaps both."

"How very Zen of you."

He smiled tightly. "Yes. But, really, this condition is not so simple. It's possible that Chie exhibits hypersexuality as a type of rebellion at the same time that she uses it for acceptance, to create the sort of emotional bond she desperately needed and never received in the past." He sat down again.

"She needs help," I said. "Probably more than I can give."

The roshi tilted his head and thought for a minute. "If you find her, what will you do?"

"I don't think she needs to be back with her family," I told him, "but I don't think her boyfriend's doing her any favors either."

"And you see yourself as a third alternative?"

I shrugged. "I haven't gotten that far." The roshi's look of disappointment told me I should have. I looked down at my hands. "In the beginning, I just wanted them to leave Yamashita alone. It was a debt of some kind that needed paying."

"And you would pay it for him?"

"Of course."

"But what has changed now?"

I picked my way carefully through my thoughts. The memory of the surreal sound of Yamashita's psychic summons still pealed in my head. But I was hesitant to speak of it to the roshi. "I dunno," I began evasively. "Nothing in some ways. But there's the sense that there's more here than meets the eye. That I'm getting played ..."

"And?" he prompted, leaning forward.

"Well," I finally said, "I don't like that. It seems to me a call to honor should be respected. I feel ..." I shrugged. "Insulted."

He leaned back and regarded me. "You've grown more Japanese than you know, Connor." He looked over at his bookcase, a casual glance like a man admiring his reading collection. His movements were slow and his voice was almost soothing. It belied the seriousness of the conversation.

"Is that all that's going on here?" he prompted, his head still turned away from me.

I fidgeted. "No, I suppose not."

"Ah," he said, nodding, his attention back on me. I could see the shadow of the therapist he had been. He waited in silence and I continued.

"Well, she's not a package is she? She's a person. A screwed-up person who maybe needs some help."

"And you can offer her what, exactly?"

I laughed silently. "I can get her out of the clutches of the creep she's with. That's for sure. Get her away somewhere where she can think."

"The knight errant storming a castle and saving the fair damsel?" His face wore a smile, but the words were pointed enough.

"Maybe get her to a place where she can ask herself what she really wants," I offered.

"Ah," he sat back in his chair. "Compassion. This is good. In Buddhism, we often say there are two important qualities to develop. One is wisdom. The other is compassion." The roshi stood up and went again to the bookcase, where Goro's packet lay. "I am not sure your getting involved in this situation is terribly wise, Connor." He turned to me, peering out from under his eyebrows. "But who am I to argue with the urgings of compassion?"

He gestured to the dark window. "Come. You'll spend the night as our guest. Perhaps you'll think more about this little mystery you've involved yourself in." I followed after him down a hall and upstairs to the dormitory. "Think about desire, Connor. About the things we want. Of the people we wish to please. Of those we wish to help. How the things that bind us together can also hurt us."

"Are you talking about Chie?"

Again the enigmatic smile. "Yes. And no."

I stopped suddenly in the hallway, holding a hand to my ear. "Hey," I said with some urgency. "Did you hear that?"

"What?"

I smiled at him. "The sound of one hand clapping." It formed a part of one of the more famous Zen sayings: *What is the sound of one hand clapping?*

"Very funny," the roshi said. "But seriously. Think on these things." He pushed open a door and ushered me into a spartan bedroom. "If you manage to find Chie, I may be able to help in some way. I know some people who could perhaps work with her on her issues." I nodded. Then the roshi drew something from the deep folds of his robe and placed it in my hands: Goro's package. I looked at him in surprise.

"Perhaps some reading will assist you in your reflections," he said.

"I thought you promised to deliver this to Yamashita Sensei."

He stood up a little straighter. "So I did. In three days. But I did not say what I would do with it before that time." He turned and started down the hushed corridor. His sandals whispered against the floor. His voice was ghost soft. "Goodnight, Connor."

And there in a monk's chamber, I opened the package and began reading.

CHAPTER 8

The book Goro had delivered to the roshi was a small one, one filled with neat, precise characters. It was a journal of sorts, a diary. And a last testament. The final page bore the seal and signature of the author, and a chill staggered up along my shoulders and neck when I saw the name: Mori.

He was a figure from Yamashita's past. They had trained together and served the Kunaicho years ago. My master had turned away from those memories with an iron resolution, and this part of his life was never spoken of. I can't know for sure, but I suspect he had traveled all the way to America to put that time behind him. Mori had never left the service of the Imperial House, and the intrigue that swirled around him eventually snared us in its grasp. I had seen Mori breathe his last as an operation he was running in the Philippines went spinning out of control. It had almost killed me and it left Yamashita in the diminished condition he struggled with today. I touched the book gingerly. I felt that even Mori's words could be toxic. I feared whatever impulse animated the text in my hands.

A small sheet of paper was inserted into the front of the book. A chill went through me as I felt the strength of Mori's connection to Yamashita. *This psychic thing could really be a nuisance.*

But I read it.

It pleases me to have finished the tale, to see the characters lining these pages like leaves carpeting the forest as winter comes on. And if you are reading it, Rinsuke, I am gone.

That pleases me too, for then I am beyond worry and free of the tangle of cares that filled my life. Understand: I have no regrets. Just relief. I have returned to the Void, a drop mingling in the immensity of the sea.

But one last story, a final spark before I am extinguished and night swallows me. I have lived too long with secrets and have seen too many of them taken to the grave. You already know part of this tale; the remainder is something I should have shared with you long ago.

Forgive me.

Or not. For by the time you read this I am beyond either scorn or approval. I have lived a life weighed down by duty, but am now as light as a feather.

—*Mori*

Mori's Journal

You came north, a promising student with the right connections. But I think the dojo was not what you expected. The winter is long in Hokkaido—the weather bites and the heavens have no mercy. I suspect that is why the old man chose to live there. He was as cold and hard as the land itself.

Takano Sho was the best swordsman of his time, a compact man with a square head and a wide, tight mouth. It was perfect for expressing displeasure. His hands were hard and his blunt fingers could grind down and find a nerve point in a way that stopped your breath. Training with him was a type of fearful revelation. In my first few years there, he stalked me even in my dreams. But he knew things, that one. And if you could stand him, if you could endure the casual brutality and endless barbs of criticism, he could polish you into something special. We all knew that. It was why we were there.

You arrived that day in 1960, eighteen years old and already marked as one with great potential. But so were we all. Nobody crossed the threshold of the dojo without this pedigree. I stood with the other students and watched you in silence. We saw the rolled-up judogi, tattered and supple from countless matches. Saw the yudansha's black belt that was wrapped around the bundle. Noted as well your thick neck and the arms strung with muscles like heavy cables. You knelt before Takano and proffered your letters of introduction. He glanced at them briefly, then tossed them to one side with contempt. The master glared at you. Then he reached out and snared one of your hands, turning it over and examining the calluses. He followed the old ways, and read hands in the same way he read faces. It was an old skill, one among many he pursued. Takano pored over the ancient scrolls, questing after arts lost centuries ago. He was forever hungry for this kind of mysterious knowledge, never satisfied. He sought more skill. More power. I think sometimes he used us like you would use monkeys in a laboratory: he tested theories on our flesh. And he was peering into the folds and creases of your hand that day, convinced he had the power to see into your soul.

Did you shiver at the experience? In my first year there, Takano terrified me in ways I had never experienced before. It wasn't simply his skill or his power, although they were overwhelming enough. When exposed to the full energy of his focus, I felt a cold, furious probing of my very essence. It was as if he were going to try to reach down and draw the life out of me.

Did you feel it that first day? The sheer, primal power of the man? If so, you gave no sign. You sat like a rock, silent under his gaze. His eyes narrowed and then his wide mouth opened slightly in a cruel grin. He had small uneven teeth, and the smile made him look even more fearsome, like some unpredictable, hungry animal.

Takano rose to his feet and gestured you up. No sooner

had you stood, then he swept you off your feet and down to the floor. When the old man threw you, he never held back. Each time, he executed a flawless technique that was beautiful to watch. Until, of course, the victim crashed down. Takano was never satisfied with the mere act of throwing; for him, the very floor was a weapon. He used it as a striking surface to pound his victims with.

You crashed to the floor and the room shook with the force of the impact. You rolled to your feet and faced him again.

He attacked once more. I saw the momentary pause in the action as you resisted and began a counter, but he flowed around your attack and drove you down. All the students watched. Our faces were rigid, but we all winced inside as we each remembered our own welcome to the dojo.

The third attack. There was a moment there when I thought you actually had Takano beaten. I saw a doubt flash across his face, but then his mouth tightened in a cruel line and he rocketed you down for a final time.

He turned his back on you as you stood up. Then he wheeled around and sat once more.

"At least," he grated, "you can fall down." He scanned the line of silently watching students. "Mori," he called, and I scampered to the front of the dojo, bowing.

"Mori," Takano said. "This is Yamashita Rinsuke. He may have some promise. You will be his sempai."

And that was how we met, with the old man making me your sempai, your senior, your special training partner. Such a long time ago, Rinsuke. We bowed to each other, our hair still black and our eyes not as guarded as they would later become. Did you wonder what you were in for at that moment? A hint was not long in coming.

"Mori," Takano said, his voice harsh like a hawser grating

on a rock, "see if you can break him."

What do you recall of those first months? When I think back, there is the memory of sweat, the unyielding surface of the dojo floor. Or the sensations of cold and wet, the smell of damp earth and pine. A place of extremes, Rinsuke. Comfort snatched in brief, furtive moments. But mostly, there is the memory of that old man, the bark of his commands and the fierce eyes that missed nothing. It was a hard place, designed to break the weak. Even those of us who endured were never the same.

We had all been tested before, of course; otherwise, we never would have been accepted as uchi deshi, live-in students. To be accepted as such by the old demon was an honor in itself. It was said in his youth he had bested all comers. He was a peerless fighter. Sword, staff, spear—it was all one to him. Take away his weapons and his broad, thick hands reached for you like claws. It was a peculiar genius, as if he were born with the memory of the old ways roaring in his blood. And we came in the hope that he would share some of this with us.

Thirty years before you or I laid eyes on him, he had been a restless youth. He loved the rough and tumble of the dojo, but yearned to make his mark upon the world. He had a good head for numbers and tried clerking. But he chafed at being tied to a desk. He taught for a time in a temple school, but he lacked the patience. Finally, he enlisted in the army and was sent to Manchuria. It was known as Manchukuo then, part of the expanding colonies of the emperor. This was before the dreams of empire began to unravel, shriveled to ash in carpet bombing, or bled white on distant Pacific atolls. This was a heady time, when our country was filled with a sense of new power and limitless ambition. In time, we learned otherwise. It was a brutal reckoning.

The old man took to military life and marched across the vastness of Manchukuo, one soldier among many in puttees and dusty tunics. Even then, he had been a noted fighter, and eventually became a sergeant. But one day, an event changed him. He was never the same. Some said it unhinged him, others that it opened a new plane of perception. I wager that both views were right.

He was at the head of a patrol, winding down a narrow canyon. The bandits, ranged out along both sides of the ravine's walls, sprung the trap. The crossfire was withering. Soldiers scurried behind what cover they could find while the bullets cracked through the air and snapped at the rocks, seeming to come from every direction. Sounds bounced back and forth in the canyon. The bandits stayed well hidden. A man would seek cover, peering out from behind a rock, only to be taken by rifle fire from another direction. The old man knew to remain in that place was not an option; the only route to safety was the offensive. He called to his men, trying to rally them. Yet they hunkered down, terrified of the crossfire. The old man stood, enraged, firing at the unseen enemy, cursing his own men.

And then, as later he explained, it was as if time slowed down. The whine of ricochets and the screams of soldiers seemed to fade into an all-pervading hum. And as he cast about, he began to see the air shimmer with the pulsing arc of bullets. He could see the rifle fire, he claimed. Knew where it was coming from and where it was going. He stood, silent and amazed in the blazing sun. He saw the flowering of a muzzle blast and a bullet ooze across space toward him. Like a man in a dream, he watched the projectile come toward him, growing larger until the blurred ocean of noise around him grew sharp and immediate again. He ducked and the bullet whined away.

His men watched him twist and whirl across the field. He grunted and foamed at the mouth like a man in the grips of madness, but he aimed and fired, reloaded and fired again. He made his way gradually up the canyon wall and, one by one, his soldiers followed in his path. He crested the slope ahead of them and was lost from sight. Then the screaming began.

In the end, they lost half of the patrol, most of them cut down on the canyon floor. But on that one side of the ravine's top, not one of the bandits survived. Some tried to surrender; the wounded dragged themselves away in the desperate hope of escape. All were dispatched, however. It was the price of failure. It was how it was done in those days. The old man wandered the field, putting them down. When his pistol was empty, he used the bayonet. When the task was complete, he sat, blood-soaked and staring into the distance.

The survivors brought him back. The officers wanted him decorated for valor. The regimental surgeon eventually recommended a discharge. The old man came home to a hero's welcome and sought the solace of the family farm. He resumed training in the village dojo that his wealthy father supported. Most of the time he was as fierce as ever. But he heard things no one else did and would unexpectedly stop what he was doing and stare off into the distance. At night he would wander the fields, returning at dawn, soaked and dirty, to collapse into sleep.

His family sent him to Hokkaido. Did they hope the wild north would somehow tame him? Or were they simply searching for a refuge where he could hide away? In the end, they got both wishes.

One day, the old man met his match. He was riding a train and was jostled by a diminutive, craggy-faced man in threadbare clothes. Words ensued and the old man reached out to teach the stranger a lesson. Amazingly, he found himself pinned to the floor, stunned and helpless. He struggled, but the stranger's grip was unbreakable. One last attempt and the shabby stranger rammed an iron-hard fist into a nerve cluster. The old man convulsed.

"Enough?" the stranger hissed. The old man tried one last time to break the hold. Again, the jolt of pain as a fist ground into him. "Enough?"

As Takano related it later, the pain of the nerve attack almost paled in comparison to the humiliation he felt. But he gave in. "Maitta," he said. I'm beaten.

The stranger stood up and stepped over him with the same casual distaste you would show avoiding manure in a barnyard.

The man in the shabby traveling kimono was a true master. He had killed men with his sword in duels, maimed students in his dojo, a man of impeccable skill and violent temperament—haughty, mercurial. In time he accepted Takano as his student. The old man drank up the lessons and merged them with his own already remarkable skill. In the heat of that cauldron, he came to an enhanced understanding of who he was and what his role in life was.

You put it best after your first year with us, Rinsuke. The dojo is supposedly a place where both skill and insight are fostered. The reality is often less than this, and more often the product is warped by the flaws lurking in both teachers and their students. Such was the case with Takano, a peerless fighter and a flawed human being. For the weaker spirits in that hell dojo, Takano's savagery was not only accepted, it was understood as an expression of his greatness and as something to emulate.

You would have none of it, though. You withstood every attack he made on you, body and spirit. You learned, but never bent completely to his will. You acknowledged his skill as a technician but never excused his failings as a man. You were his student, but never his slave. He hated you for it, but was fascinated as well. Each day the old man's eyes clicked across the dojo, searching for weakness in us all. But he watched you with a particular malevolence.

One night, secluded, the old man's students discussed their teacher's nature: was he a god or was he a devil? "Neither," you replied. "He is a genius of a type, the most gifted fighter any of us have seen. But it is a fearsome burden to bear. He is great." Then you smiled grimly. "He is also a complete sociopath."

I paused, rubbing my temples to ease the strain of translation. I paced the room in the thick hush of the monastery. There was a window opening onto the hills, but the night was dark and overcast: there was no hint of moon or stars to offer a respite from the blackness. I sighed and turned with dread back to the book, knowing I had to finish it all. Mori had much more to tell.

Sometime in the silent darkness before dawn I dropped into sleep. In the dim twilight of approaching day, faint chanting from the main hall murmured its way into my consciousness. For a moment, I was half-asleep, lost in Mori's story and its implications. I peered around, slumped in the chair, confused.

Then the sound of the chanting brought me into full wakefulness and the sounds made sense. *Dai zai geda puku*: The great robe of liberation. The opening lines of the Robe Sutra, chanted as the roshi and his monks ritually donned their clerical robes to begin another day.

I wiped my mouth with my sleeve and fumbled for the journal, which had tumbled to the floor. In the cold half-light I gathered my wits and collected my things. Time was short. I had three days to find Chie Miyazaki. Because once he had read Mori's journal, there would be no stopping Yamashita. He'd find her or die trying. It might have been selfish of me, but I wasn't ready to let him do that.

So I padded downstairs in my stocking feet. The monastery was a place with few doors and no locks. I slipped into the roshi's office and left the journal on his desk with a short note. I thanked him and promised to return.

But I was silent as to my plans. I wasn't so sure what I was about to do would meet with the roshi's approval. Or Yamashita's. But I was comforted by the sutra I had heard that morning, that spoke of a great liberation and the need to save all beings.

CHAPTER 9

Big irony: I've spent countless hours training to make my body and mind almost inseparable, but as the men who had taken me held me down, I was wishing it were otherwise. Because no matter how hard I tried to keep focused on the knowledge that they weren't going to drown me, my body was on fire with the conviction that they were, and the animal panic overwhelmed me. The brain was gone and it was body sense alone that gripped me. There was no reason, no analysis, no control, only the darkness and then choking and the curious fire of water as it smothered me and pushed its way down into my lungs.

I'd gotten back to Brooklyn that morning, my hands stiff from the tension of gripping the steering wheel of the car. It wasn't the stop and go of a typical rush hour that bothered me; it was the urgency of new knowledge that made me tense my muscles and wish I could clear the other drivers out of my way by force of will. But the commute into Manhattan is as implacable and unheeding as any force of nature. I was swept along in its own good time, one of thousands of cars carried along like flotsam in a torrent.

A very slow-moving torrent.

I reached my house in Sunset Park too late to participate in the morning parking ritual familiar to most New Yorkers: alternate side of the street parking. When I got home, the tidal shift from one side of the street to another had already occurred. I shrugged, double-parked, and went inside. The people whose car I had trapped against the curb would honk if they needed me.

There was a phone message from Owen Collins. Email from Ann. Both wanted to meet. They had some important information I needed to see. In retrospect, I should have picked up the phone then and there. Instead, I grabbed my gear bag and headed to the dojo in Red Hook to teach the morning's lesson. It was, after all, what I did.

And they knew that as well.

They were waiting in a van idling near the dojo entrance. There was enough street traffic that I didn't really notice anything special. There were deliveries being made to shops all along the street. Guys drove trucks that were scarred and crumpled like a washed-up boxer after his most recent battering. The van near the dojo entrance was no different from half a dozen I had seen that morning. It had been sideswiped a few times. Some kids had tagged it with graffiti. White exhaust ghosted out from the tailpipe, accompanied by a slow drip of water. Nobody was coming in or out of the vehicle, but that fact didn't register with me; I had other things on my mind. Students wouldn't be arriving for an hour and the building was locked and empty. I fumbled with my keys at the door and that was when they came at me.

I heard the grumble of the van door as it slid open and I sensed the air pressure shift, churned by their scramble toward me. I spun around, hands coming up, but it was too late. I had time to get an image of three men, black hair and sunglasses. Then one of them ground the prongs into my neck. The thing sparked and I was down.

Tasers. You use them right and the current flashes through

the nervous system, shorting out the pulse of muscle coordination. It's not just pain; it's the complete loss of control as the command system of the body is hijacked, spiked with static, and overwhelmed. They hit me more than a few times—these guys were not taking any chances. I collapsed. By the time I started to recover, I had been tossed into the van, where they had duct taped me and pulled a bag over my head. I rolled around slightly as the vehicle accelerated and hit a turn. Somebody grunted and planted a foot on my back to keep me still. Big foot. Hard-soled shoe. It wasn't a friendly gesture. Nobody spoke. All I heard was the distant murmur of traffic and the engine noise of the van.

It wasn't a long ride. You hear stories of kidnap victims trying to remember each twist and turn of the ride as they sit, blindfolded, the mind racing with nightmare scenarios of what the future holds. The ones who don't succumb completely to panic use all kinds of tricks to stay calm. Trying to figure out where they're taking you is one of them. But in the dark, your ability to interpret movement is compromised. You have to try to remember the sequence of balance shifts as the vehicle turns while at the same time trying to link it to auditory signals from the engine and transmission that can give you a clue about relative speed. Maybe you also focus on the sound from the tires as they hum across different types of pavement. It's probably something you can be trained to do. But I hadn't been to secret agent school. I could understand it might help kidnap victims stay calm or help them gain some small sense of control—the psychological impact of abduction, with its violent disruption of routine and total loss of autonomy, can be devastating.

But I've been trained differently. Life is as unpredictable as the next opponent, as cruelly relentless as the blade of a sword as it arcs toward you. There's no time for mind games or confidence-building tricks. You have to be fully focused on the here and now. If I spent all my energy on trying to create a mental map of the van's journey, I'd arrive at wherever they were taking me no better prepared to deal with them than I had been at the start of the trip. So I lay there and worked as carefully as I could to test the strength of my bonds without alerting my captors. I controlled my breathing and tried to assess how much of my muscle control was coming back as I recovered from the Taser jolts. I worked the angles and assessed my options.

They were slim. The bonds were tight. The hood wasn't budging. I could flail around on the floor and bang some shins. Maybe I could deliver a head butt if someone got close. But they weren't going to get close, were they? They'd eventually dump me out somewhere and watch me squirm until it got boring or I got tired. Then they'd simply haul me up and do whatever they had planned to do.

I didn't think they were going to kill me. At least not right away. They could have taken me out on the sidewalk in Red Hook without much problem. Someone goes to all this trouble—charging Tasers, getting the duct tape, finding something to use as a hood—it's because they have something more complicated in mind than simple murder.

That was the angle I had to work with. I'd be moved. They'd have to lug me around. Maybe to make it easy on themselves they'd cut the tape around my legs and I'd be able to stand. If I could stand, I could kick. If they took the hood off to question me, I might be able to bite someone.

OK, not the greatest options, but this is how it's done. You focus on the possibilities. You prepare plan A, then B, then C. And even at the very end, when the flash of the gun or the bite of the blade rides the leading edge of the oncoming wave of the Big Sleep, you die trying.

It's bred into our DNA, a biological imperative that Yamashita has refined and strengthened in me over the years. *Hakka yoi*. Hang in there. Stay ready.

The ride ended. I was dragged out of the van and carried along. There were some terse directions I couldn't make out, some grunting. I got banged down some stairs and then they dumped me on the floor. Hard and cool. I could smell the concrete. They left me alone but I could hear them moving around somewhere nearby. The thud of wood. More muffled directions. I squirmed around until I hit a wall, then worked my way up onto my knees. It was awkward with my arms pinned behind me, but I did it. Because I wasn't going to simply lie there like a piece of luggage. I made my way into seiza, the formal seated position we use in the dojo, because that's how I wanted to face whatever was coming.

It was probably as useful as trying to map the route they took while blindfolded. Probably as futile. I know. But we all get to choose our own coping mechanisms. This was mine.

I heard the scrape of approaching footsteps. More than one person. They got to either side of me and hooked my arms, pulling me upright. I got tilted forward and they dragged me across the space. My hips rammed into something hard and they bent me over it. A quick flurry of activity—a shot to my kidneys just for laughs and to keep me from making too much trouble, the bonds at my wrists and elbows cut. I was lifted off my feet and stretched out on the board. Someone tied my arms down at my side, the rope going around the surface I was lying on. They did the same for my feet. It was slanted and my feet were higher than my head.

When they pulled the hood off, I got the quick impression of a storeroom of some sort. Cardboard boxes were piled up on the periphery of my vision; there were rows of round lights protected by wire grids in the ceiling.

But then they put a towel over my face and I heard the water running.

My body jerked as the water started to flow across the surface of the towel, molding it to my face. *Waterboarding.*

I'd known it at some level as soon as they strapped me to the board, head down. There had been enough discussion in the media, enough details. Probably most ten-year-old kids in America knew how it worked. Basically, it's simulated drowning. It's been used for centuries in one form or another, and for good reason. It's an absolute nightmare. A government functionary somewhere cooked up a theory that it's not really torture. Someday I'd like to hunt him down and have him ride the board for a while. Once he stopped weeping, maybe he'd reconsider.

The flow of water soaked me, filling my nostrils. I clamped my mouth shut and tried to turn my head to one side, but hands grabbed me like a vise and forced me into immobility. A jet of nausea, the urge to puke. *Don't. You'll choke.* Which was a big laugh. I was choking already.

It's part of the technique. The gag reflex is immediate, automatic, and powerful. It tries to keep things out, but at the same time, the body is going into panic mode over the need for air. My body was quivering, burning with the need. Even with all that water, the desire was hot and overpowering. I gagged as the water surged into my mouth and down into my lungs. I retched and choked and the water kept coming.

I don't know how long they did it to me. After a while, you grow hypoxic from the lack of oxygen and the buildup of carbon dioxide in the brain. And when that happens, most higher mental processing disappears. There's simply confusion and anxiety, the crushing weight on your chest, the struggle for air and the smothering flow of water. You're simply a thrashing, desperate animal.

The towel came off my face and I could move my head again. I retched and gasped, frantic with the need to breathe. The muscles in my arms and legs were throbbing from struggling against the bonds. My heart hammered in my chest.

A face floated into my blurry vision. I tried to squint the water out of my eyes to see more clearly.

"What are you doing?" The voice said. The accent was Asian. The face was pale, the hair dark. He was still wearing sunglasses.

I couldn't speak yet. The air was rasping down my throat into lungs that were working simultaneously to get oxygen in and water out. He knew it, because it seemed as if he hadn't really expected me to say anything right away. He was content to let me choke and gasp for a while.

"We know who you are, Burke." The man seemed almost detached, his voice bored. He looked at me with all the same interest you might expend on the fish, stretched out, inert, on the crushed ice of a market showcase. He straightened up and I had to turn my head to keep him in sight. "Why were you in Lim's apartment?"

Then I realized who they were. *The Koreans.*

"What do you mean?" I managed to choke out. Playing for time. Trying to get my brain working again.

His face floated above mine once more. He said nothing

and watched me for a few seconds. Then he simply dropped the towel back over my face and it began again. The smooth, smothering flow of water. The burning and gasping. The helplessness. The terror.

When the towel came off again, I almost sobbed.

He let me lie there, quivering with greed for air. It was all I could think about for a time. There was a small, nagging voice inside my head trying to pierce the fog. The brain was still working somewhat. *They won't kill you. That's the point. They need you alive.*

It's the point of interrogation, of course. You're no good dead. That's the good news. The bad news is that for thousands of years people have been perfecting ways to make every nerve ending in a victim's body scream without actually killing him. The skilled torturer has learned to take his victim right to the edge of death if necessary. He has to convince the victim death is a real possibility. They don't want you thinking you can hold out, that it's just pain and you can get through it. They don't want you thinking at all. The key to doing this lies in timing, in flooding the victim with suffering so intense it short-circuits most rational thought. There is simply agony. Then it's gone. A question. More agony. Then it's gone. Another question, and another, and another, each punctuated by more suffering. You start to yearn for the questions. Your torturer's face floats in and out of your vision and you watch it hungrily, hoping the lips will part and there will be questions. You learn to love the face and the voice. You yearn to answer, because in those brief intervals there is freedom from the suffering. And you'll do anything and say anything to make it stop.

In the end I didn't tell them much, but it was only because I was still choking and retching from aspirating water. I've faced a few terrifying men, men with murder on their minds, men who were more than capable of carrying out that wish. I faced those ordeals and survived. But nothing has ever scared me as much as the man with the towel, and the pale, expressionless face that watched and questioned and, with a jerk of his head, had them cover my face and ply the hose again.

They were breaking me. For all my training, I wasn't ready for them. I wasn't ready for this. I've spent years pursuing an art that worships control. You meet danger with skill in the hope you will endure. But on the board, there was no skill I could use. There was no mercy there. No hope.

I don't know what was worse: the physical effect of what they did to me, or the knowledge of how close they came to breaking me. Mostly, it was the sudden realization of the illusory nature of life and how tenuous our hold. Is this the far country that Yamashita was peering into? Old age is a slower process, perhaps, but the effect is the same: it grinds you down and strips you of all pretense and all illusion of control and dignity.

Eventually, I would have told them everything. I'm not proud of it, but it's true. I had nothing to hang on to. I couldn't stall in the hopes that someone would find me—nobody knew I was gone. And I wasn't harboring some secret that would save mankind. I was just blundering around, trying to find the wild child of a Japanese diplomat.

I wasn't going to drown for Chie Miyazaki.

It's a rationalization, of course. An excuse for my weakness. And stupid as well. Which shows you just how good they were at their trade. I wasn't thinking clearly at all. Because later, once they had what they needed, they *would* kill me. It's the major escalation factor in most kidnappings; the penalties are so severe, you might as well kill the victim if it improves your chances of escape.

What saved me was a phone call. The pale face drifted over me and the lips parted for a question. Then I heard the chirp of a cell phone. Annoyance crumpled the skin around his mouth and eyes—a fleeting glimpse of the human being behind the torturer's mask—and then it was gone. The face disappeared as my torturer stood up straight and answered the phone.

The shaped charge went off at almost the same second he started to speak into the phone. The shock wave that blew in the metal door to the basement was incredible. I could feel the pressure of it in my chest.

There were some smaller explosions as well, but the noise was muffled since my auditory system was still shorted out from the first bang. The flashes of light were intense. I lay there on the board and all around me I could sense smoke and movement, but it was hard to get a clear idea of what was happening. My mouth sagged open and I turned my head from side to side. The sound in my head was like the churning roar you hear when you get dragged down into the massive swell of an ocean wave. I blinked to clear the flashes and sparks from my vision, but it was no use. All I got was a jumbled impression of motion, of shadowy forms spinning and moving.

A hand on my chest. One to my neck, checking my pulse. Another face, goggled and wearing some sort of black ski cap with a facemask, looked down at me. He pulled the mask down. I saw his lips move, but his voice was washed out by the roaring in my head. He tried to speak to me a few more times. Then he turned away.

They cut my bonds and I would have tumbled off the board if they hadn't caught me. I was way too wobbly for any real movement, but I tried, my arms and legs jerking spastically. I was desperate to get away from the board. I'll die before I let anyone do that to me again.

Calming hands. They sat me down with my back against a wall while someone—a medic, I supposed—did the usual things with a little flashlight, shining it in my eyes and doing a body inventory to look for the sign of any obvious wounds. I sat there, slumped and fog-bound.

In time, the world returned. Or I returned to it. I could smell the residue of explosives and gunfire. My hearing was starting to come back. I noted the chirp of radio voices and the terse, murmured response from men in black clothing who were still policing the area. There were other background sounds that I was struggling to make out, but I gave up. I shifted and concentrated on another ragged breath. It felt so good.

The man with the flashlight held my chin in his hand and looked into my eyes. Then he turned and called over his shoulder: "*Jefe*, he's coming around."

I made myself focus. On the room, on the moving men, on the still forms lying on the wet concrete. I tried to get my brain working again, but was distracted by a faint undercurrent of noise. I could hear a distant gurgle, and it claimed all my attention.

"Shut that damn hose off," I rasped.

CHAPTER 10

Mori's Journal

You didn't break.

As with all of us, he wore you down, but he never broke you. The lines of your face grew sharper, the bone pushing out against skin as training rendered you down into a lean, corded, lethal version of your former self. You were one of us, stoic in the face of the unrelenting demands of our teacher, your training uniform limp with sweat, battered everywhere, toes and fingers and wrists taped. Eyes wide open, wary. A predator in the making. But when I looked more closely, Rinsuke, I could see a difference.

You bowed to Takano, but you never groveled. For some of us, I expect the force of the old man was too much to withstand. The physical demands were punishing in themselves, but they paled beside the toll he took on our spirits. Takano's skill was so great, his demands and expectations so extreme, it seemed we all walked a path that would never end. In the night as we lay, nursing wounds and twitching in half-sleep as our minds and bodies replayed the day's struggles, we sought comfort in the sense that all this suffering was leading to a goal. We all cherished the idea of skill, of mastery. We had come to Takano of our own volition, convinced he had skills to teach us what we could learn nowhere else. And we were right. The stories told about him were true enough. But as the days and months churned on, grinding us down in the process, we sometimes wondered whether any of us would ever reach the level of competence he demanded, whether we would survive long enough to be granted a certificate of mastery.

For some, the combination of Takano's devastating technique and his emotional remoteness made him seem otherworldly, an ancient warrior-god looking down on mere mortals, dispensing favors or punishment with chilling dispassion. He became a teacher not merely to emulate or obey, but to worship. In some strange way, some of his disciples surrendered to him. In retrospect, it was an act of desperate self-preservation. Swept along in the current of his powers, they surrendered to the pull, no longer fighting him, but becoming one with his will. They grew to love him because there was no longer a separation in their hearts between sensei and student. They were one with Takano and so became devoted to him. It was a perversion.

But you did not surrender, Rinsuke. Your unarmed skills were already excellent, but after the first year, you were holding your own with the senior students in weapons drills, taking to the Way of the Sword as if you were born to it. By the second year, you were peerless. But to many of us, you, too, were a mystery.

I remember one incident clearly. A winter's day when Takano had worked us with a particularly savage intensity. The dojo was set on the grounds of an old monastery, high on a wooded ridge. The day was a grey swirl of icy rain and snow. Off to the west, the view beyond a range of smaller hills led to the ocean, a churning expanse of water so cold it looked almost black. We ran barefoot through the snow, down the slippery stone steps of the monastery's pathways, up hills and down. Grunting with the jolt of hidden rocks, our exposed skin needled with ice. Back to the dojo courtyard, where we stood, wooden swords in hand, our bodies steaming in the cold.

In the hours that followed, we cut the air in the seemingly endless series of practice strikes the old man called for. The snow and earth were churned up by our movements: there was the white of snow, the deep brown of mud, and the bright flecks of blood. We paid no mind. We were like machines that day. If our bodies burned, it was a fire we had all grown familiar with. Our minds floated along, empty of any thought other than the specifics of the orders the old man barked at us. He paced the courtyard, snarling corrections, watching us with narrowed eyes, the lips of his wide mouth often pressed into a thin line of disapproval. Occasionally he would stand in front of a student as an opponent, blocking the prescribed blow and countering it in turn, checking for a flaw, a weakness. But his actions were always within the parameters of the drill.

As the hours passed and the light began to fade, Takano seemed oblivious to the toll the practice session was taking on us. At any given time, some of us were injured. Bruises, strains, the small muscle tears that burned and pulled. We worked through the snag of injury, secretly favoring our wounds with slight shifts of balance, minute adjustments to movement. But as the training continued on that day, fatigue and cold made us stiffen. Our movements grew slightly less precise as we struggled to keep up. The skin on our hands felt thick as we tried to maintain a numbed grip on our wooden swords. Occasionally, one of us would slip, and the jerking struggle to stay upright did additional damage to a body on its last reserves. Eventually, someone would be seriously injured, and that would snuff out a promising career.

Surely the old man must have seen it. He was too experienced to be oblivious to what was happening. He circled us, impervious to the weather. His leathery face was streaked with freezing rain, but his eyes burned. Then it struck me: he was precisely pushing us beyond the breaking point. He wanted to winnow out the weak. It was a relative term, of course. We were, despite our injuries, in peak condition. But he was searching for flaws, the tiny shade of difference in muscle tone or ligament strength, in density of bone, differences that could only be revealed under the most extreme conditions. Takano would not rest until he had driven us into exhaustion, until we were incapable of more. Because that was when the flaws would become apparent. We all sensed this. We knew there was no escape. It was a matter of our pride pitted against his ruthlessness. And he knew exactly what we were thinking and feeling. He used our own ambition against us. We would never surrender because if any one of us stopped due to exhaustion or injury, Takano would humiliate and expel that student. And we had come too far for that. Each of us was strapped to this wheel, wondering if it would crush us before it lifted us up. Perhaps that was Takano's lesson: for the warrior, there is no real way to escape suffering.

From the vantage point of all these years, I find myself surprised by this thought. At the time, all I knew with certainty was we would hold out as a group and this stubbornness would only feed his intensity. He would continue to batter us into the icy night. It seemed utterly cruel to me then. Now I wonder whether there was a deeper point to his actions, a profound lesson embedded deep in all that agony.

Perhaps he was a god.

See what a hold he had on us, Rinsuke? Even now, the memory of his face makes me flinch, and I worry I have been an unworthy student.

But that day we endured to the point where our tendons snapped and burned. We staggered. We retched and gasped, lost our footing. Then we straightened up, took another ragged breath, and gripped our swords in anticipation of the next command.

I was leading the group, facing the rows of trainees, so I saw it all. Takano was working his way down the front line, engaging each man. His wooden sword arced up, smacking his opponent's shaft, pressing to see how firm a grip each person was able to maintain after all this time. He had just swung into position in front of you, Rinsuke, when the man to your left stumbled. Takano's eyes lit up and he began to move toward him.

But you didn't let this happen. As Takano's eyes shifted to the stumbling man, you came forward with an attack. In an instant, the old man's head snapped around, his face taut with anger. And truly, the attack was an unexpected one. You came at him as if you meant to cut your sensei down. Perhaps in that moment, you did.

It was a measure of Takano's skill that he recovered, a quicksilver shift and parry; the blow was deflected. But you pressed him, coming at him again and again. And now it was truly joined. This was no longer a simple training exercise. You meant to punish him much as he had done to us.

The twilight was upon us. The snow in the courtyard seemed to glow in the dim light. The freezing rain pelted down on us, a cascade of needles, and you and the old man snorted and cut, your swords barking out with the fury of the force you put in the blows. As you whirled, the lines we had been standing in were broken to make room for you. Your maneuvers swept you both around the courtyard and we were pushed to the perimeter to watch, slack-mouthed with exhausted astonishment.

Finally, you slipped. Or so it seemed to me at the time. It was all that Takano needed. He swarmed inside the striking range of your sword. An iron fist doubled you over—a vicious twist and your sword went flying.

Takano swept your feet out from under you. You collapsed with a thud on the wet, muddy flagstones. As you rolled over and tried to stand, he caught you in the side with his sword. It was a precise blow, one measured to inflict the maximum of pain without actually breaking your ribs. You recoiled, exposing another target. Another blow. They continued in a seemingly unending series. We stood. Mute. There was only the hiss of the ice-rain, and the meaty thwack as yet another of Takano's strikes went home, again and again and again.

And here was the most frightening thing about what he was doing: the absolute precision of the beating. We could see Takano was furious with you, Rinsuke. And the beating he gave you was relentless. But despite the rage that sparked deep in his eyes, he never totally lost control. His blows were precise and calculated, unerringly executed. Exquisite in their form. In that freezing courtyard, he burned like ice.

You had ultimately stopped moving, incapable of defending yourself, but the beating continued for a while longer. Finally, Takano raised his oak sword high above his head. He gathered himself for one last, finishing blow. I gasped out loud, certain the old man had finally lost all control and he meant to kill you.

A gong sounded from within the temple grounds and the distant chant of the monks murmured through the sound of the frozen rain, gathering in strength as the light failed. The old man cocked his head, a slight movement as if he were being tugged by its call. He closed his eyes against the sleet, then lowered his sword. He glared at us all, silent in the gloom, then spun on his heels and left us to gather you up.

You crawled to your place in the dojo the next morning, hoisting yourself upright to sit with the rest of us as we waited for Takano. We all expected your dismissal. You must have expected it as well. But it was a measure of what we had become that not one of us helped you to your place. Not one of us thanked you for what you did. Even I watched silently as the old man swept into the training hall. He sat down and glared at us. I called the class to attention and we bowed. Takano stretched his hands out in front of him on the mat and inclined his torso forward, like a rock settling into place, a slight shift and no more. If he noted your presence, Rinsuke, if he was gauging the extent of the injuries he had inflicted, it didn't show. Takano's eyes swept along the silent rows of students and it seemed to me that he lingered on nobody. He stood and nodded, grunted to me, and, amazingly, class simply began.

There was no mention of the previous day's event in the courtyard. You were not expelled for your almost unimaginable affront, for the challenge to our sensei's authority. None of us ever spoke about it. And from that day forward the old man watched you with more intensity than ever. I think he was surprised you were even able to continue. And as the months passed, he was grudgingly impressed with your ability to master the new techniques he revealed to us, despite your injuries. But more than anything else, I saw that Takano was puzzled. None of us would have done what you did. The risk of dismissal was too great. Each of us would have kept at it in the courtyard that evening until someone died. It would have been a waste of life, but that was the ordeal our master set for us. It was our duty to simply obey and endure. And we were young and ambitious and sure it would have been someone else who fell.

You shared the same confidence in your ability to endure. Certainly you could have survived whatever the old man threw at us that night, yet you chose to stop it. I wonder why.

I would have liked to ask you that question, Rinsuke, but never did. What would have been your answer? Compassion? Disgust with our master's lack of control? Pride?

None of us was sure what you were thinking. Not even

Takano. And this, I have come to believe, is what fueled his veiled, intense scrutiny. He was a man of great powers. He could see into the core of people. He knew their fears and hopes. He could measure his students' potential and their weaknesses with brutal precision. But there was a part of you that was closed off to him, and he was not used to that. The old swordsmen spoke of the need to hide something of yourself from your opponent, to dwell in kage, the shadow. But Takano had long ago learned how to pierce the barrier each of us erects as protection. He dominated his enemies both physically and spiritually.

But not you. As your training continued, he labored to fully understand you, but could not. He kept you on as a student even after your affront and it was not because he was being magnanimous. I am not sure he was capable of generosity. Everything with Takano was cold and calculated. You continued as his student, Rinsuke, because he did not understand you and could not accept that fact fully. He refused to be defeated by you in this regard.

Or so he must have thought. But while partially true, it was not the whole truth. In reality, I think he kept you close because he feared you like he feared nothing else on this earth.

CHAPTER 11

Trundled into another van, I sat there, shivering under a space blanket while the last of the men in black scrambled out of the basement. They zipped their weapons into black duffels. They yanked their hoods and goggles off and split up, some piling into the van, others into a battered SUV. Sirens wailed in the distance. Nobody said a word. The van was moving before the doors slammed shut. I looked around through the windows: cinderblock walls with graffiti tags, dumpsters, and broken wooden loading pallets. The van's tires crunched on the gravel and crud on the roadway of a weary-looking industrial park.

Part of me was expecting a crowd from Alphabet Land: FBI, NYPD, HSA. Or some group nobody knew about, a subdivision of a bureaucratic offshoot from a post–9-11 garden, buried deep in an organizational chart with an elastic budget and murky purpose.

What I got was Alejandro and a group of solid-looking Latinos who didn't say much at all. They had the thick necks and easy moves of the well conditioned. Short haircuts. No tattoos. Some were shorter and some were taller, but they all seemed the same somehow. I thought for a moment and nodded. I was picking up a familiar vibe: these guys had been trained, and trained well. It was revealed in the way they sat, almost motionless but humming with extreme focus. The only movement I could see was their heads swiveling, scanning the passing buildings and vehicles and pedestrians with a relentless precision.

I could almost hear their eyeballs clicking as they shifted and quartered the visual field, alert for signs of the next threat.

Alejandro turned to look at me from the front passenger seat. He grinned and thumbed a small earpiece into one ear, cocking his head and listening. He gave quiet instructions to the driver, who nodded. We made some smooth turns, gunned down an avenue. The sound of sirens faded.

I squirmed into a more upright position. The space blanket crinkled around me. "*Que sorpresa*," I said.

"Not what you expected?" His smile was wide. He had very even teeth.

I shrugged. I was recovering some of my composure and wanted to keep up a good front. "Yah. What you expect and what you get are two different things." I paused because my teeth were still chattering slightly. I worked to get it under control before I continued. "But I'm happy for the help. Glad to be out of there."

Alejandro nodded. "*Claro*. Who wouldn't be glad?"

I sat forward. "The Koreans again?" The minute they had snatched me, I figured it had to be somebody connected to Lim.

Alejandro pursed his lips. "Freelancers from Sunnyside. They were probably hired by Lim's people, but we'll never be sure."

"You could ask them … the ones who were down there in the basement." I remembered the raid—the explosions, the sounds. "The survivors, I mean."

A baleful look from Alejandro. "There were no survivors, Dr. Burke." He saw the expression that must have crossed my face. "Ah, my friend," he chided, "you disappoint me. These were not people who were easily subdued. And in a situation

114

like that, speed and force provide the best outcome. There was little time for hesitation. Besides, they wouldn't have known anything of real value."

His voice was matter of fact and his logic was cold. But I knew he was right. Most people don't realize just how difficult it is to take someone down without hurting him. And in a situation where guns are involved, it gets even trickier. Alejandro probably knew what he was going to do before he blew the door in. He had two goals: one was to get me out in one piece; the other was to protect his people. That meant getting in and taking everyone down who even looked like he might resist.

Besides, Lim or whoever hired those people was using them as a cutout. They'd have little knowledge of what was really going on. The people who grabbed me had been given a target, some instructions, and probably a decent amount of money. But in the end, Alejandro was right. Any way you looked at it, they were expendable. I understood the logic of it, but it chilled me just the same.

We rode along for a time. I sighed. "Now what?" I finally asked.

They got me cleaned up and into some dry clothes. I was sitting with Alejandro in the deserted basement dining room of a small Mexican place in Bay Ridge. They told me it probably wasn't safe to go home. Whoever was after me would be watching: my house, my car, the dojo. They'd have them staked out, ready to snap me up again if I showed my face.

A waiter came by and set two cups of espresso down in front of us. He stood there, hands folded on the apron that stretched over his belly, watching Alejandro, who scrutinized the placement of the coffee cups, the small yellow rind of lemon on each saucer. He picked up the small spoon and examined both sides, then nodded. The waiter scurried away.

"He seems worried," I told him.

Alejandro waited for the man to be out of earshot. "He should be. I'm part owner."

We sat for a quiet minute. "So I've ruffled some feathers with this Lim thing," I began.

He nodded. "It was why I decided to keep my eye on you."

"I didn't know you cared."

He sipped at his coffee and looked at me. "Unfortunately, my career choice does not involve a great deal of feeling. Let's make that clear. Mr. Osorio hires me to promote his interests. And that's what I am doing."

"You went to a lot of trouble to spring me," I said.

He shrugged. "An unanticipated benefit of ten plus years in Iraq and Afghanistan—lots of well-trained young men available for a certain type of work. The economy being what it is, I do what I can …"

"Still doesn't explain why." I sipped at the coffee. Dark, bitter, hot. The dining room was dimly lit. I could hear muted voices from the kitchen as they prepared for the dinner trade, the clanking of dishes and the rush of water. The liquid sound made me feel cold once more. I wanted to hunch into a small ball and get warm, but I made myself sit back and look at Alejandro. I waited until he answered the question.

"Why?" he began. "It's fairly easy. Your Japanese friends want a woman found. But the way they're doing it seems far too complex to me. And another group of people don't seem to want her found. Interesting. And then there's her boyfriend Lim. There's more going on there than what's on the surface. I think this is interesting as well. There are secrets here. Things being hidden."

"And?"

"People hide valuable things."

"The girl is valuable?"

Again the shrug. "I'm not sure of that. Whatever is really being hidden, that's valuable."

"I don't see it."

He smiled. "Of course you don't. This is not your world. But when someone wants something hidden, it's fairly easy to make money." Alejandro saw that I wasn't following him. He sighed. "You can make money by finding the valuable thing, but this is doing it the hard way. I've found it much easier to go to the people who want something hidden and simply threaten to find it. Or threaten to tell others where it is."

"Extortion."

He wagged his head from side to side. "I prefer to think about it as a type of service. I learn something and I offer to keep it secret. Surely all my hard work should be compensated, yes?"

"So why help me?"

He smiled. "Dr. Burke. You are doing the hard work of trying to find this girl. I am happy to let you do so. In the process, I am sure you will uncover the real reasons everyone is so interested in her. And that knowledge will be valuable."

"Why would I tell you?"

Alejandro finished his espresso and dabbed at his lips with a napkin. He sat back and looked at me coldly. "You're an honorable man, Burke. This Don Osorio has told me. You will tell me because you owe me. Because I freed you from that basement." He took a last sip from the tiny cup of espresso.

I sat there, and for a while, I wasn't really seeing Alejandro.

I thought of Mickey and Art telling me to walk away from the Miyazaki, of Osorio's wolflike eyes, of the strong sense I was getting in over my head. Above all, I thought of Mori's journal and the secret it contained. I came back into focus and looked at the confident, contained man sitting across from me. My stomach sank. I knew he was right. If this was the price he demanded, I would pay it. Honor binds us. But not always to the things or people we want.

The clock was ticking; that much I knew. The crew from Sunnyside had nabbed me well before noon and whoever hired them would be expecting a report, but probably wouldn't worry too much if it took a while. Khalid Sheikh Mohammed was waterboarded one hundred and eighty-three times and still didn't crack. So someone might assume I could hold out for a while. But not forever. Which meant I needed to get moving.

But where? Alejandro had tabs on all of Lim's likely hang-outs and there was no sign of Lim or Chie Miyazaki. His folks would continue to watch known locations and likely associates, but we both assumed she and Lim were somewhere else. I probably had the rest of the day and night to discover their location. Sometime tomorrow, word of the scene in the Sunnyside basement and the bodies lying there would hit the news. And then law enforcement would be all over things, gumming the process up.

I was still a little shaky. One wall of the dining room had a mirror running the length of the upper half of the wall. I looked at my reflection, taking inventory. My hair was mussed and there were dark rings under my eyes. I was slumped, lost in the folds of the limp tracksuit they had given me. I think I had seen Al Sharpton wear it years ago. Alejandro had retrieved my wallet. He had probably gone through it looking for cash as a reflex action. I couldn't even remember if there was any money in there. I did still have an ATM card, however, which meant I still had access to the money Ito had provided me. I took a deep breath and sat up a little straighter. Faced with a challenge, I did what any real American would do.

I went shopping.

I got some cash, ditched the tracksuit for some real clothes, picked up a cheap cell phone, and loaded it with minutes.

Owen Collins picked up on the first ring.

"Where are you?" I asked.

It took him a minute to recognize my voice. "Burke? Where ya been? I've been trying to get hold of you."

"Someone else did."

"What?"

I rubbed a hand over my face. *Leave it. Get a grip.* "Not important. Do you have any information for me?"

"Yeah." His voice grew increasingly animated. "Me and Annie have been working this thing and we've come up with some interesting stuff."

Annie? "Where are you now?"

"At school."

It took me almost an hour to get to him—there are over twenty stops on the R train between Bay Ridge and Fifty-Seventh Street in Manhattan. My stomach ached with frustration as the train rocked its slow way under the city. It was a relief to finally get out, and I rushed west toward Columbus Circle and then to John Jay College. It was a lurching, shambling version of a sprint; I was still disconnected, not only from the world, but also from my own body.

Owen stood up when I reached his office. "You don't look so good," he said.

I shrugged. *Better than the guys Alejandro left in the basement.*

Owen looked concerned, but pretty soon forgot how I looked as he relayed the story of the research he and Ann had done.

"We did some basic background on the family," he began.

"The Miyazaki."

He nodded. "Yeah. Very well placed—ties to the Japanese finance and industrial elite. The old man is on the board of any number of big companies. The son is in the diplomatic corps—has a long and distinguished record of service, blah, blah, blah."

"Any hint of scandal?" I was fishing.

Owen had a ream of printouts in a file he shuffled through. "Not anything that popped up. The old man doesn't seem to be well liked."

I thought of the old lizard, his wide mouth wet with spittle and fury as his son wheeled him out of the meeting room. "For good reason," I told him.

"Son's a straight arrow, well thought of in the diplomatic community."

"What's he do?"

Owen scanned a sheet of paper. "He's the Washington liaison in support of the Treaty of Mutual Cooperation and Security."

"Can you say that in English?"

He grinned. "Signed in 1960. Establishes a commitment by the U.S. to support and defend Japan. They get our military umbrella. We get bases for our troops."

"It's a point of contention for many Japanese," I said.

"Chinese aren't crazy about it either. But yeah, it's a hot

issue. There are more than eighty U.S. installations of one type or another in Japan. More than thirty-five thousand military personnel."

I thought about that for a minute. Any military base is both a benefit and a bane to a local community. Saturday night off-duty young people, freed from the restriction of military discipline, money burning a hole in their pockets. Booze, drugs, sex, assaults. Be all that you can be. Aim high. Bound to be some need for diplomacy. But it didn't seem like anything that would draw the attention of the Koreans. I left it.

"Wife?"

"Old-school. Stays at home. Appears with him at functions but spends most of her time studying *ikebana*."

Very old-school. Dutiful wife, pursuing the art of flower arranging, floating along in the traditional upper-class Japanese lifestyle where men and women largely spend their married lives apart. I almost asked if the marriage was a happy one, but stopped myself. In this tradition, marriages are valued if they are successful. Happiness is irrelevant.

"The daughter?"

Owen nodded. "Pretty much like the briefing you got: a wild child. She got her mother's good looks and her father's money. There's not much hard data, but she's clearly staking out her own path …"

"One way to put it."

"Yeah." Owen shuffled through the papers. He turned to his computer screen. "I did some analysis on the photos that were sent to her father, just to be sure."

"Whattaya mean? Sure about what?"

He rolled his mouse around, clicking here and there. Windows opened, expanded, shrunk. I got some fleeting images of

Chie Miyazaki: pale flesh, dark glistening eyes, sheets, and tangled limbs. Owen minimized them and pulled up an itemized spreadsheet. He tapped the screen.

"With any kind of digital item, you have to make sure it's really what it says it is. It's too easy to fake this stuff, so I did some analysis to see if any of it had been Photoshopped."

"And?" I had a brief moment of hope.

"There's been no doctoring of the images. They're authentic."

I settled back in my chair, deflated. I didn't even know Chie Miyazaki. Her private life was theoretically none of my business. But now, in a curious way, it was my business. It wasn't so much the Miyazaki who were pulling me in; it was Mori. I thought about his journal and what it contained. Last night seemed so long ago. Images and memories settled on me like a fog: water splashing, the desperate burn of breath. I shook my head, trying to force out the memories like a swimmer clearing his ears of water. *Get a grip, Burke.*

Owen was looking at me, clearly concerned. I cleared my throat and sat forward, pretending I could understand the spreadsheet he had created. I thought about the pictures. She was basically a pretty young woman, but as far as I could tell, porn essentially drains its subjects of their humanity. Is that what she wanted? Was she making some sort of statement? I thought about what the roshi had told me about hypersexuality: a compulsive attempt at creating some kind of connection. What was it about her life that was so terrible that she made herself an object and yet also desperately sought to create a connection? It was beyond me.

"What a freak show," I sighed.

"I know," Owen answered. "I mean, I like pictures of naked chicks as much as the next guy, but this ..." He seemed at a loss.

I didn't see that there was much more to add on that subject. "What else have you got?"

Owen brightened up. "I ran the logs and auditing function on the data from the laptop." It took me a moment to remember what he was talking about. The fight in Lim's apartment and the laptop I took seemed like another series of distant and indistinct events to me. Owen saw my blank look. "Remember you asked me if I would be able to trace where the images from the laptop's surveillance program were being sent? Connor, you OK?"

I nodded, trying to stay focused.

"There were a few locations. Three cell phones. Two are unlisted numbers, but the other one is Lim's. I pulled it off the reverse directory the cops use." He clicked open another file and pointed out various entries. "Fairly consistent pattern—the surveillance program was sending notifications to the three cell phones. Then a few weeks ago, we get a new entry, an IP address."

I at least knew what an Internet Protocol address is. It is a unique identifier provided to each computer accessing the Internet.

I leaned in toward the screen. "Can you get a real address from this?"

Owen made a face. "Not usually. Typically you can get a general location. I ran this through a geolocation database provider ..."

"And?"

Owen clicked his mouse and called up Google Maps. He entered a string of coordinates into the search box. "Presto!" he said, beaming with pride. "They're somewhere in this vicinity."

The satellite image showed woods, lots of it, with some residential roads and NY Route 97 snaking along the right side of the map.

I was deflated. "This helps me how?"

Owen clicked some more, enlarging the map. "Take a look. It's a private community in northeast Pennsylvania called Mattson's Peak. Much less densely populated than a city block or even a residential street in a suburban location. I count seven houses that could be contained within the GPS coordinates associated with the IP address."

"Seven," I said.

"Sure. But this time of the year, I'd bet not many are occupied. Summer's over and there's no snow for skiing yet."

"It's a long shot," I told him, but then I remembered the magazines in Lim's apartment. "Skiing?"

"It's a recreational-living resort. Hiking, boating, horseback riding. They've got their own slopes for skiing when the weather's right. And with just this to go on, I agree, you might think it's a long shot. Except …"

"Except what?"

"I got to thinking once I ran the logs and audits study. I took a look at the tags associated with the photos that the Miyazaki received."

I was lost again. "Tags?"

"Sure. Most digital cameras store data about pictures in the file's EXIF tag."

I held up a hand. "Owen. English, please."

He grinned sheepishly. "Just details about the image. Ya know: focal length or flash use." He saw my impatience and rushed on. "And, if the device is GPS enabled, there's also a geotag, the GPS coordinates of where the photo was taken."

"And?"

"Some of the pictures were taken with cell phones." I started drumming my fingers on Owen's desk, so he sped up. The computer screen flashed once more. A file shrank down, and another expanded. "Some pictures were taken in Manhattan. Locations consistent with her place near NYU."

"She hasn't been to her apartment in weeks," I reminded him.

Owen could sense my growing impatience. "OK, OK, but the pictures are date stamped as well. The most recent shots were a mixed bag, but there were a few that had geotags on them. Here's a sample ..." The screen filled with a new picture of Chie Miyazaki, kneeling on a rumpled bed, a short robe hanging open, her legs spread wide in invitation.

"Owen ..." I didn't want to see any more of this.

He clicked and it disappeared. "A few were sent from the same IP address we already had. Indoor shots. But at least one was taken outdoors and was sent from a phone. And the GPS code?" He highlighted a string of numbers and copied them to a blank page: 41.53592,-75.030184.

He switched back to another screen. "And the GPS for the IP address?" He copied another string and pasted it below the first series of numbers: 41.52654,-75.048766.

"What's it mean?" I said.

He smiled in triumph. "The two locations? Less than a quarter mile away."

I thought about it for minute. "You're telling me they somehow overlooked this stuff, the ..." I made a face and held out a hand, asking for him to help.

"The EXIF tags," Owen said.

"Whatever. They somehow didn't think about this? The

setup at Lim's apartment seemed pretty tech savvy."

Owen shrugged, massive shoulders surging up like a wave. "You see it all the time. There's lots of different ways smartphones and other devices store information. You could snap a picture and later, when you send it, turn the GPS off so you think you can't be traced. But the data's already been recorded. Ya gotta remember these things are designed to record data, Burke. They do it in multiple ways and it's hard to circumvent them all."

"I thought they were phones."

"They're smartphones. They do way more than that. And mostly they record information about consumer behavior. It's a marketing gold mine."

"It's Big Brother," I replied.

"It's big business," he countered.

"OK, it's Big Brother and the Holding Company." But it was a reference from another time and it flew right over his head.

We thought for a while.

"Best lead we've got," he finally said.

I stood up. "You're right." I rubbed my face, trying to line up my next moves. "I'll need a map," I told him.

Owen smiled. "I thought you might," he said, and slid a paper my way.

I checked the time, aware that my window of opportunity was rapidly closing. It would take me a few hours to get to Mattson's Peak.

"OK. I need to rent a car."

"Where we going?"

"*We* are not going anywhere," I said, and Owen's face fell. "I need you to anchor things here," I explained. "I need someone who knows where I'm going and what I'm doing. Someone who can relay information." It was true, but I also thought Owen had a promising career ahead of him and he didn't need to get too tied up in what I was doing.

He nodded reluctantly. Deep down, I think he was relieved, but I appreciated that he wanted to help out.

"I'll need you to cut class," I told him.

He sniffed. "No problem there. I'm a doctoral student. I don't go to class. I just think deep thoughts." I had a hard time picturing that. I looked at Owen. His head was big and square. His hands looked big enough to palm a cinderblock.

"How's that going for you?" I asked with more than a little skepticism.

Owen shrugged. "Some days better than others."

"A lot of that going around," I agreed.

CHAPTER 12

The sky was a smooth, milky grey and I could sense bad weather coming. The clerk in the Pennsylvania sporting goods store tallied up my purchases without commenting on them: boots, socks, a coat, canvas field pants, and a flannel shirt. If she wondered what kind of idiot would come up into the hills at the end of November in running shoes, she didn't let on. She sat on a stool behind the counter, silently staring out the front window while I shopped. But she shared my feeling about the weather.

"Snow comin'," she said when I dumped my stuff on the counter. "Ya can smell it."

I was the only other person in the store. I nodded in agreement as she continued checking out my order: hat, gloves, a water bottle, and some energy bars, a daypack. "I'm up for a short vacation with friends, but I didn't think I'd need this stuff," I explained. In reality, I wanted to distract her from the rest of the items I was buying: duct tape, a folding hunting knife, binoculars, a GPS unit, and batteries. But she seemed oblivious to what she was ringing up. Her dark hair was parted into thick braids and grey strands wound through it like new wire. She was wearing one of those knit Peruvian hats with earflaps. It had the figure of a llama woven into it. Then again, maybe it was an alpaca.

"This time of year, ya can never tell what the weather'll be like," she advised me. She barely even looked at the merchandise. Never wondered at the dude from the city and his odd collection of gear. *Duct tape?* I imagined once the winter set in, business was slow. She seemed more than happy to bag my stuff without comment and take the money. We made small talk and I paid her. I changed into the new clothes in the dressing room. She gave me a thumbs up when I emerged. "Now you're talkin'," she told me, but by the time I reached the door, she was staring out the window again, watching the sky, alone in the silent store, waiting. I drove away and, as the cold hand of the storm cell began to push down from the sky, the hills seemed to hunker down around me.

In the woods, the world was leached of color; everything was grey. The cloud cover had darkened. The trees stood naked and silent amid a jumbled field of rocks, as hard and cold as iron. My breath steamed. I could hear the wind clattering the high branches all around me. Somewhere a blue jay rasped a complaint.

Mattson's Peak sprawled across the high, uneven ground that generations of Pike County farmers had tried to farm and then given up on. It was covered in hardwood and evergreens and studded with rock. It billed itself as a vacation community, and the houses and chalets were strung seemingly at random in an appropriately leisure-community-like formation along the private roads that looped through the woods. There was lots of green space, lots of privacy. Hiking and bridle trails wound through the acreage. The main hilltop, Mattson's Peak itself, had been cleared for the welcome and activity centers as well as the ski operation. I drifted into the welcome center and grabbed a few brochures and a map. The teenage receptionist appeared relieved that I didn't want to talk with her. She was busy texting but occasionally threw a glance out the window, watching the weather. In a few years she'd be wearing a knit hat with a llama on it.

I took a drive around the area to orient myself. At this time of year the place was quiet. There were few full-time residents, there had been no snow to attract skiers, and hunting was prohibited in the community's forests. The only person crazy enough to be out in the woods that day was me.

I had parked my rental car in one of the convenient parking slips that marked all the trailheads in the community. The visitor's map made it easy enough to figure out a route that would lead me to the location Owen had pinpointed. I decided to scout on foot. There wasn't much traffic and the road I was targeting was a cul-de-sac. Driving up would be too conspicuous. The crunch of tires carried a long way up here and there was no sense alerting anyone.

But the map, as the saying goes, is not the terrain. The trail I chose wound aimlessly through the forest, the path gnarled by tree roots. It crossed and recrossed a dry streambed that was choked with leaves. Eventually, I left the path and followed the slope downhill, checking the GPS as I went. My boots thudded against the rocks, a strangely resonant sound that hinted of the dense root networks underground and a carpet of pine needles above it. I shuffled through leaves and snapped twigs, lurching through the brush. *Not exactly the stealthy woodsman.* But I wasn't too worried about the noise I was making. It was swallowed up in the general sound of the forest. Birds called. The wind pulsed and leaves rustled. The bare tree limbs groaned above me. But if noise wasn't a problem, light was.

The day was fading. This was taking longer than I had anticipated and the storm was slowly smothering the afternoon light. I moved as quickly as I could, but the footing was treacherous and the slope increasingly steep. It was slow going. *Too long, Burke, it's taking too long.* The knowledge nagged at me. Finally I picked my way down a fissured rock outcropping and the ground started to level off. Ahead, through the vertical bars of grey tree trunks, I could glimpse color and horizontal lines, the angles of a roof, the shape of a house.

I ghosted along the tree line, close enough to get a look, but deep enough in the woods so no one would notice me. Or so I hoped.

There were seven houses along the cul-de-sac, four fairly close to the main road along either side of the upper part of the lane. All four seemed empty: no sign of cars, dried leaves collecting on doorsills, the windows dark. I could smell wood smoke, though. Someone was around. Farther down, the cul-de-sac widened and there were three houses clustered there, all alike: steep pitched roofs, high decks, and sliding glass doors. Your basic chalet getaway.

It was easy to spot the house that was occupied. It was the only one with smoke wafting out its chimney, and it was coming from the house across the road, farthest from my position. The place had two vehicles in the driveway, both with New York license plates.

I looped around the rear of the three houses, double-checking one after the other for signs of life. The first two: no cars visible, nothing coming out of the chimneys, no lights on. The final house seemed like the only place currently occupied. I slowed my pace and moved farther back into the woods. Wind gusted and leaves swirled. The cold worked on my injuries, old and new. I moved stiffly and my fingers tingled despite my gloves. I felt the urge to hunker down, to fold in on myself in the effort to keep warm. *Ignore.* I let the cold roll over and through me. No sense in fighting against it. Accept it and focus instead on the things that were important. *Look. Listen. Plan.* I squatted down and watched the last house. The only one with signs of life.

It had a high cement foundation. A flight of wooden steps led to the deck and the main entrance. The deck wrapped around three sides of the building and the front door was sliding glass and faced the road. There were windows all around. No sense being in a vacation wonderland without a view. From where I crouched, I was below a direct line of sight into the first-floor windows. But lights were on. I could see that. I scanned ahead of me. The ground swelled up behind the house; they had scooped out a place for the foundation in the side of the hill. As a result, when I finally got directly behind the building, I would be able to look into the rear windows from the cover of the woods. That was my plan. Sneak up and around the back and see what I could see. *Burke. Swordsman. Scholar. Peeping Tom.*

I moved deeper into the woods, away from the house. Into the gloom. I picked my way slowly up the slope. I saw another sliding glass door on the side of the house that was nearest to me. There was a gas grill there, shrouded for the winter, and an iron circular rack for cut firewood. It was half filled. I peered through the binoculars, working the focus to see inside the glass doors. Wall cabinets. A table. The stainless steel sentinel of a refrigerator. There was a dim light on over the stovetop, but no sign of anyone in the kitchen. I slung the binoculars around my neck and kept moving.

The rear of the house had smaller windows spaced out on the first floor and a large picture window centered on the second, with smaller windows on either side. The first row of windows was blank and dark. The big window on the second floor had light coming through it.

The slope of the woods took me up higher than I needed to be. I needed to get closer to the house, following the hill down to get an angle where I'd be able to see inside. I moved slowly and took my time. In low light, movement gives you away more than color or shape. I peered through the trees, checking my perimeter, listening for any noises that might have been out of place. But there was just the wind.

I felt the snow begin to fall before I actually saw it. Flecks of cold wetness touching my face. The snowflakes were tiny, and in the fading light they didn't stand out as much as they just added to the granularity of the visual field. It gave me more confidence as I approached the house. Nobody was going to be able to spot me now. I was another shadow, a blur deep in the tree line.

I made my way down and squatted behind a tree. The snowfall seemed to be accelerating. I focused the binoculars on the window. And got an eyeful.

I had been moving around in the gloom long enough for my eyes to accommodate to the relative darkness. There wasn't that much light in the upper room, but it seemed bright to me. I could make out everything: the sprawl of the wide bed, the rumpled sheets, the pale shapes of limbs, and torsos.

Chie Miyazaki was on all fours, a short, silky robe pushed up above her hips. Lim was taking her from behind, the two of them rocking. His mouth was open and the dark eyes were vacant, turned in on the moment. A pale blur passed across the line of vision. A second man moved toward Chie. He reached a hand up and stroked her jaw. She smiled and opened her mouth for him.

I pulled the binoculars down, glad to be in the dark woods with the cold and wind and the simple sting of a snowstorm gathering in strength. I felt guilty for looking at them and angry. Angry with them all: with Chie for debasing herself, with the men who let her do it, with whoever had made her this way. I wanted to rush down there and stop it.

But I didn't. It's one of the ways I've changed. Years ago, I would have let my anger carry me down the hill and into the house. I might have blundered through the situation and come out the other end intact, but then again, I might not. And the warrior's trade is not simply about the rush to battle, but also about walking away at the end of it. Or so I thought then.

It was the "guard against impetuous courage" angle again. I've seen the effects of haste too often in the dojo. Nerves or overconfidence or sheer inexperience sometimes impels your opponent to act too quickly. What happens next unfolds with a curious, clear inevitability. You almost feel sorry for the opponent. Yamashita sums it up with a shrug: "He walked right onto your sword."

I wasn't going to do that here. I was going to bide my time and look for an opportunity. I was going to move slowly and cautiously. I was going to be a shadow drifting through the woods. At some point, I'd see a chance. Then I was going to knock some heads together.

I scurried down the slope to the house, slowly circling the property. I probably could have levered open a window lock somewhere, but there were stickers on the glass from a security response company. I couldn't chance setting off an alarm. I squatted under the deck, invisible, as the snow swirled and started to cover the ground. I waited. I sniffed the air and smelled wood smoke. I remembered the woodpile by the kitchen door. I felt the evening coming closer and the temperature dropping.

When the kitchen door slid open, I took my time. I let the man fill his arms with wood, and then clubbed him with *mawashi empi uchi*, a roundhouse elbow strike. I like the technique because it uses the density of your elbow and forearm to deliver the strike. And you don't have to worry about breaking your fingers. I slammed my elbow into the point where jawbone and neck meet, a good, solid hit. The wood thumped onto the deck and I followed through on my momentum, sliding close to him and easing him down. I didn't know whether he was unconscious or just stunned. I dragged him out of sight of the door, pulled off my gloves, and used duct tape to tie him up. He never opened his eyes. He did moan at one point, so I plastered some tape across his mouth as well.

The kitchen sliding door was open. He hadn't planned on being outside too long and also expected to have an armful of firewood. I slipped inside and rolled the door closed. I stood still in the dim kitchen, my back to the glass door. The refrigerator hummed. I could hear footsteps upstairs. Voices. A woman's low, knowing laughter. *Laughter?*

The first floor had bedrooms in a line across the back wall to my left. A hallway stretched from the kitchen to the other side of the house. It was dark. To my right there was an expanse of living area with the wide glass doors of the main entrance. The room was studded with furniture: a low couch and easy chairs facing a fireplace. I could hear the wood snapping and crackling, and shadows danced from the flames. Another man was squatting in front of the hearth, poking at the logs and embers. He was barefoot, wearing grey sweatpants and no shirt. *Probably on a break from the party upstairs.* He was young and

Asian and hunched with muscle. He glanced casually at me as I came toward him, saying something in what was probably Korean. I didn't understand it, but it had a "What took you so long?" tone. Then he did a double take, as he realized what he was seeing didn't match his expectations. It slowed his reaction time, which was a good thing. Even so, he managed to straighten up and was just swinging the wrought iron fireplace poker around in my direction when I got to him.

He didn't call out in alarm. Maybe it was because his brain was still sex-fogged or because he was too surprised. Maybe it was because he was young and strong and probably the toughest guy he knew; he had that look about him. Besides, he was swinging a heavy iron poker at me. His eyes zeroed in on me and his mouth twisted into a type of smile I've seen before. He thought he was going to enjoy this.

As he swung the poker, I swarmed in. I grabbed his jaw with my right hand and squeezed. It wasn't meant to do anything other than distract him. People don't like having their heads touched; it makes them flinch involuntarily. He did, and I used the split-second gap in his focus to reach out with my left hand to cover the hand that held the poker. I spun him around and did a short, abbreviated version of the joint lock and throw called *shiho nage*. There are a couple of ways to do it, and I knew if I changed the angle of the lock just slightly, I could shatter his elbow joint. But I didn't do that because he would scream, and I didn't want an alarm raised. Instead, I locked him, twisting shoulder and elbow and wrist joints into angles bad for him, and yanked the poker away from him.

It was simple, really. I've been taking more dangerous things out of people's hands for years. His eyes widened in surprise—I could see the gold and red of the fire in them—but then I spun him and couldn't see his eyes anymore. I reached around his thick neck. He tried to get his chin down to fight the choke-hold I was putting him in, but I had been doing this for years as well. He was big and strong, but in the end, it's not about strength. It's about getting the placement of your arms just right and exerting enough pressure on the arteries. Cut the flow of blood to the brain and it takes about three seconds for a total blackout. He grunted with effort and I held on. Then I heard the telltale sigh. He sagged into my arms. I gave him a final few seconds of squeeze for insurance and then went to work with the duct tape again.

The stairway was carpeted and I made no sound going up. There was a broad landing that served as a small sitting room at the head of the stairs. A bar of light showed from under a closed door. In the gloom I could see another small fireplace set in the wide stone chimney that rose up through the center of the building. Above me snow sifted down on a wide skylight, the whisper of flakes no more audible than my footsteps.

They didn't put up much of a fight. It was hard to recover, I suppose, from the surprise, from the effort of focusing on something other than sex. Lim was the quickest. He made a lunging dash for a pile of clothes, but I got there before he did. Found the gun hidden there and pointed it at him. He sat back on the floor, silent, his hands up, passive. I didn't buy it for a second. I glanced over at the bed, backing away to keep them all covered. The other man lay there, his eyes unfocused with whatever drug he was taking. He sprawled naked and uncaring, everything about him limp and spent.

I remember the sheets were deep red satin. It made the con-trast with flesh that much more vivid. Chie Miyazaki rose up on her knees to face me. The short robe hung open. She didn't seem to care about the black automatic I was holding. She gave me a knowing smile. She seemed to be having difficulty focusing, to be lost in some private space. *Just as well.* The room smelled of perfume and the musk of sex. A small video camera was on a tripod at the foot of the bed.

"What now?" she said playfully. She glanced over at the man on the floor. "Lim?"

"I've come to take you away," I told her. It sounded lame, even to me.

"Mmm," she said. "Yes." Her eyes narrowed slightly. "I'll play." She thrust her chest forward and the robe fell back, her small breasts pointing at me. She reached up and rubbed her nipples, eyeing me slyly.

"You'll play?" I asked.

"There's always a new part to the game, isn't there?" She sounded pleased.

"What game?" My voice was tense but it didn't seem to register with her. She was still caught in some fog. She sank back on the bed, rolling to one side so she could see Lim on the floor. She cast a playful glance over her shoulder at me. I could see the line of her waist, the round swell of her hips, the legs slender and pale against the sheets.

"Lim," she said reproachfully, "he's new, isn't he?"

"What game?" I repeated.

She closed her eyes and smiled dreamily. "Fuck your way to freedom," she said. She lay back on the bed and watched me from the distant dream she was caught in.

"He's not here to play the game," Lim said.

Chie rolled over to look at him. "No?"

"He's here to take you away," Lim continued. He sat cross-legged and calm, but I knew what he was doing. He was watching me, gauging angles and distances, watching to see how distracting Chie's nakedness would be, waiting for a gap in my focus. It's what I would have been doing.

Chie frowned. "But I don't want to go away." She swiveled her head in my direction and smiled playfully. "I like this game."

"He's taking you to your family," Lim warned, and her eyes widened as she sat up in alarm.

"Come on," I said, gesturing with the pistol at the man half-conscious on the bed. He rolled himself off the mattress and stood, blinking and wobbly. I walked him over to the same side of the room where Lim was sitting. I wanted them both together so I could cover them more easily with the gun. I made him sit and he slumped down with a grunt. Chie had gone quiet and I focused all my attention on the two men on the floor. I was trying to figure out how I was going to tie them up. Lim first, I decided. There was a sound behind me and I turned to get a fleeting image of Chie Miyazaki, about to brain me with a table lamp.

I had walked right onto the sword.

CHAPTER 13

The demonstration did not go as expected. Little did over the next few days.

It began with a strange break in routine. We were summoned by Takano without warning and filed into the temple reception hall in silence, our minds racing. What could it mean? With the old man, every day was filled with a certain amount of tension. But that was simply the stress of daily life in the dojo—the way you felt from seeing the disgusted expression on his hard face, the rush of panic he could induce merely by focusing in on you with those implacable eyes. It was even more terrible than the training itself, the relentless grind and crunch of bodies colliding. But all these things were part of our normal existence. To be called away from training in the middle of the day, however, was unheard of, and with Takano things unheard of were rarely pleasant.

But we kept our heads down and our mouths closed. Only our eyes darted from place to place, like wary animals searching for the glimpse of some unseen danger. We moved as ordered, and as we filed into the temple hall the only things to be heard were the rasp of calloused feet on the bare wood floor and the quiet swish of cloth. I knelt right next to you and listened for the faint hiss of breath that would tell me your wounds had still not completely healed in the months since the old man's beating. But you were silent; perhaps you were finally recovered.

Looking back, of course, I realize your silence was not simply the result of a type of proud discipline. You certainly had that quality, and we had all watched you as every day after that evening in the snow you set your face like stone and pushed through the training despite what it must have cost you. But this day you were focused on something other than the ache of old wounds. I was close enough to see, and I had been watching you long enough to notice the subtle change in you as you knelt before the visitors.

The temple's reception hall was broad and high, with wooden walls grown dark from a thousand years of candle soot. The wide planks of the floor had been polished to a dull sheen by the passage of untold numbers of feet. At the head of the room, Takano sat with the temple's abbot and four guests. Two were clearly female servants, who were busy assisting with the serving of tea. The sole male guest was young and hard-mouthed, unremarkable except for a settled expression of dissatisfaction with the world. But the young woman with him! A delicate thing with wide eyes set in a heart-shaped face. She sat to one side and slightly behind the young man, who largely ignored her. When a servant carefully poured tea into cups on a small lacquered tray, the striking young woman in the dark traveling kimono took it and set it on the low table, bowing toward the young man. He reached for the cup without acknowledging her, focused on the conversation he was pursuing with Takano.

Did your eyes grow slightly wide when you first saw her? Perhaps there was some dilation of your pupils. Takano had schooled us in reading body language, and we all knew an involuntary reaction like this is often a symptom of sexual attraction. But after all these years I do not recall what it was I saw. I only know the certainty of what the signs told me.

You were smitten.

It seems odd to state the idea with such certainty. Can a connection like this be formed in a heartbeat? What strange stirrings flashed between you two?

This, too, is beyond my knowledge. And in my life, I regret to say it has been outside of my own experience. I think back to this event, mystified. Saddened. But also sure you were touched deeply.

We sat in a row before them and bowed to our sensei, the abbot, and the guests. The old monk was squat and jolly. He bowed back to us, seemingly overjoyed at the rare opportunity to have us in his temple. Takano gave us a bow that was a slight incline of his torso, no more. The young man eyed us with obvious disappointment.

"These are the trainees you spoke of?" He sniffed. "Takano-san, they fail to impress. I can smell the mud and manure on them."

In truth, we had been training hard. Our uniforms were damp with sweat, smudged and worn. But we loved that old abbot and would never have dreamed of trailing dirt into his reception room. The young man was being rude and I sensed the trainees around me tensing at the insult.

Takano stiffened as well, but he was always stiff. If the jab from the young man had offended him, he gave no overt sign of it. "The smells of the north country are different from Tokyo, Miyazaki-san," he conceded. He smiled cruelly. "And I am not raising flowers here."

"I hope not," the young man named Miyazaki countered. "We went to some trouble to visit you here, you know." He craned his neck, swiveling his head around to take in the surroundings. "We would never have come so far otherwise. After all, what would be here to see? Mundane architecture ..."

"The gardens are beautiful later in the spring," the abbot offered. "It is a shame it is so early in the season."

Miyazaki rode over him, directing his words at Takano. "And I'm sure the monks are equally undistinguished. Little learning and even less piety." If Miyazaki saw the hurt he caused as it was reflected in the abbot's eyes, he did not acknowledge it. And Takano said nothing. But I saw the young woman's brow furrow in displeasure.

"We are a small, humble temple, it is so," the abbot said, almost to himself. His usually cheery expression changed. Then a spark of indignation: "and yet we serve the Lord Buddha." He sat back and said nothing more, his tea growing cold as his hands worked his prayer beads. The young woman beside Miyazaki said nothing, but looked at the abbot sadly, her wide eyes filled with apology.

"I heard your training hall preserved some of the old ways, Takano-san." Miyazaki's wide mouth stretched out in a skeptical grimace. "I thought it worth a small effort to see if the rumors were true."

"They are true enough," the old man growled.

Miyazaki brushed some invisible dust off his sleeve. "I hope so." His head moved to look at the young woman beside him. "I would not want to disappoint my new bride." The woman gave a small, forced smile, but remained silent. Miyazaki turned back to Takano. "When can we see the training?"

It was an incredibly rude demand to make of a teacher of Takano's prominence, but the old man didn't react to the provocation. For those of us watching, it was a fascinating exchange. In our world, Takano was the demanding one, the rude one. Now this visitor from Tokyo was treating him with similar arrogance and disdain. But Takano seemed to meekly accept the treatment. It was astounding.

"In three days' time," Takano said. He saw the scowl of displeasure deepen on Miyazaki's face and, as the young man drew breath to protest, Takano gave a tight smile. "We would not want to disappoint you, Miyazaki-san. A demonstration worthy of such guests will take some time to arrange." He bowed to the Miyazaki, then to the abbot, and rose. We bowed as well, and followed him out of the room in silent wonder.

The visitors from Tokyo turned the placid economy of the temple upside down. Rumors flew: the monks said Miyazaki was the scion of an old and wealthy family—descendants of the zaibatsu, the influential financiers who had dominated the business life of Japan before the war's end. In the fifteen years since the emperor's surrender and the dawn of a new Japan in 1945, the Miyazaki had plotted and worked and curried favor, eventually rehabilitating themselves and once more occupying board seats on some of the most prestigious financial organizations in the country. And the recent brilliantly arranged marriage of this young man had served to demonstrate just how far back into favor the Miyazaki family had climbed.

It was not simply that she was beautiful—although she was. We all saw that. The way she moved, her quiet and unhurried grace, spoke of the type of training and mastery of etiquette that was made possible only by an upbringing in the most prestigious of families.

Miyazaki Chika-hime, the young woman who had silently commiserated with the abbot, was a princess, a daughter of royalty, and a member of a cadet line of the Imperial House itself.

The negotiations that must have taken place, the elaborate and convoluted series of statements and regrets, the promises implied and otherwise that must have been part of the marriage proposal would have been truly astounding. I was young and naïve then, but even so I sensed that the political and financial deal that must have accompanied the betrothal was a dense, knotted tangle of actions. And when I thought of that grim-faced upstart from Tokyo and compared him to the beauty of his new wife, I did not know whether to be outraged by the marriage or simply amazed at the audacity of the Miyazaki clan and their ability to pull it off.

But here they were, newly married and traveling the country as a prelude to their new life together. And if the husband appreciated his good fortune, it did not show. If anything, he seemed to resent his situation, as if the marriage his family had worked so hard to arrange served to simply underscore how unworthy he was to consort with a woman of such a lineage and such beauty.

Takano called me to him later that day as the light faded and night approached, damp and cold. He was sitting alone, staring out into a small garden: grey rocks, raked soil, and a few gnarled bonsai. I knelt and bowed, but he sat for another long minute before turning and acknowledging my presence.

"Our guest wants a demonstration, Mori." His voice was almost dreamy. I said nothing and, indeed, it seemed to me at the time he was not really speaking to me at all. His eyes had a curious lack of focus; they were seeing something, but it was not me. His mouth twisted in a grimace and he rocked slightly from side to side. Then he brought me into focus.

"I am told he is an enthusiastic kendoka," Takano told me, referring to the modern version of swordsmanship. "He has a brutal reputation in the dojo around Tokyo." He gave a dismissive grunt. "Kendo. As if that comes anywhere close to what I am teaching you here."

Takano smiled at me then. "He will not merely want a demonstration, Mori. No. He is the arrogant spawn of a jumped-up line of clerks. Money and power have led them to expect whatever they want they can have. And he wants to be a bugeisha, Mori. He thinks he is one of us." Again, the odd smile. "Well, we will certainly oblige him. He will ask for a match to try his sword against one of ours. So be it." The tight line of his mouth curved upward at the ends, a smile of sorts, but terrible for all that.

"So ... you will prepare the demonstration." Takano rattled off a series of details about how he wanted the event structured. Then he sat back, satisfied.

But there was one detail I needed clarification on. "Am I to fight with him, Sensei?"

His eyes narrowed. "Oh, yes. But before that, a warm-up match, I think." His gaze drifted off to the side and he stared once more into the garden.

"Sensei?"

He did not turn to look at me. "Did you see him today, gawking at her?" He cackled to himself. "That idiot. Well, she will need a guide as they tour the area over the next few days. Yamashita will do quite nicely, I think."

I sat in silence, puzzled. Then Takano continued. "It was a miracle his nostrils didn't flare as he drank in her scent." His voice was dripping with disgust. "I think a day or so in close proximity to her will drive him completely over the edge ..."

He turned to face me. "Miyazaki will have two matches, Mori. First Yamashita, but we will keep that our little secret, neh? He's a peasant, but a brutal fighter from what I hear. So we will pit him against Yamashita first. I do not think his wounds have completely healed." Takano's face took on an expression of warped glee. "Even if he were to prevail, the fight will take a toll on Yamashita and he will be forced to leave. But I think it likely he will lose. This woman will distract him. And think of the humiliation as he is defeated in front of her and the entire dojo." He closed his eyes, settling back in satisfaction, completely enthralled by the vision he was conjuring. "The rest will be simple. Miyazaki will be tired. We will have had the opportunity to watch his technique. So ... when

Yamashita has failed, I will send you in to redeem the honor of our training hall." His eyes lost their focus again as he turned inward. "Yes. That should do quite nicely."

I bowed low, aghast and eager to hide that fact from him. I scurried away from that dark place, lest the madness in that room be contagious.

CHAPTER 14

Here's the thing about getting hit hard in the head: it's not the immediate burn and blackness, the taste of something in your mouth like concrete dust, that's worrisome. It's that the aftereffects can linger long after you resurface into the land of the living. Getting hit like that does things to your brain, slamming it up against your skull. And I like my brain. I was worried about it, because I was feeling nauseated and it might mean I had a concussion. I've had them before, of course. But right now, I needed my brain to help me figure out a way to escape from Lim.

He and his pals were in the downstairs living area, and I could hear the rumble of urgent conversation, but couldn't make anything out. Maybe they were speaking Korean—an entirely different language group from Japanese—so I was out of luck. Then again, maybe my brains had been scrambled so hard that everything sounded like Korean.

They had tied me up with my own tape, binding my wrists and ankles. I wormed my way into a sitting position, spit some carpet fiber out of my mouth, and blinked.

Chie Miyazaki was sitting on the bed, watching me with the cool intensity of a cat.

"Your father's worried about you," I said. I had to clear my throat to get the words out.

She looked dismissive. "My father's nothing but a suit," she said. Her English was colloquial, unaccented. "He's not worried about me. He's worried I might be having some fun and it won't fit in with the refined image—diplomats and all that."

"Your family's worried," I persisted. "Your grandfather." It was hard for me to believe that old lizard cared much about anyone, but maybe I was reading the situation wrong.

She jumped up from the bed, her body tensed as if anticipating an assault. "My grandfather!" Her eyes narrowed. "You've seen him?"

I nodded. Big mistake. It made the headache that was lurking in my skull a little sharper, a bit more insistent. Just then Lim came back in with his pals.

"Lim," Chie said, "my grandfather sent him." She was standing in front of Lim and her voice vibrated with tension.

Lim put a hand on each arm and steered her toward the door. "Go get dressed now," he said.

"My grandfather!" she insisted. I don't know what was behind the sudden anxiety. Could it simply be the knowledge that her grandfather was in the country and hunting her down? Whatever it was, it generated a fear in her that was real and powerful.

Lim's voice got a little harder. "I said go get dressed. We've got things to do." He softened slightly, saying, "It'll be OK," and gently moved her to the door. Then he looked at me. He waited until Chie was gone before speaking. He sat down on the bed and sighed.

"What am I going to do with you, Mr. Burke?"

So he knew who I was—maybe I could use that. I shrugged as if the answer was simple. "I think you're going to let me go," I told him. I tried to get my voice to sound calm and confident.

He smiled when I answered him. "And why would I do that?"

I'd been working on this little scam and was pretty proud of myself as I launched into it. "Because just before I came in the house I called my partner and said if he didn't hear from me in an hour, he should get the state troopers down here."

Lim looked at me, and for a minute I thought my threat was going to work. His expression was blank while he considered the implications of what I said, but then his eyes narrowed. "You called him from outside?" I nodded. *Ouch.* I had to stop doing that. He got up from the bed. "You made the call here, right near the house?"

"Sure," I told him. "With my cell."

Lim smiled again. This time for real. "With your cell." He bent over the bed. There was a pile of stuff there that they must have taken when they tied me up: the flashlight, some energy bars, the knife. He rummaged through the pile and found my cell phone. Picked it up and turned it on. It was a cheap folding unit. He opened the phone and turned the glowing display to face me.

"You are so full of shit," he said. I didn't respond. He waved the phone in my face. "No bars, Burke," he said. "You can't make a cell call from here. I've tried. You have to go all the way up to the top of the resort to get any reception. So I don't think anybody's coming." He paused. "And I don't think there is any partner. I think it's just you." He nodded to himself. "If you had someone else with you, you'd have used him to come in here and take us down. But you didn't ..." He looked out the window at the gloom and snow, momentarily lost in thought. "Man, it's really coming down," he noted. Then he looked back at me and smiled. It was not a happy smile. "I'd better get up to the resort. I've got a phone call to make. And you know what? I'm not going to rush. The roads are going to be slippery. And I think we've got all the time in the world with you." He tossed the little phone on the floor next to me and left. I heard some male conversation downstairs, the heavy glass doors slid open and closed, and the sound of a big engine starting.

Then they came in. Lim's pals.

They still seemed a little spaced out to me, but the anger was burning through the fog of whatever they were on. Everyone was dressed by this time. Their boots had lug soles. Just the sturdy sort of thing you need for a winter hike, but useful in other ways as well. The two guys I had taken out on my way into the house were maybe still a little stunned and maybe not at the top of their game, but they were close enough. I could see from the set of their shoulders and the way they placed themselves on either side of me that something bad was coming. I tried scrunching myself into a tight ball, but it ultimately didn't do much good. With my hands tied behind my back, it was hard to shield my head effectively. And, as Lim said, they had all the time in the world.

There was some good momentum and windup to the first kick. Maybe the guy had played some soccer in his youth. Maybe it was all that taekwondo. The end result was the same. His kick caught me high on the left rib cage and actually lifted me up off the ground. I felt something give, like a piece of plastic coated in rubber, breaking with a dull, muted crack. His second shot was aimed at the same target and I rolled my shoulder down to attempt to block it, tensing to take the impact. When the kick landed, it slammed into the meat of my triceps. But his partner was on the other side of me—the unprotected side—and saw the gift I had given him. He caught me with the toe of his boot, right in the solar plexus. My breathing stopped and my lungs burned. I gasped and tried to roll away from both of them. But I couldn't get out of range effectively. Then one of them clipped my head and the world roared and went dark for a minute. I gasped some air into me, and tried to keep moving, rolling this way and that to avoid presenting an open target. That was the theory, at least. As they rained kicks down on me, I convulsed. They laughed.

I was desperate to keep my head down and my back up, using the bone and muscle there to serve as some sort of shield. I was afraid they'd turn me over, exposing the soft tissue of the abdomen to attack. It's hard to kick someone to death. It takes time and technique, especially if the victim knows how to cover up. However, stomping someone to death is relatively straightforward if you can turn the victim onto his back. You can crush the throat or simply jump on the unprotected stomach area. Then the internal bleeding starts. It's not quick and it's not pretty, but it works.

But these guys weren't trying to kill me; it seemed they were just trying to hurt me. Payback is an international custom understood in any language. But it was hot and sweaty work, and once they were sure they'd inflicted enough damage, they got tired of it and simply left me on the floor.

My ears rang and my body was on fire. I tried to get up into a sitting position but couldn't. I retched weakly. The big muscles in my thighs were paralyzed with a scalding flood of lactic acid. I simply lay there and tried to get my breathing under control. As the roaring in my ears faded I could hear the sound of a wet animal rasping and realized it was me. I panted like a dog for some time, helpless to resist the instinct to gulp as much air as possible. I spat out the bile in my mouth in a series of weak, fluttering actions, like a faulty machine sputtering before it finally runs out of steam. But I worked at summoning up some discipline and, little by little, I pulled it together.

It is what Yamashita has taught me—the way you forge a link between body and spirit, no matter what the cost. How you work through the pain. How you endure. I'd forgotten it for a time on the waterboard. Maybe I was making up for my past failure. Maybe that beating was a perverse kind of gift, one more chance for me to get it right.

It's easy to talk about the Warrior's Way in the dojo. Training is hard, but nobody's really going to die. And you're putting yourself through it voluntarily. There's a point to it, a goal. And you've chosen the experience. You. It implies a type of personal control. All that talk about losing the ego in martial arts training is right in some ways, but really wrong in others. Because in a contradictory sense, it's all about ego, about the hard bright spark deep down that believes you're going through something that, in the end, makes you better, stronger, more complete. You choose to do it. You.

It's different when you're trussed up and helpless on the floor. Being the victim of an assault like this makes you realize just how fragile your hold on life is, the insignificance of that spark of ego, and how easily snuffed out the whole enterprise can be. Bound and helpless, it's easy to feel there is no will, no ego in control. In some ways, it's easier to surrender totally. You become just an organism. Nerves fire, capillaries fill and drain, muscles tense and go slack. You're just meat and moisture, bone and reflex. A locus of pain.

Or you can try to be more.

I may have drifted for a while. A sob jolted my broken ribs awake. Was that noise me? I rolled onto my knees and lay my forehead flat on the floor as the roaring started in my head again. I waited it out.

I got an image from my early days of training with Yamashita.

It wasn't unusual for him to cross swords with novices like me. He wasn't doing it to be nice, to give me some personal attention. He was testing my worth by simply trying to grind me down. He would do just that, of course, and, when I was gasping for breath, he'd dump me onto the floor with casual disdain. He'd nod slightly to himself as if at a job well done. Then he'd turn to go. As he walked away, I'd watch the broad expense of his back, the play of the fabric of the dark blue training top across his torso, the ridgeline where his shaved head met his neck. Sometimes I'd wonder whether I could stand it anymore. Whether I had it in me. And what he ultimately wanted from me. He'd pause slightly as if he could feel my eyes on him, as if he could sense the questions I was silently asking. He never answered them directly. Instead, he would pause, turn his head, and simply say, "Get up." It was a command as simple as it was inexorable.

In the end, I learned to fall less. To endure more. And I learned there was no real secret insight he was teaching beyond the simple act of getting up once more. Of taking it, no matter what the cost.

I rocked there on the floor, feeling the damage I'd taken from the beating. *Get up*. It was hard to gauge just how broken I was. Pretty battered at the least. But I flexed my arms and legs slightly, tugging against the duct tape. Some ability to move, I noted. So it was pain getting in the way more than any real structural damage. Good news of a type. *Get up*. I'd clenched my hands into fists during the attack and I was pretty sure the finger bones were intact. I worked my hands, opening and closing the fingers. Slow, but OK. I rolled my head to one side and squinted around the room. My eyesight wasn't the greatest— there was some swelling across my brows and the concussion made the visual field dance—but I could see. *Get up*.

It took me a few tries to get upright. I listed against the bed and just let myself breathe for a while. When they left, they had closed the door, satisfied I wasn't going anywhere. A good beating generally solves all kinds of problems and, besides, I was bound hand and foot. So they never even thought to take the flashlight and other things off the bed—like the knife.

If I could get up onto the bed, I might be able to somehow get the knife and use it to cut the duct tape. But just being on my knees and leaning against the bed made me sick. *Get up*. I wasn't sure I could actually stand tied up the way I was. My balance was too rocky. I needed my hands to help get me up. And they were pinned behind me.

But they had only bound my wrists. If they were real pros, they would have taped my upper arms together as well. But they weren't pros. At least I didn't think so. It had been too easy to get in the house. There had been no security set up. And if they were real kidnappers, how come they were all partying? Lim was going to make a phone call and I assumed it was to get some instructions about what to do with me. He might have a good idea of what needed to be done, but fortunately for me he wasn't sure. That meant he was taking orders from someone else and was new to all this. And I knew they weren't pros because, after delivering a fairly competent beating, they had made a major mistake. Two mistakes, actually.

The first was that they hadn't seriously crippled me. Lim knew my name, but clearly he and his pals really didn't know anything about me. They didn't realize after what they had done, I was going to have to come back at them. A normal person would just roll around in pain. But I wasn't normal. I knew something about pain and how it was possible to work with it.

You never really fight it; you just accept it and force yourself to function anyway. It's about will and control and how far you're willing to go in pursuit of a goal. The ego thing again.

The second mistake they made was even worse. Amateurs that they were, they had left a knife in the same room with me.

So I got up. Simple to say, but it wasn't pretty, and it took a while. I really needed to be able to use my arms, and that wasn't going to happen with them tied behind my back. I sat on the floor, feet stretched out in front of me, rocked from side to side, and worked my bound wrists under my butt, up along the backs of my thighs and down toward my feet. I've spent years stretching like this and it should have been easy. But it's hard to work against the reflex that tightens muscles when they're damaged or in pain. It takes time and concentration even in the best of circumstances. When I got my wrists down to about my heels, I almost despaired—I was wearing hiking boots with thick soles, and they added an extra few inches to the stretch. As I leaned into it I crunched down on whatever had snapped in the ribcage. There was a bright, hot thrust of pain that made me catch my breath. But I let it come. I worked on the breathing. I pushed.

And my hands came up around the soles of my feet and I got up.

I sagged onto the bed and cut the tape off my ankles, then worked carefully to do it on my wrists—no sense slicing a tendon or cutting an artery when I was so close. My arms came free and I took a deep breath. I felt dizzy and sweat was cold on my forehead. My eyes stung. Part of me just wanted to lie down and moan.

Get up.

The real question now was what I was going to do next.

Escape would be nice—he who fights and runs away and all that—but that wasn't why I had come here. I sometimes wonder whether there was only one quality Yamashita had seen in me all those years ago, and that was a simple, dogged stubbornness. He's done a great deal for me, but above all he's compressed and polished this one aspect of my personality to a hard, gemlike luster.

So there was no question of running away. I needed to get Chie Miyazaki out of the building with me. And that was going to take some doing. A number of bad schemes occurred to me. I could knot the sheets into a rope, tie it to the bed, and hang it out an open window. I would hide in a closet until my captors discovered my apparent means of escape, wait until they ran out to look for me, then slip out and find Chie. Alternately, I could brace myself up against the walls in the narrow entranceway to the bedroom and shimmy up above the doorjamb, where I could pounce on whoever entered the room. But I had left my ninja climbing claws at home.

Even with the concussion, I knew each idea to be bad. *A youth wasted watching B movies, Burke.*

New strategy. I took a deep breath and moved to the door, making as little noise as possible. I paused, alert to any whisper of external noise that might suggest a guard was waiting just outside the door. Nothing. I eased the door open and slipped out onto the dark landing. It was slow going and perhaps "slipped" is a bit too fluid a description for the way I was moving, but every second I was in motion made me feel a little more like myself—functioning, integrated. In control.

The second floor stretched across the back half of the chalet and opened, loftlike, onto the living room below. I crouched and moved on all fours, toward the loft railing, and peered down. There were a few table lamps spilling circles of warm light on the floor and the fire occasionally snapped and flickered into the general gloom caused by the snowstorm. I could hear the murmur of voices and got close enough to see three of Lim's companions on a big L-shaped couch, sitting forward, arms resting on their knees with their shoulders hunched. They didn't look happy. Chie Miyazaki sat curled up in a broad armchair, fully dressed and silent. I inched a little closer to get a better view. They seemed tense, people anxious for news but worried what it was going to be.

Finally we all heard the sound of Lim's car returning. The motor revved as he gunned the vehicle up the slight incline of the snow-covered drive. Gravel crunched against rubber. The sliding door to the house opened and I ducked down.

A quick exchange of questions, and a glance up my way. Smug assurances from his pals. Lim turned to Chie.

"We've got to go," he told her.

"Where?" She was wearing a dark ski jacket and burrowed herself deeper into it.

Lim shook his head impatiently. He moved toward her. "C'mon. Get up. We've got to leave."

"What about him?" she jerked her chin in my direction.

"Don't worry about him."

Chie got up, agitated. "Don't worry? He knows where I am." Lim didn't respond. She took a step toward him and grabbed his arm. "Lim. My grandfather sent him …" I could hear the tension vibrating in her voice.

Lim nodded and turned to the other three. A string of instructions in Korean. The men stood up slowly, nodding and blinking.

Lim turned back to Chie. "OK, we're out of here."

She crossed her arms. "What's happening?"

"Nothing," Lim told her. "Get in the car."

"Nothing?" Her voice rose an octave. "What are we going to do about him?" Her arm swept out and pointed toward the loft.

By this time the other three men were standing, rocking uneasily. Maybe they were uncertain about what they had been told to do. Or reluctant.

"They're going to take him to the quarry," Lim said. "They'll drop him off and leave him there." I remembered the map of Mattson's Peak that I had picked up earlier in the day—the remote northern edge was bound by an abandoned quarry. The trails there were marked in red with big caution signs warning against the crumbling cliffs and sheer drops.

"It's not going to change anything," she protested. "He'll just come at us again."

"He's not going to come at us again," Lim said, trying to soothe her.

Something in his expression made her do a double take. "What … Lim, what do you mean?" I could see the awareness slide over her face. She was finally getting it. They weren't going to drop me off at the quarry except in the broadest sense. What they were really planning was to drop me off the quarry cliff itself. Nice. City slicker gets lost in snow, tumbles to his doom. The fall probably wouldn't be a clean one and might explain the extensive bruising they'd find at the postmortem.

Lim grabbed her by the arm. "Don't push it, Chie. You don't need to know."

"Let go of me!" She pulled free, backing away. Lim came after her and she resisted, but it didn't seem to me that she was putting up more than a token fight. I thought back to the roshi's description of people like her: they were victims and were in some ways probably resigned to the futility of resistance. Lim gave a meaningful nod to his men and trundled her out the door.

The three men glanced at each other and slowly started to head for the stairs. One of them took out a pistol and took the lead. I backed away from the railing and pushed myself to my feet. Swayed a little. *Get it together, Burke.* I scanned the space for anything that might be a better weapon than the knife, but it was dark and difficult to see. And I didn't have time.

Yamashita trains us hard in the use of weapons, but at the more advanced levels he also works to make us see the violent potential in everything. He has expounded on the lethal uses of a rolled-up magazine, of ballpoint pens. Pillows and panty hose. It sounds creepy, but we prefer to think about it as a type of enhanced awareness, an openness to the world as it is in all its complexity. Sarah Klein said she wanted to look at the world differently. She didn't deny the reality of what I saw; she just preferred not to focus on it. Maybe it was one of the reasons she left. How can two people live in the same place and see two different worlds?

I didn't have much to work with on that landing in terms of weapons. And I had no time. I was left with the basics: the contrast between the lighted room below and the dark landing; the mindset of a group of men expecting to find me trussed up and helpless in a bedroom; the geography of a stairwell. Gravity. It was enough.

Climbing stairs requires a certain subliminal focus. You're moving forward and moving upward, but you have to be careful about leaning forward slightly to avoid tumbling backward.

You're shifting balance between each leg. Forward. Up. Side to side. We do it automatically, but nobody is at his best climbing stairs.

The guy with the gun was in the lead, of course. He wasn't expecting me, so there was a split-second pause when I swung in front of him at the head of the stairs—the startle response. The two men behind him were still moving closer, so now they were jammed a little tighter together in the stairwell. I slammed at the forearm of the first guy's gun hand, driving down like a hammer, a cleaver, an ax, going for the ulnar nerve and giving it all the savage force I could muster. I rammed my right hand into his throat. It brought his head up, disturbing the neat coordination of stair climbing, bringing his center of balance a little higher. I shoved him up and back, and he gurgled and fell backward, taking his pals with him.

I picked up the gun from where he had dropped it and stumped down the stairs as rapidly as I could. They were trying to untangle themselves at the bottom, a little confused, but they were recovering fairly quickly. The first guy was concentrating on trying to breathe, but the other two were shooting quick glances at each other, planning their next move.

I pulled the receiver back on the automatic pistol and pointed it at them. "Please," I croaked. "Give me an excuse." They slumped slightly in defeat and held their hands up.

I backed them up against the wall. One had a big hooded parka and I made him take it off. Then I had them get their choking friend upright. When I told them to drop their pants and face the wall, they seemed momentarily puzzled and alarmed. Let them worry. My thought process was simple: I wasn't operating on all cylinders and I wanted an edge. It's hard to move quickly with your pants down around your ankles.

You either pause to yank them up or have to shuffle around like you're on a chain gang. Either way, it would give me a second or two. I backed away from them and shrugged into the parka. It was the most dangerous moment of the whole thing. Gun transfer to left hand, right arm in, gun transfer back. Shrugging the coat up while keeping them covered. One of them was craning his head to see me. "Don't turn around," I said. The rasp in my voice gave a little more menace to my delivery. "If any one of you comes after me, I'm coming back and I'll shoot you all. Clear?" The head jerked back to face the wall. I could see all of their backs hunch with tension. They were probably all expecting me to shoot them anyway. At that moment, the pain of their beating still throbbing, it was an option that would have worked for me.

Outside, the snow was blinding. I got my hood up and made my way down the broad steps at the front of the chalet. Lim's car was idling in the driveway with the second car parked in a spot closer to the building. I shuffled through the snowdrift and opened the back door of the second car like I was getting it ready to dump a body into it.

Then I waded ahead to the driver's side where Lim sat. In the half-light and swirling snow I was an indistinct figure in bulky winter clothes, hood up against the weather. I tapped on the window and motioned for him to lower it.

It whirred down. I drove my right hand in and the muzzle of the pistol slammed into his temple. A shocking violation of handgun safety, since the impact might have made it go off. But it didn't, and I got the door open and dragged Lim out onto the snow. He moaned faintly. I wanted to hit him again— *just to make sure*, I told myself. But it was a lie. He was, after all, the man who was going to have someone throw me off a cliff.

To be honest, I just wanted to hit him.

But by that time I was pretty much out of gas. It took most of my remaining energy to drop into the driver's seat of Lim's car and drive off into the storm.

CHAPTER 15

Over the next few days, you chaperoned Chika-hime while I did all I could to learn a little more about Miyazaki.

The monks were only too eager to talk. They had heard of the way Miyazaki treated the abbot and seethed with resentment. Their love for that old man overwhelmed their usual reserve.

"He abuses the servants," one confided.

"This was a bad marriage," another said. "I hear the princess weeping at night."

"Truly an evil man," commented another, sweeping a flagstone path and keeping his eyes down and his voice low. "The world would be a better place without him." He saw my shocked expression and grinned sheepishly. "Ah, Mori-san, we all struggle to follow the eightfold path. And compassion is so important, yes?" He shrugged and started sweeping again. "But I am merely a monk and not a Buddha." A hard swipe of the broom sent dirt flying. "And he is still a devil."

Takano reached out as well, making phone calls, surprising old contacts around Tokyo who knew something of the Miyazaki family. The conversations that took place were cautious ones. The Miyazaki family was on the rise, growing wealthier and more politically connected by the year. The marriage to the princess had been merely the latest move in a carefully orchestrated process of rehabilitation that had been in operation for almost twenty years. But despite the caution and the elliptical responses, Takano was able to flesh out a picture of the young man who had come to a distant temple to challenge his best students.

Miyazaki's family had clung ferociously to the practice of the martial arts, even during the postwar ban on their practice. The war years had shown the world the worst aspects of our martial culture. There was no denying it. Some martial arts sensei had been enthusiastic supporters of the imperial ambitions that brought calamity to our nation, and as a result, MacArthur had banned training in the old arts, seeing them as vehicles for fostering the rabid nationalism, the cruelty and aggression, that marked the 1930s and forties. You and I know, Rinsuke, the warrior's arts can be things of fierce beauty. But if they are treasures, they are treasures passed on by people, and so can be warped and bent to bad purposes.

I do not know whether the Miyazaki family really understood the bugei in this way. Certainly from looking at their son, I doubt it. But they were shrewd enough to sense the prohibition on the old ways would pass. And they also knew something of the hold these arts have on our nation. So they clung to them, supporting the old masters through the lean postwar years with stipends, much as the old daimyo, the feudal lords, had done centuries ago. And when the ban was lifted in 1948, the Miyazaki made sure their largesse was remembered and their fidelity to the spirit of Japan was made known.

The young Miyazaki was raised in this tradition. Like many of us, he was exposed to the arts as a schoolboy. But his family insisted he immerse himself in training in the dojo as much as they demanded he excel in school. They were shaping an heir who would build a record of achievement not only in the best schools of the new Japan, but also on the hardwood floors of dojo, where tribute was paid to the old ways.

He focused on kendo, the way of the sword. We were all familiar with the art; many of us had trained extensively in it prior to arriving at Takano's door. Although a modern fighting form, it has a certain elegance and rigor that suggests a connection to the old schools of fighting. The technique has been adapted to a competitive environment that is almost sport-like, but even so, its inspiration in the way of the samurai makes kendo one of the modern martial arts forms people respect. Miyazaki grew to be quite skilled in the art and ultimately served as the captain of his university team. He achieved some distinction in prefectural competition, but never advanced in grade beyond the level of fourth dan.

The sensei that Takano spoke with did not say why such a gifted player was never promoted. But their silences and inflections, the stray hint here and there, told Takano all he needed to know. At the higher levels of rank in kendo, technical competence alone is not enough for advancement. Issues of character, of spirit, come into play. And there, Miyazaki had been found wanting.

He had cut his teeth early on in training with old-time instructors who still followed the practices of prewar kendo. Even today kendo is an aggressive, austere art, but the old-school players were noted for their no-holds-barred approach. It was called gekken, severe sword, and its ruthless savagery fit Miyazaki's personality perfectly. He was able to rein himself in when required, but his practice never lost a certain savage quality. He was a particularly brutal team captain at university, and there were rumors that he was personally responsible for crippling more than one novice in hazing rituals.

After college, although concentrating on the family business and political interests, he still trained. But he drifted from one dojo to the next, sometimes of his own volition, at other times because he was banned from further play at a specific location. He sought out the schools with the toughest reputation, always looking to prove himself and to wipe away the shame of his lack of promotion.

It was why he had come to see Takano. If he had heard the same stories we had heard about the old man, ones that told of his mastery, his rock-hard fidelity to tradition, and his brutal insistence on perfection, it was no wonder Miyazaki was drawn to the small dojo tucked away in a small temple far to the north of Tokyo. Miyazaki must have thought Takano was a kindred spirit. For his part, the old man saw Miyazaki as an answer to a prayer. Takano may have had distant dreams of the way in which an association with the Miyazaki family would advance his fortunes. It was rare that he acted without more than one motive. For the most part, however, I think Takano saw Miyazaki's visit as a way to humiliate one of his most troublesome students.

Takano had tried to break you, Rinsuke, but he could not. It rankled. We all knew this. Why did he hate you so much? After all these years, I am still unsure. He was a master of his art and had not been bested by anyone for decades. Perhaps he expected such dominance to be his in all things. You accepted him as teacher, but never acquiesced in the submission he really craved. You never became a disciple. He wanted you to be his man, not your own, and you could never bring yourself to give in.

You were always hardheaded, Rinsuke. I say that with admiration, even now, even knowing what it cost you.

And then again, as I look back all those years, I wonder whether Takano was really afraid of you. I wonder whether he saw the potential in you to exceed his own skill and could not bear the thought of the student eclipsing the sensei.

The motives for what he did were never fully revealed— Takano would not have been a master if he were that easily read. But his plan was clear.

He had in Miyazaki a savage fighter itching to prove himself. Takano had sensed your attraction to the princess and arranged for the two of you to be constantly together. Your focus would be on the woman. Miyazaki's would be on the fight. Takano would use the visitor from Tokyo to teach you a lesson, to humiliate you in front of your peers. That you were perhaps not fully healed from the beating he had given you made your defeat almost certain. And, the old man planned that I would watch the match between you and Miyazaki, and in the process I would learn enough to defeat him in the inevitable rematch to salvage the honor of the dojo. With Yamashita broken and Miyazaki humbled, Takano would, in one stroke, rid himself of a hated student and ensure the reputation of his training hall.

With the passing of time, it all seems so petty. I hated Takano for it for years, but now my anger has faded. Is it wisdom or simple weariness that comes with age? Even now I am unsure. You and I have trained all these years to develop a type of focus, to acquire an ability to see things as they really are. The old masters talked about "Enzan no metsuke," the ability to gaze at things and see the big picture, as if looking at a far mountain. They cautioned us to be aware of, but never distracted by, the obvious. To see through petty distractions and the illusion that is life. But how often have we been deluded? We hoped for clarity always, but for me, I remember as many foggy days in my life as bright ones.

I was a dutiful student, and for that I am ashamed. Despite my insight into the real motivation behind Takano's plan, I could not disobey him. Even for a friend like you, Rinsuke. I rationalized my actions, and even now, as I finish this last message to you, I half believe it. My life's path had been set. I would serve. I always would serve, no matter what it cost me. You know of the life I led after leaving Takano, of my service to the Imperial House. You know what I say about my choices is true. Yet I imagine you reading these words and smiling ruefully. If I were sitting there before you, there would be only silence. But your face would slowly form a look that cut through all my rationalizations. Thinking about it, I hang my head in shame. You know me; the odd combination inside me of ambition, practicality, and pride. What could I do? If I refused Takano, he would deny me my certificate of mastery and all the training would have been for nothing. If I refused, another one of us would have volunteered for the match. And if you were doomed to be defeated by Miyazaki, I believed I was the only one who stood a chance of beating him.

So I trained. I burned, stoked with shame and anger and resignation. But I prepared for the match.

The day before it was to take place, the old man ordered me to go get you. The Miyazaki had taken residence at a local ryokan, an old-style inn that perched along the rugged seacoast. It was their last stop on the scenic tour of the province. Although they had left their retinue of servants behind, Takano had insisted you accompany them as a "sign of respect." In actuality, the old devil was simply playing with you. And now he had decided to bring you back, supposedly because you would need to prepare for the demonstration the next day. In reality, it was one more move to throw you off balance.

He could have telephoned and ordered you back; instead he sent me, on foot. The rural road that led to the sea took the long way around. There was a shorter trail up through the woods and across the rugged hills that lay between the monastery and the coast. This was the route I was ordered to take. It was eight grueling miles of rock and mud, gnarled roots, and the damp, silent presence of ancient trees. In the years since, I have wondered why he went to such elaborate lengths for this errand. The old man never did anything without some ulterior motive. In the end, I think it was because he could. He could order me up the slope and across country to do his simple bidding. He would watch me disappear into the rocky woods and his wide mouth would spread wider into a grim, contented smile. He was the master and I was the servant. It was something I believe he never tired of experiencing. But there was more: I would appear to order you back, and there was the possibility that perhaps you would resent the messenger as well as the message. As I stumbled down one slope and up another, I could imagine his satisfaction at that.

Early spring is a changeable thing on the northern coast. The thin sunlight that had hinted at warmer things to come appeared briefly, and then vanished. It was overcast and damp, and as I climbed higher into the hills the temperature dropped. On the ridgebacks, the wind was stronger, and I could feel the iron touch of a sea that had yet to shrug off winter.

The snow began so gradually, the flakes were so tiny, that it snuck up on me. I was trudging along, head down, carefully making my way across the slick, dark earth, the twisted roots and rocks. Occasionally I would glance up, and the light seemed dimmer, the air less clear. But I was in a hurry. It was only when the snow began to cling to the ground that I really noticed it. I crested the last ridge and gazed out onto the wide expanse of ocean that heaved behind a curtain of snow that blew in from the continent and loomed across the gloomy sea.

By the time I reached the inn, I was soaked with sweat, my face and hands burning from the cold. I stood on the wide porch while the innkeeper brought you out. You took the summons from Takano calmly enough; maybe you were expecting it.

"He wants me back," you said. "Right now?"

"Right now," I said, nodding.

"It would have been too easy to send a car, neh?" There

was nothing to say to such a comment. I slumped down, enjoying the sensation of being at rest, even for a short time, and waited.

"We're taking the trail back?" Again, I said nothing. Just nodded in weary resignation. You snorted, asked the innkeeper to fetch me some tea, and disappeared inside. I could hear you explaining your departure. A man's noncommittal response, a woman's objection. Then you were back, lacing on your boots and shrugging into a coat.

"Let's go," you said. And we headed off.

The snow was falling heavily by then and it made the switchback trail up the hill treacherous. We paused halfway up. You turned to look down on the inn. It was a sign, I thought, of where your emotions lay. You gazed out onto the shallow bay, a fishing trawler, rocking at anchor in the choppy water. You squinted, as if the action could help you pierce the thickening snow.

"What kind of fisherman is out in this weather?"

"A foolish one," I answered. "Much like anybody who's hiking out in this ..."

You didn't smile at my joke, but kept looking out into the bay. You pointed. "They've put a boat off ..."

I was tired and wanted to get back to the task at hand, to hurry up across this ridgeline in the hopes it would shield us from the worst of the storm. But the tone of your voice made me look. Like you, I squinted. I watched the small motor launch make its way toward the shoreline near the inn. The wind blew a momentary hole in the veil of snow and I felt a sudden spasm of alarm. The boat held five or so men and they appeared to be carrying weapons.

You had launched yourself down the slope before I had fully grasped the implication of what I was seeing. No words were necessary between us. We were both certain.

It was only years later that the world learned of the periodic raids the North Koreans would stage along Japan's coast, abducting innocent farmers and fishermen. They may have been looking for intelligence, for information about the outside world that was hard to come by in their isolated land. Or they may have done it simply because they wanted to.

This was the early part of the sixties, when the war in Vietnam was ramping up and the renewed presence of the United States in the East was making the Chinese and Koreans anxious. Anxious men do stupid things.

Like that landing on a storm-battered coast. An isolated place with little to recommend it, except the presence of a member of the imperial family. A prime target for a kidnapping that could be of some use in whatever diplomatic maneuvering lay before them in the tumultuous years ahead.

How we both knew it, I am not sure. But I followed you back down the trail a split second after you started, convinced, as you were, that we were the only thing between Chika-hime and abduction.

CHAPTER 16

She didn't scream, which was a real plus. My head was pulsing with pain.

Chie Miyazaki was pushed up against the driver's side door instead, her face pale, eyes wide. I ignored her and got the car rolling even before my door had closed, one eye on the snowy road ahead, the other focused on the black rectangle of the sliding doors to the house. I gave the gas pedal a nudge, and when we hit the end of the driveway, I yanked the wheel and the sedan slid into a sloppy turn. I gunned it and the tires whirred in the accumulating snow. Traction was an on-again, off-again thing, but I kept at it, willing us up the slight incline of the cul-de-sac. I hoped the main ring road was in better shape. I was worried about many things: the pain that gripped me in spasms and what that said about whatever damage the beating had done; the deteriorating weather; the long-term plan about what I was going to do with the woman in the seat next to me. Mostly, I was worried about putting as much distance between us and Lim and his pals as I could.

Because in all the excitement I had forgotten to get the keys to their other car.

I got Lim's car up the hill and felt at least a little relief. The main road had been plowed and sanded sometime earlier, and even though a new layer of snow was already smothering the road surface as the storm gathered strength, I was able to pick up speed. I thought of the layout of the roads at Mattson's Peak, laid down in crisp lines and neat curves on the map I'd used earlier in the day. It seemed like a long time ago. The woods were dark along the roadside and the snowfall covered the terrain, making it all a series of soft, humped, and unfamiliar features. The world was all black trees and a sky gone gunmetal dark, and against that backdrop, the snow seemed to glow in the fading light. There is a term for it: albescence. I laughed. It was the type of weird observation that drove my brother Mickey crazy. I'd been beaten to a pulp, had probably just crossed some legal line that made me a kidnapper, and my brain was playing Trivial Pursuit.

"How can you laugh?" Chie Miyazaki's voice broke my reverie. She may have been quiet, but she was watching me closely. "You killed him!"

"What?

"Lim. I saw you." Chie's voice wasn't shrill, despite the accusation. She seemed stunned, withdrawn. It was probably just as well. I needed her docile so I could concentrate on driving.

"I didn't kill him," I told her. I had wanted to, and part of me worried whether I'd regret my restraint later on.

"How can you be sure?" Out of the corner of my eye I saw her hand creeping toward the door handle. I hit the button and the car's electric door lock engaged. The thud of the mechanism startled her. The first real reaction she'd had.

"I'm sure, OK?" It was hard to explain: the amount of force I'd used, the feel of the impact, the way Lim's body reacted when I dumped him in the snow. My voice was testy. I was mapping out a route, struggling to keep the car under control, gaming my next moves, and fighting the urge to vomit. I wasn't up for conversation. But I needed her calm. "Trust me," I said, swallowing. "I know these things. He'll need some medical care, but he'll live." *A lot of that going around.*

I saw the turn I was searching for and pulled into the small parking area where I'd left my rental car. It was a snow-covered lump, but I was glad to see it. I had rented a small SUV and it had all-wheel drive. I'd shoved the keys and my wallet up under the front bumper when I'd left it there earlier in the day, following the basic rule that you should only carry what you need to do a specific job and never carry ID when planning on committing a crime. I scrabbled around in the snow under the car's front end, grabbed the keys, and dragged Chie into the SUV. She didn't put up a fight, just drifted along as if the entire process was inevitable. I thought again about my conversations with the roshi, about her psychological issues. Maybe for Chie Miyazaki the key to survival, to acceptance, was going along. I shrugged. Best to think about it later.

I swept what snow I could away from the windows and off the hood using the length of my arm as a brush. As we pulled out, I lobbed the keys to Lim's car into a snowbank.

I drove down the mountain, grateful for at least the suggestion of increased traction from the all-wheel drive. But the roads were a mess, the snow kept coming, and there was only so much the SUV could do. I drove as fast as I could, desperate to escape but afraid the twists and turns of the narrow road would dump us into the deep culverts that lined either side. At the beginning I was glad the ride was all downhill, but it didn't take long for that feeling to leave me. The road snaked down a narrow track whose borders were increasingly hard to see. There were points at which I had the brakes locked and the SUV just kept going, sliding and unresponsive as I madly turned the steering wheel, hoping to reassert control. By the time we bottomed out on the feeder road that would eventually lead us to the interstate, I was drenched in sweat and my hands ached from clenching the wheel.

The snow kept coming, a manic swirl of flakes that danced in the headlights. The temperature was dropping outside; I could feel the cold seeping in through the windows despite the fact that the defroster was going at top speed. The wipers thudded back and forth, the snow building up on them and then sloughing off at random. The windshield was streaked with ice and foggy with condensation. I was breathing so hard I was creating a small circle of water vapor on the inside of the windshield. Fortunately, there were virtually no other cars on the road. I had stopped checking the rearview mirror for pursuit. It was taking all my energy simply to drive.

My eyes burned. The blizzard was growing denser and the car was cocooned in falling snowflakes. They glittered and shone in the headlights, but everything outside the arc of the lights was black. There was a hypnotic quality to the bright flakes that streamed in from the deep darkness and danced around the vehicle, only to disappear as if a curtain had been drawn behind us. I found my focus shortening until I was looking at the bright swirling points of snow. For a moment, I felt the shock and disorientation of vertigo. I wasn't sure where I was in relation to the road. I shook my head and the pain made me wince but also got me focusing once again.

We slid on toward Route 6.

Chie had remained silent after her first outburst. Maybe she was picking up on my tension. Maybe her heart was jumping up into her mouth every time we hit a slick spot or I lost control of the steering. I know mine was. But once we were headed out on Route 6—a broader road surface bearing the signs of recent plowing—she could probably sense me calm down a bit.

"Why?" she asked.

"Why what?" Maybe I was calmer, but driving was still no picnic. And I had just remembered the approach to Interstate 84 was a long, long downhill run. The dread made my voice tight.

She put her head in her hands. "Oh, please." Half plea, half sarcastic retort.

"Your family …"

"Really does not give a shit about me," she finished. Her face was pale with the dashboard lights, but her eyes glittered in resentment.

I shrugged—a cautious movement. I felt the tug of damage along my ribs. "Well I think the picture thing got their attention."

She slapped her hands on her thighs. "I told you I don't know what you're talking about."

"The pictures? Of you and Lim … and whoever."

"I like a good time," she retorted. "So what?"

A plow truck came hurtling down the road on the other side of Route 6. As it passed, it tossed a wave of snow in front us. I gripped the wheel a little tighter and felt the momentary lack of traction as the wheels slid across the extra snow.

"Look," I said, "whatever you do is whatever you do. But sending the pictures to your father? That was cruel." I winced at the judgmental way I sounded. Not because I didn't think she was screwed up, but because I had forgotten it would probably be best to try to keep her docile.

It was too late; she was angry. "'Look' yourself, you … complete asshole! I don't know what you're talking about. I never sent my father anything like that."

"Some of the shots came from your own cell phone."

"Bullshit." She rummaged around in her pockets, but then

gave up. "I'm always losing the fucking thing. Lim holds on to it for me."

"Lim," I said. "What a guy."

"What do you know about him?"

A state trooper passed us on the rutted left-hand lane, his lights flashing. I instinctively slowed down. The last thing I needed was to get stopped. I had a handgun in my pocket, the marks of a severe beating, and an unwilling passenger beside me. It would take about three seconds for them to decide to cuff me. But the trooper was focused on more pressing business ahead and as he passed us my hands relaxed slightly on the steering wheel.

I focused back on Chie. "Lim's got a street rep as a low-level dealer and party boy. But his apartment tells a different story."

"What are you talking about?"

"You've probably never been to this place." I told her the address. She looked confused. "It's very neat. Very serious. Not the kind of place you'd expect."

"So what?" *Did I hear a defensive note creeping into her voice?*

"And when I visited the place, I got a surprise visitor." I turned toward her to see her expression; her face was impassive. "We didn't talk much." I remembered the sound of our banging around the hallway, the thud of blows. "But guess where he was from?"

"My father?" she guessed.

I smiled bitterly. "Nope. Someone from the frozen Choson."

"What?" I glanced at her and saw the slackness of confusion as she tried to process my statement.

"Yep. Lim's pal was some kind of operative from the Democratic People's Republic of Korea." I looked at her again. "You know, our friends north of the thirty-eighth parallel."

"Bullshit," she said. But her voice didn't carry much conviction.

"You know, Chie," I told her, "you need to get your head straight on this. I'm not sure how everything fits … what it means. But trust me, something is going on and it's bigger than just you and whatever issues you have with your family."

That struck a nerve and I regretted the words almost the second they got out of my mouth.

"What the fuck do you know about my family?"

I tried to make my voice calm. "Some things I know … some I don't. And I know, in some ways it's none of my business." Which was a lame comment, since I had just kidnapped her. So I kept talking.

"Here's what I've got, however. Your family is worried about you and your involvement with this guy Lim. The pictures you sent …"

"I didn't send the fucking pictures!"

I winced at the shrillness of her voice. "OK, you didn't send the pictures. Doesn't it worry you that somebody did? Your old man's some kind of hotshot diplomat, right?" She nodded grudgingly. "And when I start poking around, I find out the hard way that some people really—and I mean really—don't want me to do that. Including your boyfriend Lim."

That got her back up again. "You broke into the house and attacked us!"

Technically, of course, the door had been open, but I thought I shouldn't point that out. *Maybe I'll save that thought for my trial instead.*

"So why didn't he call the cops?" I asked her.

"Lim told me my family had sent someone to look for me. He was afraid the cops might be in on it."

"How'd he know?"

"Know what?"

"That your family was looking for you?" Silence. I pressed on. "How'd he know my name? I didn't tell him and I had no ID on me." The windshield wipers thudded back and forth and the car rumbled across the ruts in the snow. She said nothing.

I let her sit there for a few minutes. Finally I spoke up. "Chie." She stared straight ahead. "Chie, look at me. Look at the beating they gave me. What was that all about?"

"We were angry," she said.

"And Lim's phone call?"

"What do you mean?"

"I show up," I explained. "You clock me across the head and he's got me all tied up. Best thing to do at that point would be to cut and run. It wasn't like I was going to be able to follow you."

"So?"

"So," I countered, "what does your boyfriend do? He ducks out to make a phone call. Who's he calling, Chie? It wasn't the police. Why's he calling?" She had no answers. But my voice was rising with indignation. "You don't know. I don't know either. I do know I got the crap beat out of me." I thought of how she had looked when Lim was sending his henchmen upstairs after me. "And we both know what was going to happen to me after he made that call."

She turned her head away, staring into the blackness. "No," she said in a tiny voice. I wondered what she saw out there in the night.

"Yes," I said. "They were going to toss me off a cliff."

I let that idea float between us for a while. I concentrated on driving down the long approach to Interstate 84. There was

180

more traffic on the road now and it made the going both slower and more treacherous. We finally made it, though. By that time I was spent. There was a gas station and convenience store off to our right, an island of bright white light in the swirling darkness. A team of heavily muffled guys with shovels was trying to keep the areas near the pumps clear. They weren't doing too well.

I slid into the parking lot, and Chie Miyazaki and I sat in the relative silence of the parked car. The wipers thumped back and forth. The defroster fan worked with the resignation of a forlorn hope. A snowplow rumbled by, followed by the hiss of a sander. Yellow flashing lights, car doors thudding closed, the sounds of cars growling through the snow.

"They were going to toss me off a cliff," I told her again. "And I want to know why."

She sat there, silently gnawing on her lower lip. The two of us stared straight ahead, watching the occasional battered driver stagger into the bright refuge of the convenience store. I hit the electric lock and got out of the car. I scooped a fistful of snow off the hood and pressed it against the side of my face. It burned for a moment; then the cold began to numb my skin. I waited, looking expectantly at her through the windshield. Finally she shrugged and got out.

Inside I pointed her at the restrooms. "Pit stop," I told her. Her eyes drifted around the store—a heavy middle-aged guy behind the counter, a few other rumpled pilgrims grabbing Slim Jims and sodas. I knew what she was thinking. I put my hand in my coat pocket and touched the pistol, shook my head at her. *No.* She got the message, sighed, and headed off to the bathroom.

I grabbed some painkillers, some granola bars, and a big bottle of water. The beating I had taken was putting a strain on me. The body needed rest, but it wasn't getting any. I figured hydration was the next best thing. Finally, I picked up a Trac-Fone and got it loaded with minutes.

The guy behind the counter looked at my face, wet from snowmelt.

"What happened to you, man?"

"Fell down," I told him.

"Must have been some fall."

"Yeah," I told him. I scooped up my purchases. *Thanks for bringing up such a painful memory.*

When Chie came out, I jerked my head at the door. She walked out, hunkered down in her coat, walking with the stiff look of a person moving against her will. Nobody gave her a moment's notice. I brushed the snow off the windows and we rolled out again into the storm.

Interstate 84 was going to be our best bet. I needed to get into New York and head down to a place where we could be safe. Someplace I could think through my next moves.

The road was wide and well graded. Highway Department trucks moved in tandem, giant plow blades angling across the road surface. Sanders came behind, yellow lights whirling. Hard ruts were building up on the edges of the lanes. It tended to lock you into position, since switching lanes forced you across the ruts and the tires planed across the snow and your stomach flipped as you sensed you had lost control and were hurtling down the road in an out-of-control missile. Lots of fun.

I drove for a while, putting some distance between us and the interchange—there were too many cops floating around back there. After a while, I pulled into a rest stop and fumbled with the phone. It took me a few times to get the number right. My head felt like it had been packed with wool. Finally, the phone chirped on the other end. I was tired, so I put it on speaker and set it on the dash.

"Collins," he said.

"Owen, it's me."

"Burke?" The next words sounded fainter. "Holy shit, it's Burke."

"Who's with you?"

"Annie," he said, sounding faintly guilty. I heard a voice fluting in the background. "She wants to know if you're OK."

"I'm OK." It wasn't entirely true, but I wasn't dead and that was rapidly becoming my basic criterion of OKness.

"You kinda dropped off the grid there for a bit," he told me. "People were starting to worry."

"People?"

"Well, me and Annie ..."

"And?"

"And ... well, your brother called me."

"What did he want?"

"He was trying to get hold of you. He left a message."

"And?"

"He said, and I quote, 'Tell my brother to stop dicking around and call me.'" I said nothing, and he continued. "Your brother is one cranky dude, Burke."

"What else?"

"He wanted to know what you were up to ... he seemed to know you were working for the Miyazaki. Trying to find the nympho ..."

"She's sitting right next to me here, Owen."

The line went silent for a few seconds. "Ooohkay ...

Anyway, Annie and I had been doing some more digging about the family …"

"Go on."

"Her father's been involved in some high-level stuff down in D.C. Hard to pin down what it is exactly, but it looks like he got pulled off his usual beat."

"This helps me how?" I was probably sounding testy, but the snow was pounding down, my body ached all over, and I couldn't see how any of this all fit together.

"I dunno, Burke," Owen sounded defensive and hurt. "We're doing our best at this end."

I took a slow, deep breath, trying not to involve the ribs too much. "Yeah, I know. Sorry. I'm a little fried from driving in the storm."

"No problem."

I sat for minute. "OK, here's a question. Can someone find out where I am when I use this phone?"

"Sure," he said. "They can usually triangulate the location from multiple cell towers."

I was worried about that. This is something you'd only normally worry about with law enforcement, but there was no telling how many favors a guy liked Miyazaki could call in. I thought for a minute. "OK," I finally said. "Here's what I need you to do. I've got a draft in my email that has a phone number in it. It's for a guy named Ito."

"OK …"

"Call him. Tell him I have Chie and she's safe. Tell him everything you know. And tell him I'm not bringing her in until …"

"Until what?"

It was a good question, but I hadn't thought through that

far. I gave Owen my login information. "Tell Ito I'll check in with him tomorrow. Right now, I need to get Chie somewhere safe."

"Where ya goin'?"

I ignored the question. It was best he didn't know. "Thanks, Owen. I'll call back tomorrow." I shut the phone down.

I pulled out of the rest stop and headed back out on the road.

"You're not taking me to my family?" Chie said.

"Not exactly," I said and gripped the wheel a little tighter.

CHAPTER 17

Mori's Journal

We went through them like fire. There was a guard at the entrance, but he was facing outward, toward the road. We came across the snowy fields to his rear, working through the grounds of the inn, unseen, our footfalls muffled by the thick snow. There was a gardener's shed, its flimsy door hanging open to the weather. Snow spilled into the dark interior. You paused there, grabbing a long brush knife and an ax. Even in the breathless haste, Takano's lessons held us: no matter your skill, better armed than unarmed.

The sentry started to turn toward us at the last minute. Perhaps he sensed something; maybe he was simply scanning the area. It made no difference. The ax bit deep into the side of his neck and he collapsed, breath and blood hissing across the snow.

The storm muffled sound, but we could hear the progress of the raiders inside, the thud of footsteps, the crashing of doors. Their passage was punctuated by shouts and the occasional scream. But the snow drew a curtain across it all. The inn looked dark and blurred through the storm.

I grabbed the fallen man's pistol. We churned through the snow and up the steps. The inn had two parallel wings stretching back from the front entryway. From the sounds coming from inside, the raiders had split up and were working their way through both sections simultaneously. It was a mistake. In situations like this, better to concentrate your forces and overwhelm the opposition.

Unless, of course, they knew there would be no opposition.

186

It was a thought that occurred to me later. In the investigation that followed, the source that led the raiders to that remote inn was never definitively identified. The wall that protected the imperial family reared up, thick and forbidding. Years later, when I worked inside those walls, I searched for clues to what had happened. But there was no conclusive finding. Officially, a minor secretary to the Miyazaki family died shortly after the incident, late in the summer when he appeared to fall into the path of an oncoming train. It was a day without rain, yet he slipped on a crowded platform. I admired the economy of it: the family spared a scandal and the leak plugged with finality. It was the sort of thing I learned to do myself in a long career of both finding and hiding secrets.

But whatever the reason, we were grateful our opponents were divided. You had the advantage of knowing where the Miyazaki were staying. In the main reception area, two ancients were collapsed on the floor, the woman cradling the bloody head of a white-headed man. We didn't stop.

Down a long corridor, we could hear guttural commands. The higher fluting notes of a woman's voice came to us as well. It spurred us on. We made our way down the passage. Like many traditional inns, the wing was a series of rooms facing an interior garden. The hallway ran down the outside of the rooms, with the interior wall made of dark wood that rose three feet to meet rice paper shoji screens. Internally, each room opened onto the next, the flimsy paper screens providing minimal barriers. A door stood open, spilling light into the dim hall. You held up a hand and we paused, listening. I could hear Miyazaki's voice. He sounded angry. He sounded afraid.

You held your head close to mine. "I will go in this room," you said, nodding your head at the dark chamber just before the room with the voices coming from it. "When I break through, you come in through the door."

"I don't like it," I hissed. I didn't see how this was a safe plan.

"There is no time. The others will be here soon as well. I will crash through the shoji. While they are focused on me, shoot them."

That was when I realized you weren't thinking about your own safety. You would do anything to save the princess. I always admired that about you, Rinsuke. You had the real warrior's spirit. It made you extremely dangerous. Even to your friends. I shared your concern for Chika-hime, I suppose, but even then, I was thinking not only about getting in, but also about getting out.

You stared at me in that hallway, your eyes bright. I took a breath to protest further, but we could hear voices from the other wing of the inn growing louder as they approached.

You shoved me in the direction of the open door and gave me an indisputable command. "Go!" Then you disappeared into the dark room.

I edged toward the open doorway, fearful the old wooden floorboards in the hall would give me away. Somewhere in the room, a woman squealed.

There was a snapping of wooden laths and the tearing of paper. I knew you were through the door and I made my move as well.

There were two of them in opposite corners of the room. Right inside the door, Miyazaki himself stood, his hands raised in the air in surrender. A gunman stood to my left covering him. Just over Miyazaki's shoulder I could see Chika-hime in the distant corner. A raider had his fist bunched in her hair and was twisting her head to force her to move.

I shouted as I came in the door—a strong kiai of the type Takano taught us. I know some sensei think of the shout typically used when striking someone as a way to focus the spirit or demonstrate resolve. Takano would snicker at the idea. In his dojo, focus and resolve were expected always. The importance of the kiai, he explained, is simply that, done right, it can assist in overloading the nervous system of an opponent. It is a fleeting phenomenon, but the split-second pause it can create offers a priceless advantage to an attacker. Years later, we would use flash-bang grenades to greater effect, but it is the same principle.

My shout and your sudden crash through the shoji made them pause. Although there were two of them, each was focused on a hostage, and now they had two more people to worry about who were entering the room at two different points. They should have simply shot us all. But they had been ordered to take hostages and it impeded their effectiveness.

But only for a second. The gunman to my left recovered first. His pistol came up, but strangely enough he pointed it toward you. Perhaps it was because I was partially blocked by Miyazaki, who stood there, hands pathetically raised in surrender. I wasn't sure I was going to be able to get to the shooter in time.

Miyazaki lurched forward across the line of fire as the gun went off. He collapsed, but his fall cleared the way in front of me. I shot the man to my left. I was new to firearms then, and nervous. I wasn't sure I had hit him, so I decided to make sure. I shot him again.

The pistol's report was loud in the snow-hushed world around the inn. I could see Chika-hime struggling with the other gunman—she had more spirit than her husband—but the pistol reports made my ears ring and I couldn't hear any other noise. I gaped at the two bleeding men at my feet.

By the time I looked up, you had swarmed across the room. Another pistol shot rang out, but it appeared as if you somehow danced around it. I am not sure, even now, what really happened. All I know is the gunman tried to shoot you at point-blank range and failed.

Were you even aware of the danger? I wonder. You were moving so fast and with such focus. You closed the distance. The pistol flew out of his hand and you were on him. I saw your arms clamp around his neck, noted the quick, powerful thrust and twist. You snapped his spinal cord and he was done.

My hearing was coming back to me. I could hear the shouts of other men coming closer. You looked across at me, hefted the ax and knife, and plunged back into the hallway. I started to call out, to tell you take a pistol, but you were gone before I could utter a word.

I knelt by Miyazaki, who lay there without moving, his skin the grey color of putty. There was blood seeping into the straw matting of the tatami floors, pooling around the two men. I felt it soak through the knees of my trousers as I knelt there.

I couldn't tell if Miyazaki had a pulse. The gunman's legs jerked in a series of small, diminishing spasms. He was finished.

Chika-hime came to stand beside me. She had picked up the other pistol.

"Is he …?"

I looked up. "I cannot tell."

Shots exploded from somewhere in the inn. I heard shouts, cursing. A shrill wail of pain. I knew we should move, but didn't want to leave Miyazaki if he could be saved. I look back now and wonder how things would have been had I left him there to bleed out on the floor.

An old man's regret, Rinsuke. Too much time has passed and what happened, happened. But I want you to know if I could do it again, I would have left him. Some small admission of regret on my part after all these years.

I stood up shakily. I hadn't yet grown accustomed to killing. I looked at the princess. "We need to get you somewhere safe."

Chika-hime looked at her husband on the floor, then gazed toward the dark doorway you had disappeared through. She bit her lip, hesitant.

You loomed up out of the darkness and took her by the arm. I saw the relief flood across her face, followed by concern. Your hands were dark and slippery with blood. Even in the dim light, I could see the fine crimson spray that had dotted part of your face.

I looked at you. You gestured out into the garden. "The back. It is our best chance."

"The others?"

You grimaced. "One made it to the road. I was too slow. He used a flare gun. I got to him, but it was too late. There is another boat coming." You looked at Miyazaki on the floor and your face was flat but your voice had a touch of confusion in it. "He took a bullet for me."

The three of us looked at each other, each registering a type of amazement.

I shrugged. "He may still be alive. I can't tell …"

You grimaced with impatience. "We have to get her out of here. That's the most important thing."

I nodded. "You take her up into the hills. Use the track I came in on." Outside the snowfall had intensified; perhaps we could put it to good use. "There's a logger's hut off a side trail a few miles up into the hills. Take her there. It will shelter you overnight. The snow should hide your tracks if you hurry."

I watched you consider the plan for a split moment. "You?"

"I'll head cross country to the village. It's not that far. Someone there will have a phone. The prefectural police will send help. They may even arrive in time to save Miyazaki. Either way, it has to be done."

You nodded. "Agreed." You turned toward Chika-hime, regarded her for a moment, then stripped a coat off the body of the man whose neck you had broken. You held it out to her and she flinched, uneasy at the idea of wearing a dead man's coat. "Put it on," you said gruffly. Then your voice softened. "It will be cold in the hills tonight, Himesama. Please put it on." She reached out reluctantly. You looked at me.

"Be careful, Mori." You turned to go, but my voice made you pause.

"The other men," I said. "How many?"

You looked befuddled for a moment, as if you didn't know what I was asking or had put it so far out of your mind that it took an effort to recall. "The men?" A pause. "Three."

"And you took them all? All three."

You nodded. "I had to chase the last one."

"Three," I repeated. "All armed."

"Not anymore," you said, and disappeared into the storm with your princess.

CHAPTER 18

It was like driving down a long tunnel that never came to an end. The snow caught the headlights and swirled around us. It was exhausting. The eyes kept wanting to focus on the tiny flecks of bright snow, but I had to keep squinting into the darkness beyond them instead. I ached. My eyes burned and I felt my focus slipping.

"Talk to me," I told her.

"What? She had been lulled by the steady thump of the windshield wipers and the drone of the tires on the snow, and now she was wedged into the corner where the seat met the car door, staring out into the night. She faced me with a look of startled anger.

"I'm falling asleep," I explained. "Talk to me."

"What the fuck do you want me to say?"

I sighed. "I don't know. Anything. Tell me about yourself."

She wiggled into a more upright position and I could feel the anger pulsing off her. "Tell you about myself! I'm Miyazaki Chie and I've been kidnapped. I'm trapped in a car at gunpoint, stuck in the middle of a snowstorm. How's that, you asshole!"

I grimaced a small smile. "It's a start." She had started out calmly enough, but the last few words came out in a loud shriek. It made my head throb. *You asked for it, Burke.*

I wiggled around in the seat and worked the pistol out of my coat pocket. I handed it to her.

"Here."

She started to reach out, then hesitated as if it might be a trick. I put the weapon in her lap. She hesitated, then snatched it up, pointing it at me.

"It's empty," I told her. "I threw the magazine away with Lim's car keys."

"You bastard."

I shrugged. "I don't like guns much. Don't know enough about them to really be comfortable with them around. It seems to me a loaded gun is just a small disaster waiting to happen."

"But at the rest stop …"

I waived a hand. "I just didn't want you to cause any trouble there."

"You lied to me." She sounded strangely petulant.

"You're not used to that by now?" I said. I regretted it as soon as the words came out of my mouth. *When would I learn to keep my mouth shut?* She didn't answer. She had lowered the pistol onto her lap, but kept a grip on it. The muzzle was pointed my way. Maybe she thought I was lying about the bullets. I got the sense she didn't know much about guns either. Maybe she was hoping there was a round in the chamber. For a moment I felt a stab of anxiety—did I clear the action when I threw the magazine away? I couldn't remember. I took my eyes off the road long enough to get a fleeting look at her: eyes narrowed, shoulders tense, hand gripping the pistol. And I knew she had seen the doubt flash across my face.

She waived the gun slightly in a tight circle. "You're not really sure it's empty, are you, Burke?"

I just shrugged, a gesture that could have meant anything. I figured I needed to bluff this one out.

"Basic rule is never point a gun at someone unless you intend to use it," I said. The wipers thudded back and forth. The tires growled through the snow. I was weary.

"If you're gonna shoot me, Chie, let me know so I can slow down a bit," I told her. "That way at least one of us walks away."

We had come off the interstate and were navigating a series of state roads that trended south in the narrow river valleys of upstate New York. The hills shielded us from the worst of the nor'easter. But these roads were plowed infrequently and they rose up and wound down the hilly terrain, forcing me to reduce speed. But I was pushing it as hard as I could, still feeling the drift and slide in the turns, worried I'd put us in a snowdrift in the middle of nowhere. I checked the mirror for any traffic coming up behind us, but there wasn't a light to be seen. We were alone out there, two crazy people on the road. She didn't say anything and I took my foot off the gas. The car slowed down and eventually crunched to a stop. I left my hands on the wheel and turned to face her.

Chie kept the pistol pointed my way. Then she made a small growling noise of disgust, thrust the pistol at me, and turned quickly to face the front of the car. I shoved the thing back in my pocket. She crossed her arms in front of her, angry, cold. Maybe both.

"Where are we?" She was still angry, but resigned.

"We're back in New York State."

"Heading south toward the city?"

"Yes."

"Good." I heard her swallow. She licked her lips and I felt the skin on my face puckering: we were both getting parched from the car's defroster. I handed her the water bottle I had bought. She sipped at it cautiously as if she were afraid it, too, was part of my plot. "You're not going to make me go back to my family?" She said it quietly, as if afraid of the answer she might get.

I had been mulling that precise question over for a while, arguing with myself. I had agreed to find her and to get her out of Lim's hands. To make sure she was safe. I'd done that, after a fashion. Now the real question was what would I do next. I was pretty sure the Miyazaki wanted Chie back in their custody. But she was a grown woman. Ultimately, she could do what she wanted. Actually, I thought ruefully, she already seemed to embrace that concept fully. It was none of my business. But I did have an obligation to see her safe. Whatever the specific details of the Miyazaki family's expectations, certainly just making sure she was safe was the core of what they wanted. So if I could determine she was basically OK and get her away from Lim, hadn't I fulfilled the essence of my commitment?

I was splitting hairs. I knew that. The family would not be pleased. But I had made a minor career of frustrating people's desires for me. Generating disappointment was a type of Burke art form. And part of me remembered Mickey and Art and their warnings. The Miyazaki proposal was one that, if fulfilled, would make me a kidnapper. I had no desire to go to jail. And, more importantly, I didn't think that would really help her.

Besides, there was more to it than that. I knew things now that I hadn't when I started. I had an extra obligation to do what I could for her. I wasn't sure how much I would ultimately be able to help her, but I had to try.

"No," I finally answered her, more a sigh than a statement. "I'll get you back to the city. That's all. Away from Lim."

If she was relieved, she had a funny way of showing it. She turned on me, furious again. "What's your issue with Lim?"

The energy from her anger filled the car. The force of it was startling; it made me momentarily stupid. I shrugged defensively. "Well," I said, "for one thing, he's a creep."

"You don't know the first thing about him!"

"He's using you, Chie."

"Ohh … bullshit." She braced one hand on the dashboard and the other on the seat, pressing her torso all the way around to confront me. I'd stirred her up and now she was completely out of her reverie and back in full furious mode. "Did it ever occur to you that I was using him?"

I nodded, remembering the roshi and his talk on hypersexuality: rebellion and connection in one muddy, tangled package.

"Works that way in a lot of relationships," I said, with more confidence than I really felt. "But there's more to it than that …"

"Oh, please. Now you sound like a shrink."

I smiled at that thought. "I'm about the farthest thing from a shrink you could find."

She eased back away from me, her eyes narrowed. "So … who are you? And," she slammed herself back into the seat, eyes rigid on the road, "what the fuck is this all about? Can you just answer me that?"

"Well, yeah," I said quietly, "at least partly."

So I told her about me, how study in Asian culture had gotten me hooked on martial arts. How I'd eventually worked my way through a Ph.D. and slammed around dojo. "I used to think I was a scholar with a unique research specialty," I told her. "Now I realize I'm just a dojo rat with an advanced degree."

And then, I explained, I met Yamashita and my world changed. It wasn't just the things he could do, the things he taught me; it was the sense of being part of something special, a tradition that stretches back centuries, an organization where membership is open only to those with the will to endure a harrowing apprenticeship and the ability to absorb its lessons. Some people thought it was delusional, a lifetime pursuing skills that were largely irrelevant two centuries ago. I'd had a woman in my life once who saw the dojo as some sort of psychic black hole sucking me in deeper and deeper. I had a family that shook their heads in consternation at my life, even now. But it was a place where I belonged, I lamely concluded, a life that gave me a sense of meaning.

Chie didn't know what to say to that. "The martial arts …" She shook her head. "Back home it's for the old-timers, traditionalists who can't let go of the past and the jocks in high school and college who can't let go of the present …" She glanced at me. "It's weird, Burke."

It was an accurate characterization of my life. I was in a car in what the radio was telling me was the worst snowstorm since the 1800s, traveling with a drug-abusing nympho whose dysfunctional family had hired a complete stranger to kidnap her. She may have been right.

"Probably like a lot of people's lives," I said. "I'm not asking you to live it. It just makes sense to me."

"And that," she said, smacking the dashboard with a palm, "is precisely what I think. It's my life, right? Nobody needs to approve of it but me."

I frowned, realizing I had walked right into that one.

"There's a bit more to it than that," I started to protest.

"Oh bullshit," she spat. "My family doesn't like the fact that I party too much, that I fuck whoever I like? Tough shit. It's my life. They've got no business butting in." She crossed her arms and finished. "And neither do you, Burke."

I took a breath. Concentrated on making the correct turn on the road ahead, slid through the process, and got us on the last leg of the trip for the night. "Fair enough," I admitted. "But hear me out." She started to talk, but I held up a hand. "Just let me finish. There are some extra pieces to this."

She wasn't particularly receptive. "Like what?" Grudgingly, looking out the side window to show just how little interest she really had. She couldn't be seeing much: the bluish wash of snow and dark forest, the reflection of the instrument panel on the glass. Maybe the ghost image of her own face.

"Well, first off there were the photos of you ..."

"I told you I didn't send them!"

"I believe you," I replied. "But someone sent them ..."

"So what? It's my personal life."

I didn't rise to the bait. "Yes. But someone sent them. Based on the analysis I had done, it was someone who had access to your cell phone and someone who also had Internet access from the place at Mattson's Peak." She said nothing.

"It was Lim, Chie."

Now it was her turn to shrug. "So?"

"So why would he do a thing like that, I wonder. Just to get to your father?"

"He doesn't even know my father."

"Hmm. But he knew how to get in touch with him, didn't he? Talk about weird ..." I let the statement hang in the air for a time.

"Why would he do that, Chie? What did he want?"

"I told you," she snapped. "Lim doesn't know my father. He wouldn't have wanted anything."

"Yeah, I wondered about that. I figured your family is rich, so maybe it was money he was after—a simple extortion case? The more I poked at it, the more I wondered. And then there's the whole Korean thing."

"I told you I don't know anything about that."

"Yeah, and again, I believe you. But from what I can tell,

Lim has some connection with these people. Serious people, Chie." I looked at her and, for the first time, she met my gaze. "Serious as in 'throw Burke off the cliff' serious, Chie."

She mulled that over for a while. "So why," she began. "I mean, why get involved?"

I shrugged, feeling the ache in my neck and shoulders. "In the beginning, just to do an errand that would keep people from bugging Yamashita. But then it got more complicated in a hurry …" I thought for a moment. "Neither of us is going to be safe until I get to the bottom of it. And besides, there's something else."

"Ooh," she said. "That's so fucking cryptic. What do you mean?"

So I told her.

The rest of the trip was quiet. For most of the drive I had been feeling my way along, having a general sense of where I needed to go. Now that I was getting closer, the roads were familiar and I could relax. The snow was still coming down—the radio said it would most likely continue for at least another day and the entire Northeast was shut down—but by this time the demands of driving through it were familiar. We were almost at our destination.

I knew that we'd never be able to reach Manhattan. Roads and bridges were closed; the main arteries open only to emergency vehicles. But I wanted to get us both somewhere safe where we could ride out the storm and where I could figure out my next steps. It occurred to me that the roshi's monastery would be perfect: isolated and remote, a few hours' drive from the city. Plus, I needed to see Yamashita. I had something for him.

The monastery has a broad parking lot carved out in the side of the road and a winding path that leads onto the grounds and the main hall. The lot had a few cars in it, all of them smothered in snow and now nothing more than vague, rounded domes. The area had been plowed early on in the storm but was filling up again and the snow had drifted across the main entrance. I didn't so much park the car as I gunned it up and over the drift and aimed it toward a distant berm, burying the nose of the vehicle and lurching to a final stop. I shut the wipers down and snowflakes slid across the glass, stopped, reached out to others, and started to create a fuzzy, opaque web that thickened with each second.

Chie and I waded our way toward the entrance. The snow was up above my knees and in places the drifts reached Chie's waist. We were both winded when we reached the wide covered porch of the main building. I rang the bell and when the door opened, we practically fell inward.

The receptionist didn't act particularly surprised at our presence—we weren't the only lost pilgrims blown their way that night—but he took one look at me and called the roshi, who arrived in short order with a gangly man wearing a scraggly ginger beard and the dark grey outfit of a novice.

I handed Chie over to the roshi and the thin man had me sit down on a bench. He pulled off my boots and removed my coat with an easy, efficient technique that suggested lots of practice. He noted the extra weight in my pocket and removed the pistol, raising an eyebrow. He didn't say anything, but he racked the action back, noted the missing magazine, and double-checked to make sure that there wasn't a round left in the chamber. Then he smoothly hit the safety and the slide sprung home. He set the gun down and looked at me.

"Sig Sauer .45. Modeled on the old 1911 Colt," he said. He saw my expression and smiled. "I wasn't always a Buddhist, you know." He turned my head this way and that, shining a small flashlight in my eyes.

"I could tell," I said. The light made my head hurt more.

He watched my pupils for a few seconds, then nodded. "Tenth Mountain Division," he said, answering my unspoken question.

"Light infantry," I commented through gritted teeth. He was poking my ribs.

"Medic," he added. "Afghanistan."

"That must have been a learning experience," I added.

He nodded. "Uh, yeah. Learned lots of things. Mostly I learned I never want to go back to Afghanistan again. That's for sure."

He stopped jabbing and probing and I sank back against the wall and closed my eyes.

"Somebody gave you quite a beating," he said. He wasn't surprised or even curious. It was a diagnosis, a flat statement of what was. I just nodded. "From what I can see you may have a minor concussion. Probably some fractured ribs. Extensive bruising." He gestured toward the door and the storm beyond it. "Best place for you would be a hospital, but none of us are going anywhere tonight. I can tape you up so you get a little relief from the ribs. We'll get some fluid into you …" He hesitated for a minute. "You ever been hurt like this before?" When I nodded, he seemed relieved. "OK, then you know what's up. Rest, fluids, painkillers. But basically …"

"There's not much for it except time," I finished for him. "I'll feel like the walking dead for a week or so, but it will get better." He nodded. We both knew the drill. Contrary to the movies, nobody takes a major beating, manfully wipes the blood off his lips, and limps away with determination that grows as the soundtrack swells behind him, basically shaken but OK. Ask any boxer: even the fights you win take a toll.

He reached out. "Let's get you into bed."

"In a while," I told him. I asked where the roshi had gone and they took me to his office. It was empty and I sagged down into a chair. When he entered, his face was filled with concern. "Connor," he said, and reached out to touch my shoulder.

"It looks worse than it really is," I assured him. He seemed skeptical. "Chie?" I asked.

"She's settling in upstairs."

"Yamashita?"

"In the far rooms by the garden. Reading," he told me with a look filled with significance.

"I need to see him."

"Yes," the roshi said, although he did not sound happy about it. "Chie as well, I assume."

I nodded. "Me first, though."

They gave me another of the grey novice's uniforms to wear. It was cut in the traditional Japanese manner: drawstring pants and a top that wrapped closed. It was like a karate gi and I felt at home in it. I shuffled down the quiet corridors in my socks, listening to the wind whistle and the grainy wash of snow against windows. The storm pushed at the building, but it held steady—a rock, a refuge.

Yamashita occupied a suite of rooms at one end of a wing of the building. I found him in a type of sunroom. Broad French doors opened onto a garden that was now just a white space with indeterminate humps that lay like victims smothered by the blizzard. He was kneeling, a long swath of rice paper before him, and the tools of the calligrapher's trade lay alongside him. I knocked on the doorjamb and he sat back and set the brush down carefully.

I bowed. "Sensei."

He swiveled and his usually remote face brightened for an instant, then darkened with concern. "Burke," he said, gesturing to a spot next to him. "I have been thinking about you."

I came into the room and saw Mori's journal resting on a table beside a chair and a floor lamp that spread a warm pool of light across the floor. I knelt down and bowed again to my teacher.

He bowed slightly in response and reached out to turn my head back and forth, letting the light play on the damage. His touch was light, but authoritative, much like the medic from the Tenth Mountain Division.

"I see you have been busy," Yamashita commented.

I closed my eyes and nodded in agreement. Then I opened them and glanced at Mori's journal. "Sensei …," I began.

He cut me off, gesturing at the calligraphy drying before him. "I thought we might benefit from some new inspiration at the dojo, Burke." He sat back. "You are familiar with the saying?"

"*Enzan no metsuke*," I read out loud. "Looking at a far mountain."

"Just so," Yamashita commented. "How often have we heard that, over the years? The warning to keep focus on important things, to not be distracted …"

"Sometimes easier said than done," I told him. We were both looking toward the table and Mori's journal now, talking about it without talking about it. I shrugged. "It's why we keep training."

Yamashita didn't seem comforted by that idea. "And when the training comes to an end? What then? When we look back at the long path we have walked?" I had never heard him like this before. Was it the product of the meditation? The days of introspection? I wasn't sure but it struck me for the first time that my teacher sounded old. Yamashita let the question dangle there, and then smiled wryly when he saw the look of consternation on my face. "But at least you have learned this, Burke: you endure well."

He stood up and I followed suit. We both moved like men with injuries, old and new.

"*Honto desu*," I answered. *It's true.*

"It takes a toll, does it not, Burke?" He almost sighed. He seemed lost in thought. If I didn't know him better, I would have wondered if he were experiencing regret. It was a side of my teacher I had rarely seen.

"You've taught me that there is always a price to be paid, Sensei. And sometimes, it brings reward …"

The roshi knocked and came in, Chie at his side.

I bowed to her and to my teacher. I swallowed, suddenly nervous to say the words. "Yamashita Rinsuke, Miyazaki Chie. Miyazaki Chie, Yamashita Rinsuke."

I looked at my teacher. "Meet your granddaughter."

CHAPTER 19

Mori's Journal

The world was nothing but different shades of white and grey. The snow filled the air and blanketed the land; the roads were indistinct, virtually impassable. The sea was gone from sight and even the sound of the waves was muffled under the relentless weight of snowfall. I staggered through it, a dark smudge lurching across a world without hard edges or landmarks to guide me. I finally collapsed on the veranda of a house on the edge of a village. They took me in and thawed me out. The skin on my face felt stiff and made it hard to talk. My fingers and toes burned.

A neighbor had a phone, and in time the prefectural police arrived, swaddled to the eyeballs: thick suspicious men who weren't sure what to make of my tale. My urgency seemed only to confuse them more. They radioed their superiors, who in turn made further calls from headquarters. My clothes thawed and dripped and I pleaded for action. But the policemen stolidly waited for direction from their superiors.

In the meantime, the storm raged. It would not let up for days.

When the orders eventually made their way down the chain of command, I could hear hysteria in the voice on the radio, even at a distance. The two local policemen looked startled, guilty, alarmed. They gazed out through windows that were sheeted with ice, felt the wind rocking the building, and then gave a shrug and headed back out, wading through the drifts to their patrol car, taking me with them as a guide. We were a long time gone.

We reached the inn eventually, but night was coming on.

They called for an ambulance. Not so much for the old couple that ran the place; it was obvious their instructions were focused on Miyazaki.

I led them to the room where he lay. One policeman checked Miyazaki's vital signs and began a frantic conversation with his dispatcher. Someone was reluctant to send an ambulance out in the weather. Other calls were made and the heavy hand of higher-ups intervened. The ambulance was on its way.

The other policeman had checked the two other bodies we had left there. "Tell them no need to rush for these other two," he told his partner. They began what first aid they could on Miyazaki, trying to staunch the bleeding, working to keep shock at bay.

I was amazed he was even alive. When you disappeared into the snow with Chika-hime, we all thought he was dead. By this time I had digested the rumors about an unhappy marriage. I had felt something between the two of you. It was obvious in the way the woman clutched at you as you headed out into the storm. So perhaps the idea that Miyazaki was dead was all wishful thinking. I know it was on my part.

The ambulance arrived with nightfall. The attendants trundled him out into the dark, ramming the gurney through the snow. I asked one of the policemen whether Miyazaki was still alive. He said nothing, but looked at his partner, the senior man, whose reply was not encouraging.

"Still alive? Perhaps. Perhaps not." He peered outside, where the storm gave no sign of abating. The ambulance's flashing light whirled faintly, almost smothered in the driving snow. "Even if he is, the ride to the hospital will probably kill him."

"And his wife is out in this," the other policeman commented, shaking his head in disapproval. "Your friend should have known better."

I looked at the two of them. "When do we go after them?"

"We don't," the senior man replied. "We wait for first light and see."

I argued with them, but without success. Priorities had been established: they were to do what they could to save Miyazaki. But they were not about to risk themselves any further. I thought it curious that there was not more concern for the princess. But I was naïve then. I did not realize the extent to which the imperial family was wrapped in the strong, thick coils of a system designed to keep them remote and uninformed and powerless.

I had also not come to realize just how powerful the Miyazaki had become, and how their responses could outstrip the speed and efficiency of the very government.

First light brought no pause in the blizzard. It was another whole day before they were able to bring a ski rescue team into the area. In the meantime, the police fidgeted, uncomfortable with inaction, but dreading the fact that some higher-up might eventually order them out into the hills to search. So they took my statement of what had happened. They were polite, but skeptical. They took careful notes and left me for a time. Then they returned and started with the same questions all over again, asked in different order. Who did I think the men in the boat were? Why would they be here? What did they want? How had you and I managed to overcome an armed party?

They questioned me on where I thought it likely you had gone. I traced the path into the hills on a survey map for them. They asked about the terrain. Any survival equipment you might have carried. They all shook their heads, resigned to eventually having to head out into the storm but not optimistic about what they might find. They were politely concerned for you and the princess, Rinsuke, but it was a professional's concern: little real emotion, even less optimism. They weren't looking forward to searching for anyone in this blizzard; they were not very hopeful that any good would come of it. But they would do their duty. Yet from the looks they gave one another, they were certain it would not be enough: I think they were worried about having to report failure to their superiors.

Because now officials were said to be on the way from Tokyo.

The police used the inn as their command post. Men trooped in, stamping the snow off their boots and glad to be out of the weather. There was tea and quiet talk, the endless smoking of cigarettes. Occasionally, someone would get up to check equipment that had been checked multiple times already. I sat with them and listened to the crackle of radios. The wind howled. Night came again. There was no word on Miyazaki. There was little hope the ski patrol would find you alive the next day.

In the end, the storm blew itself out. We woke to silence, the world shrouded in snow and frozen fast. In time, the sun came up over the mountains, dawn a late arrival on that coastline. But light eventually came and the sky was revealed: a hard blue like deep and ancient ice.

The search party would not let me go with them. They strapped on skis and slowly made their way up into the hills. They pulled sleds that carried emergency clothing, food, and shelter. They also carried long, bright yellow rubber bags. For the bodies. I watched the team disappear into the tree line, wondering how long they would be gone. How long it would take to find two huddled forms, stiff and motionless in a drift.

They were, in fact, only gone for three hours when the police radios crackled to life, the silence thawing with the heat of excitement. The words coming across were indistinct, but the tone was one of amazement, incredulity. There was a small crowd of policemen in the inn gathered around the communications station, and I pushed my way through. The radio operator looked up.

"They found them. Alive. They're bringing them down."

It wasn't quite true, of course. You found them, Rinsuke, not the other way around. And you carried the princess back down, in much the same way you had carried her up. You both seemed dazed, and your movements were robotic, like a man unsure of the ability of his limbs to fully respond to the command of his will. She clung to you, even then. I remember that. Eventually, the two of you sat, collapsed in the warmth of the inn. You looked at me, your face red and abraded from the cold wind. You reached for a proffered cup of tea, but your fingers moved stiffly, still reluctant to acknowledge the ordeal was over. Slowly, the innkeeper's wife pried Chika-hime away from you, cooing about a hot bath and a change of clothes.

"Come," the old lady said. "We need to make you presentable when you visit the hospital."

The two of you were stunned and remote, as if the time in the storm had taken you to a place where the world of people and warmth and shelter was nonexistent, a backdrop of vague forms and distant sounds. Your universe seemed to have tightened down to just the two of you.

I watched Chika-hime processing the old woman's comments, saw the world slowly thawing its way into her awareness. "Hospital?" the princess whispered.

"Ah yes," the old lady said, smiling, her skin wrinkling in pleasure. "To see your husband. He's asking for you."

You cast a despairing look at me, Rinsuke, and it was then the princess fainted away.

CHAPTER 20

I left my teacher with his granddaughter and made my way to my room. The roshi sat with me for a time. The monastery occupied territory with a thick past. It had been in stuttering procession: an obscure boarding school, a seminary that grew increasingly empty and forlorn over time, a failed conference center. As a result, it had no shortage of places for guests. The room they put me in had a small closet with a fabric curtain, a desk, a brutally designed hardwood chair, and a narrow bed pushed against one wall. Who knew the Buddha and the Spartans had so much in common? I sat on the mattress, my spine digging against the hard wall. The bedsprings creaked when I moved. My body creaked as well.

"I wasn't sure what to do exactly," I explained. "So I brought her here."

He sat quietly in the chair, his face impassive. The storm howled outside. We could hear it tearing across the roof.

The roshi nodded. "Yamashita was expecting you."

"Really?"

"Indeed." He raised a hand, his index finger pointing up. "Almost to the hour." He saw the look on my face and smiled. "Your sensei is a man of many talents, Burke. Surely you have felt the connection between the two of you?"

I remembered the experience back in Brooklyn of Yamashita's voice calling me, a summons that was bell-clear for all that it was entirely in my head. I nodded.

"Besides," the roshi continued, "he read the journal that was

left for him. I explained your involvement with the Miyazaki."
He paused and waved an arm around us. "And then this. The
storm. Where else would you go?"

"Home," I suggested.

His eyes crinkled. "Precisely." He saw my confusion and his
expression of amusement deepened. "Home is the place that
nurtures us and gives us meaning, Burke. It is not so much a
place as an experience. And for you, now, that experience is one
linked to Yamashita more than anything else."

I wondered about that, struggling against the roshi's words.
I had a home, I thought. *I wasn't raised by wolves.* I had parents
and brothers and sisters. Good memories. My dad was gone,
but my mom was still alive. I thought of Mickey, my brother.
My sisters. Their spouses, and my nieces, nephews. A sprawl-
ing, messy Irish Catholic clan, fruitful, and dutifully multiply-
ing. I was awash in family.

But the life I had chosen created a distance between us.
Maybe "chosen" is the wrong word. Perhaps my life is not so
much the product of a conscious choice as it is the result of a
stumbling pursuit of half-seen goals, of options pursued in the
moment. And distance? Not a good characterization either. I
think I am still bound to my family. Emotion and experience,
the years shared, all of this can't be easily dismissed. But I also
realized I had changed over time. The pursuit of Yamashita's
art created a mindset that viewed the world and the people in
it in their essence, stripped of affection and pretense. My life is
one focused on motion, angle, velocity. The potential for attack
and the variations of response. It is critical, evaluative. And if
my vision is clear and razor-sharp in some ways, it is as if it has
been bleached of some of the gentler colors in others.

If home is the place where you see yourself in others, then

maybe the roshi was right. Home for me was the dojo. But more fundamentally, it was anywhere Yamashita was. I remembered the scroll in the training hall: *Be in the dojo wherever you are* …

"Are they still talking?" I asked him, meaning Chie and Yamashita. The roshi nodded in answer to my question but didn't offer a comment. It seemed as if he were waiting for something else from me.

"Did you get a chance to talk with her much?" I finally said.

"Some," he replied. Again, the silence.

"What do you think?"

"I think right now she is exhausted," the roshi told me. "She is angry and confused." He smiled grimly. "From what you told me about her before, I would say confusion is probably a central condition of her being." The monk looked at me to see how well I was following him. I realized my eyelids were drooping.

I stirred on the bed and the springs creaked. Various body parts ground together and the spike of sensation woke me up a little. I thought about Chie and what I had seen through the windows at the chalet before I had broken in. The pictures sent to her father. The mystery of Lim and what he was really up to.

"She's not sure who she can trust in this world, is she?" I said. "I mean, she's conflicted about her family, rebellious. She connects with men mainly through sex … a way to create connection without intimacy." I looked at him to see if I was getting it right.

"She is trying to make her own way through life," the roshi commented. "She thinks she is breaking free of whatever conditions in her past shaped her. At least she thought that … until you came along and ruined everything."

The comment made me sit up straight. "What!" I winced at the stabbing pain in my ribs.

The roshi held up a hand. "This is what she thinks ... what she feels, really."

"I'm trying to help her!"

"She didn't want your help." His voice was quiet and measured. He watched my body language: the frustration, the denial. He waited until I settled back against the wall. "You have to understand, Connor. Whatever you or I may think about her life, it was hers to create. We may both agree that Chie's choices are not healthy ones, but they are her choices anyway. That's the important point for her. She got to choose. Not her family. Not you. Not me."

"It's an illusion," I protested.

Again, the wintry smile. One of the roshi's eyebrows rose and his long face was all amusement. "Now who's being all Buddhist?" he commented.

I waved my hand. "You know what I mean."

His smile collapsed. "Oh, I do indeed. But people come to recognize illusion at their own pace, Connor. Forcing it on them ... never a good idea."

He let that sit for a while and finally I stirred.

"So ... she resents me." More a sigh than a statement.

The roshi nodded. "Yes. You broke into her life. You've laid bare some things she didn't know. Probably things she didn't want to know. And it was all done so suddenly."

"It seemed like a good idea at the time." Even as I said it, I knew it was a lame defense, but the roshi had the kindness not to point it out. Besides, it was one of very few, yet well-respected, Burke family mottos.

"A young woman with trust issues. With control issues. Identity issues. You barge in, unwanted, unknown. And." He paused, then sighed. "You kidnap her."

He didn't need to say any more.

We sat there for a time, listening to the blizzard scouring the hills outside.

"How do I fix this?" I finally asked.

"I am not sure you can," the roshi said.

It was obviously a widely shared opinion.

"Connor," my brother Mickey said, his venom crackling over the phone. "I mean, what the fuck is wrong with you?" It was a rhetorical question and he plowed right on without waiting for a response. "Didn't we tell you to leave this alone?"

"Well, yeah, but …"

"But nothing. You complete moron." He fumed into the receiver on his end for a time, then was rendered temporarily mute from anger and disgust. I could imagine him sitting there on Long Island, his grey eyes hard enough to strike a spark, his free hand gesturing wildly.

"Hey, come on," I protested. "I mean, I got the girl. We're safe. And there's more going on here than I thought." It didn't seem to calm him down.

"You. You complete dickhead … Whattaya think it means when ya say, 'I got the girl?'" My brother has a pretty strong Long Island accent and the impressive engine of his temper was cranking out a thick, coiling verbal cloud of run-on words, vanishing *r*'s and flat vowels. And he wasn't letting up. "I'll tell ya what it means. You just kidnapped someone. You unnerstand? You moron! As in a federal offense. Jesus Christ!"

"Mick," I protested. "It's more complicated than that …"

"You want complicated? Try doin' hard time in the federal pen."

But now my temper was up. "Will you shuddup?" *Geez we*

almost sound identical. "I'm trying to tell you the boyfriend was up to something."

"I'll bet he was." The sarcasm was heavy.

"No, really. Look, she wasn't sending pictures to her old man. As far as I can figure out, he was."

"Yeah, so?"

"So, the father's a diplomat, Mick. He's got a history of working as a liaison between the Japanese government and our military." I closed my eyes, trying to concentrate, dredging up information Owen had given me over the phone. Between the beating I had taken and the drive through the storm, I wasn't sure I remembered all the details and I was still trying to process them fully. But as groggy as I was, a pattern was starting to emerge.

"Yeah. Miyazaki the diplomat. This I know," he told me. I should have wondered how he knew and why, but I was not exactly razor-sharp at that point.

"He's up for a new post, Mick. That's why he's here—visiting D.C. I don't have all the details, but it's all involved with the whole pivot-toward-Asia strategy Washington's cooking up."

"More," he said, the detective part of his brain sputtering to life, the mixture still too rich with anger, but slowly smoothing out and coming back on line. "Tell me more."

"And the boyfriend," I rushed on, sensing an opening suggested by the change of Mickey's tone. "He's a complete lowlife."

"He's a lowlife with a really unusual set of friends," Mickey finished.

"You know about the Koreans?"

"I know about the Koreans," he told me, sighing. "Do you want to know how I know about this … this incredible shit storm you are wading through?"

"Uh, yeah."

"Charlie Wilcox."

"Charlie Wilcox!" He was a guy we had grown up with who had somehow managed to get himself made an FBI agent. When we were in high school, Charlie was a real loose cannon whose major claim to fame was being shot through a windshield in a car accident and having to get his ears sewn back on. It seemed to tamp down his taste for the wild life, but still. At the time, nobody I knew was even sure he could actually read. But the years passed and something must have clicked. The last time we had seen him, Mickey had managed to wheedle some bureau surveillance data on the Chinese secret service's activity in Manhattan. Charlie resented having to do Mickey a favor and was pretty clear that he was looking forward to never seeing the Burke brothers again.

"So," my brother began, "Charlie is doing his usual boring analysis of surveillance photos of thugs from the Chinese consulate. He also dabbles in tracking Koreans from the UN. When lo and behold, a series of shots from a stakeout of an apartment of a suspected agent shows some interesting footage. Wanna guess what it was?"

"Me," I said sheepishly.

"Correct." He paused for effect. "You total idiot! Connor Burke, rogue operator, rolls up to the entrance of this place with some slick-lookin' Hispanic dude. The two of you go in. He comes out and has a smoke. You are still rattling around in there, doing God knows what. Meantime, who rolls up but another car with one of the bruisers from the Korean mission. You know the type? Thick neck. Flat face." I closed my eyes and there was the ghost memory of the fight I had with the Korean in Lim's apartment—the set of his shoulders, the ferocity of his attack, all of it compounded by tight spaces and desperation.

"So," my brother continued, "the stakeout team is having a field day. The motorized drives on the cameras are whirring and they're happy as clams, snapping away at the new faces. A few minutes go by and the Hispanic guy goes back into the building. Then you both tumble out and away you go. The stakeout team makes a call and sits around with their thumbs up their ass, waiting for authorization to break cover and enter the building. They're still waiting when the Korean stumbles out, looking a little shaky. He staggers to his car and boogies.

"This is the most excitement the stakeout guys have had in months. They're pissed that they didn't get to see what happened, but hey—good news—they have photos of all these new friends to look at. They run a match on the plates of the car you're in, but guess what? They're stolen. So they start shopping the headshots around and eventually, you—did I mention you're an idiot?—you end up in an eight-by-ten on Charlie's desk."

"And he called you?"

"Of course he called me. Charlie is not really crazy about either of us, but he's still not a complete pinhead. He gave me a heads up and also told me you'd been flagged as a person of interest."

"What's that mean?"

"What it means is that you're on their radar. And they know something we don't know about this guy Lim and his friends from the UN mission."

"So?"

"So now we both know what you said is true—there is more to this than meets the eye. And we start putting the pieces together and it is not good."

I sat back and sighed. The building was full of night sounds: the creak of heating units, distant hushed voices. Above it all, I could hear the snow blowing across the roof and feel the pulse of the storm as the wind pushed and pulled at the building.

"So what are we dealing with, Mick?" I said it quietly, as if I somehow hoped he would not hear the question and not give me an answer.

"Hard to say exactly," he said. I could almost hear his shrug over the line. "My guess is you are right—please note that it pains me to say that—and they were probably trying to set Miyazaki up for some sort of extortion. Ya know, racy pictures of his crazy daughter … the sense that maybe she might make him a security risk …"

"He'd want to protect the family from disgrace," I said.

Mickey snorted. "He'd want to protect his career. Ya ever wonder why, if this chick was such a wild child, they never did anything about it until now, Connor? They've probably been covering for her for years. I think the reason they wanted to get hold of her now had nothing to do with the family. It had to do with keeping her old man's career on track."

I wasn't so sure. There's a whole rich dimension of shame and honor and family reputation to consider in the Japanese psyche. "I'm not sure you totally get the Japanese, Mick."

"Ya know what I get, Connor? I get the fact that sometimes you are so into this martial arts stuff that it blinds you to the obvious. I mean, come on. If the Miyazaki wanted to lay their hands on the chick, these people are wired through the diplomatic corps … they could have had some calls made and someone from state would reach out and the problem would have been solved. But they didn't do that because it would have raised flags and ruined his chances for the job. So what do they do? They reach out to you in the hopes that you can get her roped in, but do it on the QT."

"Which I did," I protested.

"Yes," he agreed wearily. "Through some sort of complete moronic convergence you manage to pull this off."

"So then what's the problem? I did good, right?"

There was silence on the line as if Mickey were completely stupefied by the comment. "Buddy boy," he told me, "since when is it ever just about doing good?" The sadness in his voice reminded me he had been a cop for more than twenty years.

"I don't get it, Mick."

That comment seemed to revive him somewhat. "Of course ya don't get it." His voice was rising. "That's the point."

"I got her," I said. "She's out of the clutches of Lim and safe and sound. Nobody knows where we are."

He laughed. "Connor, everybody knows where you are."

"How so?"

"Because you are only ever in a few places. Most of the time, you're way up your own ass. If you're not home, you're at the dojo. When's the last time you taught at NYU?"

"It's been awhile," I had to admit. I had been what's known as an adjunct professor there. Overeducated and underpaid, I worked on a class-by-class basis. Like all adjuncts, I was cheap and docile labor, but I'd gained a certain notoriety from some of the scrapes I'd been in. The dean eventually thought my continued employment might not be contributing toward the image the university was trying to project. So the sputtering little biplane of my academic career had carved a painfully erratic but low arc across the university skyline and eventually augured in with a muffled thump.

"Yeah," Mickey commented. "So I gathered. One less variable to consider. So if you're not at home, not at the dojo, and not at NYU, and not in transit between any of these points, where are you?" I took a breath to answer and he interrupted me with mockery. "No, please, let me guess … you're at that Zen place upstate where Yamashita spends so much time."

"I'm that obvious?"

"Connor, you're off on some wild-goose chase up in the Poconos and then are trying to head home in the worst snowstorm in a century. They're closing the highways; Amtrak and every other form of mass transit is frozen in place. The entire East Coast is in bed and pulling the covers over its head. Where else ya gonna go?"

"I guess …" I said grudgingly.

"And here's the kicker," he said, and his voice once again began to grow in intensity. "Once they lost track of you, it wouldn't take them long to figure out your next step. They just stake out likely places and wait for you."

"You think they're waiting for me here?" The possibility rocked me. I had thought the monastery was going to be the place we could hide for a time from all the different storms swirling around us. But the storm had stranded a number of newcomers. Could some of them be waiting and watching for me? I remembered the ease with which the ex-medic had handled the gun in my pocket. Was he one of them?

"If it was me, I'd a had someone there," Mickey said with total conviction.

"Shit," I breathed over the phone.

"Yeah. Shit. But there's good news and bad news."

"What's the good news?"

"Whoever is up there is probably just someone to watch

and notify the Koreans when you show up. Whoever it is probably won't try something on their own."

"OK ... bad news?"

"Bad news is they've already made the call and the Koreans will be trying to get to you."

"In this weather?"

Mickey laughed. "Connor, they're North Koreans. Weather like this, I'm not even sure they'd bother to put on a hat."

"Oh."

"Oh," he echoed. "Although I think they're gonna have a hard time getting to you anytime soon. The city is closed down and nobody's being allowed on the bridges."

"So, good news, yes?"

My brother sighed, as if I had finally worn him out. "Good news, then bad news. Then good news. But now ..."

"There's more bad news."

"In my experience, there is never a shortage of bad news. And here's the thing I want you to hear clearly, Connor." The fuming and rage were gone from his tone and he was speaking clearly and quietly. You rarely heard Mickey this way and when you did, it meant something very, very serious was about to happen. And in my brother's world, serious things were always dangerous things.

"The blackmail scheme has been blown all to shit, since now we know about it."

"That's good, right? It only works if there's a secret to be kept."

"It's good on one level, but not for you."

"Whattaya mean?"

"Right now, you got these Korean goons trying to erase their tracks. If they get blown as operating here, they get sent home. In disgrace."

"To Pyongyang," I breathed.

"The armpit of East Asia," he agreed. "Ruled by a bunch of maniacs with an intelligence service that has never bought into the whole 'forgive and forget' approach to management."

It began to dawn on me then. "So they would seriously like all knowledge of this little scheme to … go away."

He gave his evil cackle. "Go away … you are so cute. These guys are fucking serious, Connor. Killing serious. And they'll try to eliminate everyone who's a direct link to the scheme."

"Lim," I said. "Chie …"

"Forget Lim," he told me. "Forget the chick. Worry about yourself."

"Unh," I said. *Burke, the master of the quick comeback.*

"That's all you've got to say? Unh? Do you realize what you've stumbled into? And how really serious this is? I can't believe we're even having this conversation. After all this time … all the other shit I've had to bail you out of. You keep living in this weird little fantasy world. Yamashita and the martial arts and the code of the warrior. And now you're in way over your head. It's the North Koreans and these guys are not foolin' around." He had slowly ramped himself up into a new rage. But he got it under control and his last words were tight and precise and scary because they were so quiet and so matter of fact. "You really piss me off, Connor. And do you know why?"

"Why?"

"Because," he screamed into the phone, "they're coming to get you and I'm stuck here in this fucking storm and I'm not sure I'll be able to get up there in time to help. YOU ASSHOLE."

The line went dead—probably overwhelmed by brotherly tough love.

CHAPTER 21

We were comrades, Rinsuke, but there were always parts of you that you tried to keep hidden and inaccessible, even to me. But truly, while you were in some ways distant, you were never hard to understand. We returned to the training hall, numb and only foggily aware of the whirl of activity surrounding us. Most thought it was the aftereffects of the incident and the storm. But I knew better. We never spoke of it, but the looks I had seen pass between you and Chika-hime told me all I needed to know. The connection created between the two of you was powerful. I imagine it took all your discipline to hide it from sight.

At the time, I wondered what this would cost you, what price you would pay for the love affair between the two of you. Now, of course, I know. But at that time I feared if you two were ever together again, the world would see what I had seen and you would be destroyed. For the relentless machine of the dynastic ambitions of the Miyazaki, combined with the stone-hard honor of the Imperial House, would crush you both and grind you up. I was sure of it. You could not see it, lost in your love and your misery. But I could see clearly.

You moved through the next few days in a type of trance, seemingly engaged in the mundane challenges of movement and speech, but on closer inspection you were a man who had removed himself from any true engagement in the here and now.

The story of the North Korean attempt to kidnap the princess grabbed the public's attention. The details of our fight at the inn were embellished in the telling until I barely recognized it.

Takano drank in the attention, smugly nodding at the wonder with which our exploits were greeted. His statements were humble ones, but I caught him in more than a few unguarded moments. At those times his mouth would tighten in a grim, satisfied line and his eyes would gleam with the sure knowledge that his fortunes had been made. It was, after all, his skill that had shaped the two trainees who fought off the kidnappers. This was how he spun his version of the story. Within weeks, the leading families of Japan were begging him to accept their sons as trainees.

But the greatest accolades were saved for Miyazaki himself. In this version of the story, his selfless act of leaping in front of one of the Korean gunmen was what allowed the two of us to rescue her. It was a tale rich in scenes for public consumption: the loving husband willing to sacrifice himself for his bride; the scion of a distinguished family willing to show how he valued honor and duty more than life itself. If those who knew him best wondered at the characterization of Miyazaki as a paragon, they never spoke publicly. Nobody ever protested that he was, in fact, an arrogant and cruel man, a selfish human being and an abusive husband. No voice ever registered complete amazement that he would do such a selfless thing. No person ever speculated on the real motives for an act that seemed so at odds with the personality of the real Miyazaki.

He himself could shed no light on his actions. The doctors would later describe it as trauma-induced amnesia: Miyazaki could remember nothing leading up to and including his act of courage. He never would. But he held on to the story tightly; even as the diagnosis of paralysis was delivered, he wrapped himself in the tale of his honor.

You and I listened to the other trainees talk of it, but

refused to discuss the matter. We left the story as it had been presented in the newspapers. For you, I imagine it felt like the final disastrous event, the keystone that fell into place and locked your destinies into its structure.

You and the princess had both hoped to be rid of him, but Miyazaki lived. Worse than that, he had sacrificed himself to save us. The actions demanded respect. And if it was a reaction privately tinged with stunned incredulity that so flawed a human being could rise to such heroism, it demanded to be honored nonetheless. You saw that. Whatever wild hopes each of you may have harbored about your future, they were smothered in the fact that Miyazaki's courage now bound the princess to him forever. And you were honor bound to agree.

Two nights later, you came to me. You were dressed for travel, a small scuffed suitcase stuffed with clothing at your feet along with the canvas bag that held your training weapons. Our conversation was stilted; there was so much to say and few words could carry so heavy a load. You told me you were leaving and I asked where you would go.

"South," you said. "Away."

"Tokyo?" I asked.

Your face was rigid with shock. "Never." It was where they would live together. Miyazaki and his wife. You seemed as if you were afraid the mere fact of being in the same city with her would be too much to bear.

You gave me a note for her, wrapped in a bamboo tube. You asked me to see that it reached her hands. That only her eyes would see it. I only nodded. We were seated in a small, dim room and darkness was falling. I lifted the note in its container and marveled at how something so light could, in fact, be weighed down with so much importance. I looked at you. Your eyes glittered. Perhaps it was tears. Perhaps just a trick of the light. I set the note down in front of me and bowed low to you. I tried to make that bow sum up the sadness I felt, the understanding of what you were doing and why, and the deep regret I had.

When I straightened up, you were gone.

I delivered the note to your princess, of course. And from that moment we had a special bond. She never asked me about you or where you had gone. She only asked that I watch out for you.

Which I have done for all these years.

Before the year ended, the princess gave birth to a boy. People thought it must have been a comfort to Miyazaki, one last gift from a time before his body was strapped to a wheelchair. I saw the child some time later and thought I recognized a familiar shape to the head. The princess caught my eye and we said nothing. There was no need.

Your son grew up in that household, never knowing of his origins in the storm.

But I knew, and I carried that guilty knowledge with me over the years. The princess and I kept the secret locked tight, knowing family honor required it. But she had charged me with caring for you, Rinsuke, and I did. I entered the service of the Imperial House and used my connections to smooth the way for you in various places. I eventually brought you into the Kunaicho as one of my most trusted assistants. You might wonder whether I simply did it for her, but that would not be entirely true. You were, in fact, tremendously skilled, and we put your abilities to good use over the years. This you know.

But if the truth be told, and now there is no reason to hide it, I did it for myself.

I had hoped for great things in my life. But when I saw you, I knew I could never be your equal. It was not simply your skill, but your sense of self. I watched you struggle against Takano's will, against his abuse, and triumph. If some of his trainees thought he was a god, I looked at you, Rinsuke, and saw a true master in the making. And when you fell in love with the princess, as sudden and inexplicable and unlikely as the event may have seemed, I feared for your happiness. For this love could never be allowed to blossom. I knew that.

The North Korean plot, in an odd karmic way, could have been a blessing. If we could rescue the princess, and Miyazaki could perhaps fall as a casualty …

It seems cold-blooded, does it not? But even then, I had the ability to spin events to serve varied purposes. He was a despicable human being; if he fell, the world would be better off. But mostly, I feared he would see what I had seen, and know that you and the princess were in love. I had no illusions about how he would react. He would destroy you and her life would be an endless round of humiliation and abuse. His death, I decided, was a necessity. It would not make you happy, but it would at least keep you both safe.

Understand my intentions were good.

I laugh as I write that line. It may well be the epitaph for us all. Indeed, it may be the only one possible. We struggle and plan our way through this life, staggering under the weight of duty and desire. What does it get us? At the end, who of us can look up and know that in that last moment, our actions have created more good than suffering?

I know I cannot.

But I do know in that moment at the inn, I wished you both the best. I saw a chance to rid the world of an odious presence and perhaps shelter your love from the harsh storms of a demanding world. In the end, I failed. Miyazaki did not die, but emerged a hero. His wife was bound to him in honor, reminded every day of his sacrifice by the sight of his wheelchair. Two young lovers forever parted. And your child was raised as another man's son.

Forgive me. It seemed such a simple thing.

When we burst into that room at the inn, I saw that your plan would not succeed: sometimes, like our master, I could experience real clarity at moments of danger. The Korean gunmen would begin firing at any moment. What could I do? In that second I made the decision. I refused to let either of us sacrifice ourselves for such a man. So I did what I thought best.

I had come to care for you and the princess too much. Forced to choose, it was an easy action. You may say it was a move without honor, but I think love is stronger than honor. And in my own way, I loved you, and the princess. In any event, I have spent the rest of my life atoning for my actions in that one second, serving the Imperial House. And yet I will always regret what it did to your lives.

Miyazaki did not jump in front of the gunman to save you, or me, or his wife. He was not thinking of honor or sacrifice or duty. He was not thinking of these things at all.

The truth is simpler than that, a straightforward act that fell into the still water of our lives and sent waves pulsing through it, changing things forever.

I pushed him.

CHAPTER 22

The roshi's place was technically called a zendo and it was part monastery and part Zen education center. At any given time, there were transient visitors mixing with the residents, people coming for a day or a weekend or longer, for the purposes of exploring Zen meditation. The roshi welcomed them all with open arms and without judgment. Yet his compassion had many permutations and, while his smile was genuine, I knew now that he saved his most troubling insights for those he thought capable of withstanding them.

Not that this little realization made me feel any better. I was mostly focused on the situation at hand and how I would deal with it. I wondered who among the strangers in the zendo tonight might have been watching for my arrival with Chie Miyazaki. You'd think someone like that would stick out, but I wasn't so sure. The visitors were a real mix. Some were jittery and ill at ease, victims of too much caffeine and too much career, who were trying to slow down their lives but were really uncomfortable with the simple experience of silence. Others were painfully sincere—people long on enthusiasm but short on discipline. They came looking for refuge or for instruction or enlightenment. Most found the work too hard, the challenge too great, the task too daunting. They came for a time and left. It occurred to me that they weren't so different from most of the people who drifted into a martial arts dojo—we just tended to have thicker necks. But I had learned from years of trying to predict who would stay and who would go that it was an imprecise science at best. The zendo was no different, and if I were to spot a mole, I would need to watch everyone at the monastery carefully.

The monks, regulars, and other hard-core types were a generally quiet bunch—maybe because they were introspective, maybe because the morning bell would summon them for dawn services while the sky was still dark. I thought right now, this late in the evening, I would have the chance to meet some of the newcomers to try to get a read on them: there were occasional late lectures and social hours for visitors. But tonight the place was buttoned up, as if everyone were like Mickey had described: in bed with the covers pulled over their heads, listening to the blizzard batter the landscape.

The hallways were dim, with nightlights softly glowing at long intervals along the walls. I poked my head out of the bedroom, thinking I had heard the whisper of feet along the floor, but the corridor was empty. I was weary, but at the same time I was so wired I couldn't rest. I kept reliving different conversations I had been part of during the day: those with Chie, with Yamashita, with the roshi, and with Mickey. I played them and replayed them in my head like some audiophile stuck with a record collection he didn't particularly like, but felt compelled to listen to anyway.

I shambled down the corridor in my socks. The floor was cold. I felt stiff and off-balance and old. I knew it wasn't permanent—just a result of the beating—but I didn't like it. It made me think of Yamashita and how he struggled against the onset of old age. It reminded me of how the years were passing for all of us. More significantly, Mickey's warning had made its impression on me. I needed to be as sharp as possible. So I thought I would wander downstairs and maybe spot a suspicious character or two. More realistically, I thought I would drift by the kitchen and see if I could get a banana— potassium for the muscles. Then, having exhausted my plans, I would sit for a time in the *hondo*, the main meditation hall, and wait for an idea, confident that nature abhors a vacuum.

The hondo was a cave, a bunker, a cathedral. The walls were grey worked stone, and at night the clerestory windows were blind eyes, the thick stained glass covering them like dark cataracts. The hall's ceiling vaulted up into the darkness, where broad old wooden beams crisscrossed space—solid, silent guardians watching from on high. Candles flickered in that room and a tapestry with the Buddha on it hung against the stone wall. In the comfort of that space, I was hoping I could see my way clear of this mess.

It was a tall order. The whole string of events had never been particularly straightforward to begin with. I knew that. There was something wrong about the Miyazaki and their odd proposal, something wrong about the way Ito rode herd on the whole project, but never really provided much help. He had given me an envelope with some electronic files, some money, and a warning. It occurred to me that everything else he had done was designed to allow me to blunder around while he got to keep his hands clean.

Did he know about Lim and his connections to the Koreans? Had an attempt already been made to make Chie's father provide Lim with classified information? Or did the Miyazaki plan on short-circuiting that scheme by having me do their dirty work and get rid of Lim?

I could believe that last idea. The family was an ambitious one, jealous of its prominence in business and diplomatic circles. But there had to be more to the whole arrangement. Mori's journal laid bare a secret he had kept for decades, a scandalous situation where the son of a powerful and connected Japanese family was revealed as the offspring of a youthful tryst between my teacher and Miyazaki's young wife. How had that horrible old man dealt with the news? Was he sitting somewhere in his wheelchair, seething at the discovery of a long-hidden betrayal by his dead wife? Had his original plan been to get Yamashita involved in the attempt to kidnap Chie and then somehow betray him to the authorities? If so, then why rope me in? It would seem a petty type of revenge to frame me for kidnapping: too indirect and besides, I believed they sincerely wanted Chie out of Lim's clutches.

It was very likely there were at least two and maybe three parallel schemes at play. The fact that the Miyazaki wanted to control Chie to protect her father's career didn't mean the old man wasn't also trying to rig something that would blow up in Yamashita's face. That I could deal with. What really worried me was the additional dimension Mickey had surmised. By ruining the Korean blackmail scheme against Chie's father, I had also inadvertently ripped the cover off it. And that set alarm bells ringing. I thought back to the men who had snatched me off the street and their interrogation. I shivered in the darkness of the monastery, blaming it on a nonexistent draft, or on exhaustion, blaming it on everything but the memory of the experience on the waterboard that even the Buddha's calm couldn't tame. I shrugged to myself: *Life is suffering*. The roshi preaches what are known as the Noble Truths. He never said they were easy to deal with.

So … the Koreans. I had ruined their plans and now they were scrambling for cover like bugs. And the bigger and nastier of them were wondering whether they couldn't pull the rock back on top of the plot—they'd be back in the dark and hopefully Chie and I would get crushed in the process.

The kitchen was empty and still. The condenser in the big industrial refrigerator clicked on, but it only made the room seem more deserted. I filched a banana from a bowl of fruit that had been left on the table, and peeled it slowly, sitting on a stool, lost in recrimination. I had thought I was being so clever. Keeping Miyazaki, Goro, and Ito away from my sensei, trying to shelter him from being used. And I had been so proud that I had endured, that I had tracked Chie down and gotten her away from Lim. It seemed so straightforward in that sense, so right.

But the roshi had let me know life is more complex than that. I had been looking at things from only one perspective, and I had let my own sense of honor and duty and the need to do what I thought was good lead me to a series of actions that spawned unanticipated consequences. I thought of Yamashita sitting there with his calligraphy. *Enzan no metsuke* warned us against concentrating on one perspective and losing the bigger picture.

By this time my thoughts had made me lose my appetite. I ate the banana anyway. I wasn't really tasting it, but it was still fuel for the machine.

Nobody was going to thank me for this one, I realized ruefully. Chie was pretty clear on that subject. I had no right to force her to live a different life than the one she wanted. And, strangely, the roshi agreed with her. From his perspective my actions were fueled by ego, pure and simple, clouded with foolish ideas about right and wrong, damsels in distress, and the warrior's path. He hadn't lectured me, but I knew the Eightfold Path of Buddhism started with Right View, the need to understand and see things as they really are. In the roshi's eyes, no matter the sincerity of my intentions, I was fundamentally deluded.

I sat up with a start, my ribs sparking with pain, as I realized this was what Yamashita had been telling me as well. It was a subtle message. The calligraphy *enzan no metsuke* was both a rebuke and a lesson, and both actions were themselves wrapped up in a test. He was waiting to see whether I would be self-aware enough to realize what he was trying to tell me. It was the typical, maddeningly elliptical way the Japanese went about things. It was also a compliment, I realized.

In the old days, when I was new to his dojo, Yamashita was all thunder and direct instruction, a teacher as hard as the oak training sword he carried like an extension of himself. If I did something wrong, he would come straight at me and give me a lesson by stripping the sword from my hands, or by dumping me on the floor and humiliating me in front of everyone. Silent, yet oh so effective. But over the years the lessons grew more complex and the corrections more intricate and subtle. Lessons were learned in different ways, not all of them overt.

And how had my actions impacted my teacher? I brought his granddaughter into his life, but did Yamashita even want this? Was the revelation contained in Mori's journal too painful to confront this late in my sensei's life?

I eased myself off the stool and out of the kitchen, my ribs complaining. I was concentrating so much on moving carefully, watching each step, that I didn't even notice someone paused at the foot of the staircase leading up to the sleeping area.

"You are one hurting puppy," he said. My friend from the Tenth Mountain Division. I smiled, but in the back of my mind I heard my brother commenting on the likelihood that

235

the Koreans had an informant at the monastery: *If it was me, I'd a had someone there.*

"I'll be OK," I said and started to move around him.

But he seemed like he wanted to talk. "Crazy storm, huh?"

"Storm of the century," I agreed, parroting something I had heard.

"I've been out with a few folks trying to keep the parking lot clear and the paths open. But it's too much. Better to let the storm blow out …"

"Any sense of how long that will take?"

He shrugged. "They say at least another day. Maybe tomorrow night or early the next morning."

"That long?"

"Yeah," he said. "None of us are going anywhere for a while." In the dim light his face was covered in shadows and I couldn't tell whether his expression was carrying some more sinister meaning or whether I was imagining it. I smiled noncommittally and shuffled away toward the hondo.

The empty room was vast, dark, and chilly. I could feel the rumble of the heaters in the basement struggling against the blizzard. I sank down wearily and focused on my breathing, hoping the discipline of stillness would lead me to some insight. I closed my eyes.

The training tells you to let your mind "bubble off." Don't fight the busy thoughts, but rather let them come, and let them go. Acknowledge them as they pass, but try not to hold on to them. You let the rhythm of breath calm the beast, let stillness seep into the muscles, until you sink to a place where the distractions of the rushing world are distant and you are simply present.

Burke. The summons once again, clear and immediate, my

master's voice coming as if he were standing before me. *Burke*, it came again.

I opened my eyes and he *was* standing before me. Chie was at his side, looking pale and as worn out as I felt. I got to my feet, my body grinding and complaining like a rusty machine. Yamashita watched me, his face revealing nothing, his eyes taking silent inventory of my condition.

"We should plan, Burke," he said. I nodded in silent agreement, sagging, feeling momentarily deflated. Then I took a breath and straightened up. I looked at Chie.

"I meant the best," I told her, "but I was wrong to take you." She just stood there. A sudden storm gust rocked the world outside; I could feel the shift in air pressure even behind those stone walls. Chie just watched me, and it seemed as if her silence, her calm, had within it a disgust so deep it robbed her of words.

I nodded as if hearing her silent rebuke. "As soon as the storm blows itself out, I'll take you back to the city."

That got a small rise out of her. "To my family?"

"No," I said, "back to school. Back to … your life."

Yamashita's eyes narrowed. "It is not as simple as that, is it, Burke?" He smiled grimly. "Chie and I have been talking, as you may imagine." He sighed. "I do not have all the pieces of this puzzle put together, but I think this is more complicated than you may have originally thought."

"It is," I agreed. I looked directly at Chie and held up my hand. "Whatever you may think, the information I have is the people Lim was working for are angry …"

"You've contacted your brother?" Yamashita asked, and he grunted in satisfaction when I nodded yes.

". . .they're angry because I've made enough noise to alert

people to what they were trying to do to your father."

"So," she said, shrugging. "That's their problem, isn't it?"

I squinted in thought. "Yes and no." She folded her arms impatiently and I rushed on. "These are the kind of people who work in the shadows, Chie. If they're known, their usefulness is at an end. And when that happens …" I looked at my teacher for support.

He nodded. "Their masters will not be pleased." Yamashita pursed his lips, considering. "Standard procedure with issues like this is to try to cover them up. It usually involves the elimination of witnesses."

It seemed to break through the subtle air of disgust Chie wrapped around herself for protection. She swallowed. "Like me?"

"Like us," I said. The two of them stood there, silent as the stones all around us. Easy to see they were related. I held a hand out. "I'm sorry, Chie." Yamashita was watching the two of us—our body language, the way we related to one another.

"Enough," he said. "Whether you caused this situation or whether it would have unraveled on its own is neither here nor there. Really, Burke, after all this time …"

"What?" I said, a tone of annoyance creeping into my voice.

"When the sword is drawn …" Yamashita began.

"There is only the sword," I answered with a resigned sigh.

Yamashita nodded. "The roshi is focused on … other things, Burke. You and I must be focused on the here and now."

I took a breath. How many times had he called me to attention over the years? I could hear the echo of the dojo command, *yoi*. In my mind's eye a row of swordsmen in blue stood a little straighter, quivering with anticipation at the command to get ready. They were human springs tightening down and eagerly sensing the approach of some sort of release. And I was one of them.

"OK," I said quietly.

"We are here," my teacher said, waving his hand around the room. "It is only a matter of time until they realize this." He smiled. "But the storm that traps us here also keeps them from reaching us."

"For a time," I added.

"Oh, certainly." He looked at me, a hint of wryness on his face. "Nothing lasts forever, Burke. But it does give us time to prepare." He looked around the dark meditation hall and his black eyes glittered with candlelight. "They think they have us in a box, *neh?* In reality, it is a maze. A large building with many rooms and hallways. We should use that to our advantage, Burke."

I nodded my understanding. "They say the storm will last all through tomorrow. It should give us some time to prepare … maybe hunt up some weapons."

Yamashita smiled grimly. "A zendo—probably not a place rich in weapons, Burke. But we will do what we can." Chie was pale with tension and exhaustion. My teacher nodded in her direction. "For now, I think some sleep. The two of you have had an interesting day."

"And you?"

"Oh, my day has been interesting as well," he admitted. "But it is not over yet. I think," and he paused here, gazing off as if he could see through the walls, beyond the storm, to the forces that would converge around us. "I think I will go to the kitchen."

Chie stirred. "How can you think of eating at a time like this?"

Yamashita looked at me and smiled. It was a look I had never seen on his face before: amusement blended with deep affection, as if to say, *my granddaughter, she's so cute.*

I didn't respond, just smiled back at Yamashita, a silent message passing between us about how little the different generations understood each other. I took Chie out of the room and up the stairs. She let herself be led, one more silent form drifting down the cold hall of the zendo. I put her to bed and never told her why Yamashita was going to the kitchen.

It was where they kept the knives.

CHAPTER 23

The monastery clicked and creaked in the darkness. Outside the snow sifted down and smothered everything in its path. I lay on the narrow bed, eyes closed. The barometric pressure danced along with the storm. I slowed my breathing and gradually worked on letting the tension seep out of me. I ignored the aches and worked on softening, feeling my body's warmth grow around me while cool air lay across the blanket surface, held at bay for a time. I was eager for sleep.

But something was wrong. The sense of unease was real, but its exact source was difficult to articulate: a subtle shift in the sensory field, stillness where there had been sound, or a spike in sound where there had been the steady hum of night noise. My eyes flew open and I knew there was someone at the door before the knob even started turning.

It was Chie, draped in a blanket, looking small and lost and incredibly sad.

"Burke," she whispered, testing to see if I was awake.

I sat up and the soft, warm cocoon dissipated, sliding off me along with the blankets. "Yeah." I rubbed my face in my hands, the skin ripped-feeling and tender to the touch.

"I don't like this place," she said. "The noises." She slid through the door and closed it behind her. "There's someone watching."

That made me sit up straighter. "You saw something?"

She shook her head. "No. Just a feeling."

I nodded. "Strange building. Lots of noise. It's easy to get spooked."

She came and sat next to me. "Can I stay here tonight?" She bit her lower lip as she asked, looking all innocent and defenseless. Part of me wondered how much of it was an act and how much of it was genuine. But most of me just wanted to go to sleep. "Sure," I sighed. "But I'm not sleeping on the floor."

She gave me a small smile, and her eyes showed a knowing glint. "I don't take up much room."

I sank back on the bed, pretty sure I had been conned. But maybe on some level her fear was genuine: she went to the door and fiddled with the knob. "The doors don't have locks here," I told her. "It's a monastery."

"It creeps me out," she said. "I mean, what if someone tries to get in during the night …"

I sighed and got up. The floor was cold against my bare feet. I took the wooden chair and wedged the back of it up against the doorknob. "There," I told her. "That should do for tonight." I climbed back into bed and pulled the covers up, lying on my side with my back almost touching the wall. She lay down next to me, wrapped in the blanket she had come in with. Small adjustments and the faint creak of an industrial mattress. The distant hum of the blizzard. Eventually we settled down. Her breathing grew quieter. But she must have been cold, because she moved closer. Her hips moved slowly against me.

It may have been almost a reflex on her part. She may have been genuinely frightened, but then again she was also someone who compulsively used her body to get what she wanted. And I wasn't made of stone. *Yamashita's granddaughter*, my conscience reminded me. *The nympho*, reminded another part.

"Chie," I said in whisper. "Enough." The movement

stopped and I tried to move even further back against the wall, but there was only so much mattress space, and it was hard to avoid touching her. Her small body lay there next to mine and the world moaned and creaked around us. Eventually, I heard her slip into sleep, but I lay there with my eyes open.

In the darkness, I sensed something once more. I watched intently. The knob turned with painful slowness until the latch gave. There was a stealthy push, as gentle as wind, and the chair rose up, jamming itself against the knob. The door settled back and the smooth pattern of nighttime resumed. I eventually slept, but it was an agitated rest, threaded with a recurring dream that I lay there awake, waiting for dawn to come.

The morning was dark with a snow that seemed like it would never end. The roshi was worried about the oil burner, a massive block of iron and valves that rumbled on its basement slab like an archaic locomotive straining to leave the station.

"We've been using the fireplaces to take some of the pressure off the system," he told us all in the morning gloom. "We'll need to clear the paths to the woodpile." Fortunately he was well supplied with cut wood. The roshi systematically harvested the property's forests, creating a sustainable source of income for the zendo. There were mounds of neatly stacked hardwood under lean-tos behind the main building. All we had to do was tunnel through what looked to be at least four feet of snow.

There was sweet hot tea and oatmeal for breakfast. We sat together, monks, visitors, and castaways, on long benches that paralleled a long, scarred wooden table. The roshi and his monks had already chanted the first office of the day, but instead of donning their robes they were dressed in baggy heavy pants and sweaters that drooped around them like the inescapable gravity of the mundane. After the Robe Sutra, when their voices moaned with longing for enlightenment, they now began the search for snow shovels. Was it Thomas Merton who described monks as in the world but not of it? Today, they were in it for sure.

A bright-eyed middle-aged woman bustled around the room, ladling out globs of oatmeal. I sat there, hands wrapped around a mug.

"Hi, I'm Sue," she said. I looked up. She was middle aged and carried about thirty extra pounds on her, but it was packed on evenly and she moved with lots of energy. Her blue eyes twinkled.

"Hi, Sue," I said and introduced myself.

"What brings you here?" she asked, cocking her head. "Blown in by the storm?" She was nice enough not to comment on the condition of my face.

I smiled. "Sort of yes, sort of no." She waited, ladle poised. She was one of those people who seemed genuinely interested in other people and their stories. Go figure.

"I know Yamashita Sensei," I explained. I'm not much of a conversationalist in the morning.

"Oh, the old Japanese gent," she said, her eyes round with amusement. "He's the roshi's special guest."

"What brings you here, Sue?" She was so chipper; it was forcing conversation out of me.

"Oh," she waived the ladle. "Just searching … I spent some time at Tibet House in New York, ya know?"

"Sure," I said. The Tibetans and I were old friends. "*Sustainable Happiness*," I told her, and her face lit up. It was the title of a book written by one of the teachers there. It was a good one.

"Yes," she said. "Great stuff. But the Tibetan approach is sort of …"

"Dense? Complicated?" I supplied.

She beamed at me. "Exactly. So when I heard about the zendo here, I thought why not check it out? Seems a bit more straight-forward, ya know?" I smiled at that. In my experience the search for enlightenment was like the search for cold fusion: simple in theory, difficult to achieve. "Anyway," she continued, "I decided to come up for a short retreat. Who knew I'd get snowed in?" Something started gurgling over on the stove, her head jerked up, and she was gone. But she left a smile on my face.

The guy from the Tenth Mountain Division came in and grunted himself onto the bench. He explained to me the plan of attack for the day. The main building was like a broad, asymmetrical V with the point flattened out by the main entrance, the shorter left arm thickened by the hondo and the suite of rooms where Yamashita stayed. The longer arm of the V contained the monastery's offices and classrooms, the roshi's quarters, and the bedrooms on the second floor. The interior space of the V was a series of outdoor meditation spaces and the meticulously tended rock gardens that Zen temples are famous for. Now it was just an expanse of white, with the occasional dip and hump suggesting whatever was buried beneath it.

There were paths that stretched from the building at each end of the V's arms, both slanting up at an angle toward the woodsheds. At least that's what he told me. It was a good fifty yards from the doors to the woodsheds, all of it thick with drifting snow. We were going to clear both of the paths. There was a lot of snow, and it was still coming down. Dry and feather light, it would be relatively easy to shovel. But there would still be a great deal of work. There was a lot of snow to move, and there was so much of it that we would have to clear wide swaths for pathways, otherwise the drifts created would start to sift and tumble back in on us.

I rolled my shoulders and my body clicked and groaned. I flexed my fingers, anticipating the heft of the shovel in my hand. *I hope we get more than oatmeal for lunch.*

Yamashita sat beside me. Tenth Mountain gulped his tea and left. My teacher watched me stretch and take inventory. "How are you?" Yamashita asked. He wasn't making conversation. It was an operational question delivered in a quiet, matter-of-fact way. We both knew he wasn't wondering how well I'd be able to shovel snow.

"I'm good," I told him. I saw the skeptical look in his eyes. He had an intimate knowledge of the toll a fight takes on a body. I shifted on the bench and amended my reply. "Well, I've been worse … it should be OK." He gave me one of his penetrating looks, but then nodded. We both knew the reality of a fight: it's not being ready so much as it is being willing.

We sat for a time, shoulders touching, watching the monks organize for the day. It was comforting to sit like that for a moment. I could feel the warmth of his body next to me, the solid presence of him. I sat up a little straighter, feeling more confident. He had that effect on people, Yamashita. When I first met him, I was simply captivated by his mastery of a martial art. Over time I learned perhaps his greatest skill was not what he could do with a sword, but how he could enthrall people and call out the best in them.

"Someone tried the door to my room last night," I told Yamashita. I said it quietly so as not to be overheard.

"Mine as well," he murmured back. "They want to know where we will be located during the night. This is good."

I looked at him. "How's that good? It means there's someone here, on the inside, keeping tabs on us. And we don't know who it is."

"True. But their activity tells us things, *neh?*"

I considered what he was saying, then smiled. "It tells us they'll plan on attacking at night."

"Yes," Yamashita said. The room was getting crowded as more people drifted in for breakfast and he spoke in a murmur. "It's not terribly original, Burke, a night attack, but at least we know we have some time before we have to worry about anything happening."

"And the storm is going to delay their response," I added, "so we may have another day or so."

Yamashita pursed his lips. "It is possible. But I am not counting on it. They probably think the storm has trapped us here, but I think the snow can work to our advantage." He gestured to the monks as they began handing shovels out. "The snow will erode their ability to move. The paths you make today will most probably channel them into predictable vectors of attack." His eyes crinkled with pleasure and he sipped at a mug of steaming tea. If you didn't know better, you'd think he were one of the monks: placid, otherworldly, and harmless. But you would be wrong. He shared something of their focus and their immediacy. But his air of contentment had other sources, including the stout butcher knives he had liberated from the kitchen the night before. "What a great gift to know when and where an attack will come, don't you think, Burke?"

"*Hai*, Sensei," I said, smiling.

We moved snow all day, taking shifts with the limited number of shovels available, grateful for the breaks when we could stand up and massage lower back muscles that were rigid and burning with hard use.

There was an undercurrent of mild hysteria as the snow continued: would the oil burner hold up? Would the food run out? When would the roads be plowed? Some of the visitors looked at each other and I could tell they were regretting whatever had motivated them to come to the monastery in the first place: *We wanted to get away from things for a while, not be trapped here.* On the bright side, it made them eager to take their turns with the shovels.

And this was a good thing because, truthfully, the monks were not the best shovelers in the world. They were diligent and mindful as you would expect, but a life of meditation and prayer does not build strong bodies twelve ways. So over time those of us with more aptitude or simply more claustrophobia took over for increasingly longer shifts. We split off into two groups: one focused on getting to the woodpiles, the other working out from the main entrance toward the parking lot.

Toward late afternoon the wind started to die down. It was a relief because until that point the wind had constantly shifted and blown fine snow crystals in your face and down your neck. Some people wrapped themselves in scarves and hats, only slitted eyes peeking out between the wool. But I knew despite the cold they would eventually be sweating with the effort of shoveling, overheating, and tiring themselves. I opted for a light jacket, some thick mittens, and a hat. It meant the skin on my face burned from the icy needles of windblown snow, and when I slowed down, the cold started to seep into my bones. But I endured the misery in the pursuit of a greater goal. It seemed, it occurred to me, to be a recurring theme in my life.

Late in the day, I called my brother.

"What's up?" I asked him.

"Whattaya think I'm doing?"

"Shoveling snow."

"Hah. No way I am touching a shovel until the fucking snow stops falling." I could see him, holed up in the converted garage space he uses as a home office. It's covered in cheap sheets of dark paneling. There's a dilapidated, stained couch and a few listing easy chairs. A pressed-wood desk warping under piles of paperbacks and knickknacks. Mickey's room is where old furniture is banished in disgrace—too ugly to live but too stubborn to die. There are family photos framed on the wall, along with newspaper clippings from some of his more famous cases. There's even a signed dust jacket from the book a crime reporter wrote about us. Our fifteen minutes of fame got Mickey a crimson book cover. The black lettering of the title was shaped like it had been sliced with a knife. It was inspired by reality: there had been fighting with blades and at the end of it I got to go home from the hospital with a long scar down my back.

"Still coming down?" I was wondering whether the weather was breaking further south. It might mean help could get to us. Then again, it might mean someone else could get to us as well.

"Yah. You?"

"The same. We're digging out a bit, but the roads haven't been touched."

"Yeah," he said dismissively. "Enough with the weather report. What I'm doing is working the phones for you, you dope. Trying to get a sense of when the weather will clear. The storm will probably break tonight. But then the real fun begins. The word is that nobody should expect much until sometime late tomorrow at best," Mickey said.

"And … so?"

"Charlie Wilcox and his guys are trying to keep the Koreans

buttoned up. The good news for you is the surveillance shift got snowed in along with everyone else. They got nothing to do but keep an eye out."

"So how do you think it'll play out?"

My brother grunted. "We can probably slow them down a little, but if they have other assets we don't know about ..." he let the implication dangle.

"That's what I'm wondering."

"Yeah. And the highways will get cleared down here first. Means they can probably get to you sooner than you can get out of there."

"You got any contacts up here?" It hurt me to ask; my brother has made a minor career out of bailing me out of jams and he never lets me forget it.

"Not in your area. Whatever juice I once had with the PD is starting to evaporate. I talked to some people, but no dice. Everyone's got their hands full with first-level emergency response. Even if they could get to you, they got bigger fish to fry. It's like the end of the world all along the Eastern Seaboard."

I sighed. "Call me if the Koreans roll."

"Will do." Neither of us sounded particularly happy. Neither of us could figure what else to say and the silence on the phone stretched out.

I gazed out the window: snow, the black trunks of trees. The cloud cover was still dense, so there was no sunset, just a thickening of shadows as the light went blue and grey and seeped out of the world.

Eventually, Mickey's voice called me back from wherever my mind was wandering. "Ya got a plan, Connor?" His voice was quiet and bled of hope.

"Survive 'til dawn," I said.

CHAPTER 24

Sue the Kitchen Lady put a bowl down in front of me. I poked around in it. "Steak in here somewhere, right?"

She laughed and wagged a finger at me. "Vegetable stew, Connor. Compassion for all things …"

In all honesty, it was pretty good: hot, thick with potatoes, and filled with garlic. I wolfed it down. I should have been grateful for it, but was feeling ornery. *The Burke luck holds true to form: I'm here in tofu land while somewhere out there somebody had been snowed in at an Outback Steakhouse.*

It had been a long day and even though there were other people outside with me at various points, nobody had much energy for talking. The bruises on my face were also turning all sorts of colors. Probably discouraged small talk from strangers. Except for Sue.

I didn't mind. It gave me plenty of time to think, and I had come to some conclusions. Not about how I was going to solve this mess, but rather about my role in creating it. The roshi and Yamashita both had rebuked me. Just thinking about that fact made my ears burn. But if I have come to admire men like the two of them, I've also learned in the end they are just men. They were wise and accomplished. But fallible, like us all. I thought they were wrong.

I went to see the roshi. He called me in when I knocked on the door and I found Chie sitting with him.

She stood up, as if alarmed. "I'll go," she told the priest.

I held up a hand. "No need. I want you to hear this." The

roshi was back in his robes and he sat in a chair, fingering his *mala* beads, his eyes calm. "Please join us, Connor. Sit. Please."

There was an empty chair, but I ignored it. "I wanted to let you know I've been thinking about things," I began. The roshi's face had a half-smile on it. He nodded encouragement. "You were right … I wasn't thinking clearly about what I was doing." Chie didn't say anything, but the subdued snort she gave was eloquent commentary: *No shit*. I plowed on.

"At first, I'll acknowledge, it was just a way to prove myself." I shrugged. "Ya know, be as good as my teacher. Ito, the guy from the government … he played on my vanity. I see that …" I swallowed. I took a breath. Another. "But it's more complicated than that now, isn't it?" I looked for acknowledgement in the roshi's eyes, but he held himself very still and I couldn't read him.

I waved a hand. "The whole Miyazaki thing … the horrible old man in the wheelchair. The uptight father worried about his career." I looked directly at Chie then. "And you. And Lim." Another wave of my hand. "The whole situation. And then I read Mori's journal and it got even crazier. I mean, the fact that you are Yamashita's granddaughter." Finally I sat down, leaning forward with my forearms resting on my knees.

"I had to do something," I said. "For him. For you." I looked up and she smirked at me.

"Sure," she said. "Your motives are so pure." She wiggled her bottom on the chair and arched her eyebrows. "Remember last night, Burke?"

I felt my face burn, but I sat up straight. "I never said I was pure." My voice was cold. "I said some of my motives were good ones." I looked imploringly at the roshi. "You were a shrink. Since when does anyone ever do things for one simple reason? Aren't we all a ball of tangled-up emotions and ideas?"

"True," he said. But the word came out reluctantly.

"OK. Well what I'm telling you …" I paused and looked at each of them. "What I'm telling both of you is I thought Chie at least deserved the chance to meet her real grandfather."

"I wasn't looking for a new family," she said tightly.

"Like the one you got is winning any prizes," I said and regretted it the instant the words tumbled out. *Still working on that keeping-my-mouth-shut skill.*

She sat forward, tense. "It's none of your business, Burke!"

"Maybe so," I admitted. "But I made it my business, and you know why?" I looked quickly from one to the other. "Cause your life is a fucking mess, Chie. And I thought you deserved to know there is something else out there. Something better. Another way."

"I'm not looking for another way," she hissed.

I stood up and felt tremendously weary. "I realize that now." She said nothing, her face narrow and closed off. I tried one more time. "I thought you were worth the try, though. Still do." The roshi watched Chie carefully, but made no sound. I hoped he would break in on the tense silence, but he said nothing. I started to turn away from them, but paused. "You know what the saddest thing in the world is, Chie? Not the people who don't find themselves. It's the ones who've stopped looking." I glared at both of them, then shuffled out of the office and closed the door softly on the room.

"You are angry," Yamashita observed when I joined him and gave him another version of the same speech. I shrugged, but said nothing, all the steam bled out of me. "I do not need you angry now, Burke," he continued. "I need you focused." He was in his room, kneeling in front of the French doors. We shovelers had cleared a path all the way to this spot and the small patio outside was gradually filling with snow again, the mounds of the drifts we made rising up along the trench to the woodpile, their tops softening with new snowfall. "Come sit beside me," he said quietly.

"I'm trying to do the right thing here," I told him.

He smiled then, a rare thing for Yamashita. "Of course you are, Burke. It is one of your most endearing qualities as a person."

"So why is everyone giving me such grief?" I demanded. It just popped out, and I felt embarrassed. *Want some cheese with your whine?*

"Why do you need other people's approval if you are in the right?" he asked, his head tilted to one side, faintly amused in that infuriatingly dispassionate way he has.

Where do you begin with a question like that? The beginning, I guess. I'd been raised that way: the Catholic universe of hierarchy, of sin and grace, and the weird moral mathematics of confession every Saturday. The Irish American compulsion to obey the rules, the feverish hope in the possible that warred against the ancient Celtic voice deep within that whispered the deck is stacked against us all.

There are two schools of thought in Zen about coming to awareness. The Soto sect thinks it comes after long effort and discipline. The Rinzai sect thinks with the proper guidance enlightenment comes upon you like a sudden storm. I realized at that moment they were both right. I'd been moving toward answering Yamashita's question all my life, but it was only now that a type of clarity rushed in on me.

I thought about Yamashita's question and what he was

getting at. I suppose I've been looking for approval every day of my life. I grew up in a home with lots of kids and not much in the way of resources. Every day was a scramble for my folks, and each of us had to scramble in turn for some small slice of their attention. I did it through toeing the line, with being good, with succeeding at school. And it was a hard habit to break. I grew up and when my parents' hold on me as authority figures waned, I found new ones at graduate school. I put myself through the rigors of a Ph.D. program not just for the joy of learning. It was the emotional roller coaster of challenge and struggle, occasional success and the distant approval of my professors that I was really craving.

I sat there in the snowbound monastery and snorted in amusement at myself. If you had asked me earlier, I would have said the whole graduate school experience was a cerebral one. In reality, I saw now that all those years were ones laced with emotion, with the fear of failing and the need for approval.

I looked at Yamashita sitting next to me, silent yet forceful, his dark eyes watching me, judging me. The martial arts, the Way I had chosen, were simply an extension of the same childish urges: the need to prove myself; the emotional connection to a distant authority figure; the need for approval and a sense of belonging that only came with conformity.

But I also realized I struggled against conformity as well. If I was good at school, I nonetheless chose pathways that were slightly odd. My mother wanted me to become a lawyer. I completed a degree in Asian history with an obscure research specialization. If my brother Mickey proved himself through a stint in the Marines, I spent decades on the hardwood floors of martial arts dojo, pursuing arcane skills from another world. My father put a picture of Mickey in his dress blues on the living room wall. When I told him I had earned a black belt, he just shook his head and said "nice."

Mickey had the same stubborn rebellious urges as I did, but he had managed to channel them into a career as a cop. I, however, charted a path with little likelihood of gainful employment, cobbling together a living as an adjunct professor, never fully a part of academia. Always a man apart.

So Yamashita's question reverberated through my head. This was the life I had created. It was time to admit it, to accept it. *Time to grow up.*

I took a breath. "It doesn't matter what anyone thinks," I said as I stood up. "I thought it was important that the two of you should meet. She needed to see you … to know …"

Yamashita blinked, then nodded. "Chie has spent years creating a certain life for herself." His voice thickened with sadness. "I wish it were otherwise, but I think a sudden conversion is not likely."

I opened my mouth to protest, but he held up a hand. His palm was wide and his fingers thick from a lifetime of gripping a sword. "Please, Burke …" he said. He sighed. "You have read it. The journal." I nodded and heard his voice tighten. He swallowed. "Years ago I walked away from someone … I will not do so again." He smiled, but it was a melancholy expression. Then he bowed slightly at me. "Thank you for giving me this last opportunity to make amends, Burke." I should have picked up on the subtext of what he was trying to say, but only remembered it in retrospect.

He looked up at me. "And do not be too disappointed with the roshi. He is a good man and very often wise. But truly, he is out of his element here. I think the fear of violence coming to the zendo clouds his understanding." Yamashita's next sentence was uttered as if to himself. "He is as fallible as any of us." Yamashita looked out into the darkness where the lights from the room threw a circle of brightness across the stone patio. He squinted and I could see him come back into the here and now. "The snowfall is slowing."

"'Bout time." I was relieved for the mundane conversation.

"It means things will begin. And these are things only you and I can deal with, Burke." He smiled tightly again. "The roshi envisions a world of compassion, but what would happen if people arrive to take Chie?"

"He would try to reason with them. Appeal to their better sides."

"Yes. But extortionists are not renowned for their altruism. So what would happen?"

"They'd take her."

"And how would he feel about that, the roshi?"

"Sad, I guess ..."

"But?"

I sighed. "He's one of those people. You know: 'The moral arc of the universe is long, but it inclines toward justice.'" Yamashita looked at me flatly. "Martin Luther King," I added.

"I am familiar with the quote." Some asperity in the voice. "I would have preferred a shorter arc for King's sake."

"I guess that's what we do," I said. "We try to shorten the arc."

Yamashita rose, and if the movement was not as smooth as it once was, there was still that sense of grace and control and latent power. He bowed slightly and I bowed back. "Truly, Burke," he said, and the lesson was over.

My teacher looked around at the room, taking stock. "Now I need your help with rearranging the furniture."

As night set in, people clustered around the fireplaces, huddling together from deep instinct, faces crinkling in the fire's heat and backs turned toward the cold and scary dark. Everyone was weary: weary with labor, weary of the storm. The wind had gone and the deep snowdrifts muffled all sound. You'd think the end of the storm's battering would have been a relief, but the silence was complete and unnerving.

The roshi brought Chie to Yamashita's suite, asking her to stay there for the next few nights. She looked at me with an expression of surly triumph: *Enjoy the night alone, Burke.* Maybe she thought that the roshi wanted to keep us apart in the interest of purity, that the carnal seed of doubt she had tried to plant had taken root in someone's mind. I shrugged it off. I knew this change of her location was Yamashita's doing. If we were expecting visitors, and we both thought there would be more than one, it would be best to know exactly where she was. We would have enough to do without having to find her too.

As the night wore on, the knots of people around the fires drifted off to bed. I could feel the drop in temperature outside. The cold seeped in through windows and was carried along the hallways by drafts. I brought more wood in for the fires, pausing outside to gaze into a night sky gone suddenly clear, the wash of stars astoundingly dense and bright.

Chie went to bed. Yamashita and I talked quietly, taking inventory, discussing possibilities. He had spent the day rooting around, scoping out hiding places, and looking for weapons. He had a good idea where he could stash Chie to make her hard to find while we dealt with any intruders. To do that, our arsenal included two knives, an old ax handle, some rope, a rusty ball-peen hammer, and a wardrobe mirror on a floor stand.

My teacher sat in a chair for once, his back against the wall to one side of the double glass doors that led onto the patio. There was a small reading lamp on a table at his side, throwing yellow light across him. It made him look old. He sat very still, and the shadows made it hard to tell if his eyes were open or closed.

I sat for a while, then got up to pace when I started to feel drowsy. Finally I sank to the floor in seiza and began the series of exercises he had taught me years ago on another night when we were expecting danger.

My hands flowed through the sequence of gestures, the cadence of my breathing linked with the silent words that sounded in my head. I felt myself simultaneously rising and falling. My eyes grew wide and I felt the press of sound and stillness all around me.

I waited and outside the stars wheeled in cold formation.

In that state there was little sensation of time passing. But eventually I rose, working my stiff legs and glancing at my teacher. *Something.* Yamashita's head swiveled slowly in my direction and our eyes locked. I made a gesture and he nodded.

I slipped out into the hallway, through the hondo and into the main entrance hall. I paused, straining to catch a repetition of the sound I had just heard. I eased the front door open and peered down the wide irregular pathway that cut through the snow like a trench. Nothing moved. No lights, no sound. The cold was a jagged thing and I closed my mouth to breathe, feeling the air cutting at my nostrils.

I watched for a time, then headed through the first floor of the right-hand wing of the building toward the kitchen. One path to the woodpile began at Yamashita's room; the other began at the kitchen. Yamashita had the one covered. It was my job to secure the second. The kitchen had a long drying rack piled with clothing: hats and gloves and scarves, as wet and limp as their owners sleeping upstairs. I pulled my boots on, shrugged into a coat.

The drifts from the path we had shoveled closed in on either side of me, higher than my head. I moved slowly down the trench and everything around me was the ghostly grey-blue of nighttime snow. I swiveled my head back and forth, scanning for sound. But whatever I had heard—if I had heard it—was gone. I reached the broad lean-to that sheltered the firewood. The stacks stretched out on either side of me. I knew the left-hand path that led to Yamashita's door was there somewhere, but I couldn't see it for the drifts. I paused in the shadows under the lean-to roof, waiting. I caught a sense of something—a muffled thump, the sibilance of displaced snow—and crouched down.

He dropped down into the trench and a small cascade of snow slid down with him. A dark figure, muffled against the cold, wearing a facemask and goggles. He was wearing snowshoes and had a rifle strapped across his back.

He paused, still crouched, and peered up and down the trench. I looked away as his head turned in my direction. The old sensei say people can sometimes feel another's gaze on them. I wasn't too sure, but I wasn't taking any chances. I held my breath, just one shadow among many in the woodshed.

He took another slow look around, then started to undo his snowshoes.

I came churning out of the woodshed at him, drawing my knife, my feet digging for purchase in the snow. He heard me coming and stood up, kicking the snowshoes away and reaching around for his rifle. But there was no time. I was moving too fast. He must have realized it at the last moment because he brought his arms out in front of him and threw himself to the other side of the trench. The slight change in trajectory I had to make threw me off. My boots slipped in the snow. I hit him, but not as hard as I wanted to. He slammed down at my forearm. My nerves buzzed and he slammed me again and the knife was gone from my hand.

We hit the sidewall of snow and he struggled free, backing up toward the woodpile. He needed the space to bring his gun to bear, I knew that. I had to stay close, to keep on him. He backpedaled furiously and stumbled across the floor of the lean-to. I heard the dull ring of dried wood as logs rolled off a stack. I peered into the shadows looking for my target.

He came out with an ax in his hand.

He knew what he was doing with that thing; I'll give him that. A single-bladed ax, a woodcutter's ax, has got a heavy poll so it can bite deep. It's meant to be swung hard at stationary objects. A heavy head and a long handle don't make it the most nimble of weapons. He was a big guy, but not big enough to fight gravity and mass and turn the ax into a rapier.

So he used it as a bludgeon. He came at me, thrusting the top of the ax head at me, using the tool like a battering ram. I dodged him and circled to my right. He came at me again, driving me back against the stacked cords of wood. He feinted at my face, and when my hands came up, he reared back and took a swing.

I pushed in toward him, desperate to get inside the blade's arc. I headbutted him, slamming up against his chin. It hurt me, but probably hurt him more: I heard the chill click of his teeth snapping together. The ax buried itself in the wood behind me and I slipped away.

There was a hatchet hanging on a peg on the wall. I had

used it for chopping kindling earlier in the day. It was an old tool, the wooden handle worn smooth over decades, the metal head old and dark. But it was sharp enough. I knew that.

I fell against a post and snow spilled down from the roof above us. My hands scrabbled desperately, closing around the hatchet just as he reached me. I could hear the whoosh of the ax blade coming at me. I sank down under the attack.

There's a real danger of emotional paralysis in these conditions—the desperate alarm that someone is coming at you to snuff your life out, the urge to somehow stall and play for time: *Maybe he'll change his mind.* It's one illusion I've set behind me. If anything, the little voice inside me was shrill and insistent: *Finish it! Finish it now!*

Because here's the thing about fighting in general and fighting in the snow in particular: Time is your enemy. Your heart is racing and you're panting. The lactic acid is building up in your muscles, slowing you down. And in the snow your footing is never certain, all the cold-weather gear protects the targets, and the cold stiffens the fingers and makes your grip weak. I knew it had to end soon. We could flail around for a while, hacking at each other like inept Vikings, but sooner or later one of us was going to drop a weapon and then it would be over.

There was no time for finesse, no big swing leading to a final payoff. It was all going to be short, furious, and brutal. It had to be.

I was moving down and to my right and the ax tore a chunk out of the pole where I had been just a moment before. He loomed up next to me, dark and thick, swaddled in some sort of insulated jumpsuit with heavy boots. There were only so many good target options, places where a blow would do some damage. I scrambled to get to one side of him and as I did I backhanded the hatchet against his knee using the blunt end.

He grunted and one of his hands left the ax handle to reach for his leg. It was a reflex move, but the type of opening I needed. I straightened up and slammed the head of my weapon down on the ax handle. I could hear the buzzing resonance of the blow along the wooden shaft of his weapon. The ax pinwheeled out of his reach. *It's the cold, buddy. Makes it hard to hang on.* He backpedaled as I swiped at him with another backhanded blow, abandoning the ax that lay there in the churned-up snow. His goggles had somehow gotten pulled down and I could see his eyes glinting at me. They flicked toward the corner—where the ax lay. In the clear cold air, my world slowed down for me in the odd, languid unspooling of time some sensei say you can experience in a fight. I saw him reach back and fling a piece of wood at my head. It arced lazily toward me and I pivoted away from it with ease. He feinted to my right, but I knew what he was doing. Time dragged across the world and I stood there, in the still space between one of life's pulses and the next, and waited as he dodged one way, then the other, driving left toward the ax.

And then in a flash, I stepped in, bringing the blade down on his exposed neck. Time resumed its normal pace.

He collapsed with a sigh and I smelled the blood, hot spray in the frigid air, and heard my own desperate and labored breathing.

Off to my right, there was the flash and boom as a shotgun lit up the night in Yamashita's room.

CHAPTER 25

It was like one of those nightmares where you are running and don't seem to be getting anywhere. The long snowy trench hemmed me in on either side as I scrambled toward Yamashita's room. There had been more than one shot, a scream, and crashing noises. I worried I wouldn't get to them in time.

I scrambled and slid along the snow-covered path, the high drifts throwing the sound of my breathing back at me. Lights were coming on in the monastery and I could hear far-off voices shouting in alarm. The sky was slowly bluing above me and dawn was creeping into the world. When I skidded to a stop, the French doors to Yamashita's room were wide open. There was a form crumpled on the floor in the dark. Apprehension rippled its way along my gut. My fingers played along the smooth wood of the hatchet and I realized with some surprise I was still holding it.

Lights came on inside. I glimpsed shattered glass and wood, smelled the acrid sting of gunpowder, and saw a body on the floor, covered in a thermal jumpsuit. Yamashita slipped into view, the ax handle gripped casually by his side.

Our eyes met. "You good?" I gasped. He nodded. "Chie?"
"Fine."

I gestured at the broken glass on the floor. My hand was still holding the hatchet. In the strengthening light, I saw the blood on the blade and dropped it in the snow. "I see your little trick worked."

Yamashita had set the dressing room mirror up to reflect his seated image through the doorway. The two of us had worked to make sure the angles were correct, that the line between mirror and chair and mirror and doors created the illusion my sensei wanted. When we were done, anyone coming up the entrance in the dim light would see Yamashita sitting in a chair, facing out through the doors. Now he nodded to me in satisfaction.

"I can't believe it worked," I told him.

He squatted down to examine the body in front of him. "In moments of stress, people see what they want to see." He tugged a shotgun out from underneath the body. It was a lethal-looking black pump model with combat grips and no shoulder stock. Later I learned it was a Remington Model 870 MCS and the company's website said it was "the ultimate choice for virtually any close-range scenario." But not this one, obviously.

"How'd you do it?"

Yamashita straightened up and handed me the weapon. "I left the door open. He came through and shot at the reflection in the mirror." My teacher held up the ax handle, a shaft of wood about as long as the wooden bokken we use to train. "The rest was fairly straightforward."

"I heard at least one other shot."

"True. He was swinging toward me and I could strike at his left arm only. I knocked the barrel down but he managed to jerk the trigger." Yamashita gestured into the room where there was a chewed-up spot on a rug. "He was not a particularly good assassin. More dangerous to the floor than to people."

By this time the roshi had arrived, his face pale and appalled. The guy from the Tenth came up behind him and squatted, checking the body for a pulse. After a time, he looked up at us.

"There's another one out by the woodshed," I told him.

He swallowed. "Like this?"

"A little messier." It was callous and I saw the roshi blanch.

Yamashita took my arm and led me outside. "This is but the first wave, Burke. We can expect ..." his words were cut off by a loud crash and all the lights in the building suddenly went out.

"Get Chie," I urged. "Move her into another location."

He nodded and handed me the shotgun. "Work the perimeter, Burke. They will be focused inward." He reached into his robe and brought out a handful of shells. He saw my look and shrugged. "I went through his pockets before the roshi arrived." Then he disappeared into the dark building.

I moved down the trench, thankful that the snowdrifts blocked the ability of anyone on the first floor to spot me. I saw the small cascade of snow that marked the spot where the man with the shotgun had dropped onto the path. Like the other man, he had been wearing snowshoes. I put them on, fumbling with the unfamiliar bindings, my fingers stiff with cold. Then I climbed up into the snow and rolled away from the building.

The sun was rising but the long row of hills to the east meant the sunlight was just touching the higher parts of the trees, a warm rose color in that world of white and frigid blue. Much of the monastery's grounds were still in shadow. I followed the tracks into the tree line and found the snowmobile that the two of them had ridden in on. I realized it was the sound of the approaching four-stroke engine that had alerted me to the attack in the first place.

I left the snowmobile huddled in the woods and worked my way around the building's perimeter, crouching low and searching for signs of anyone else. It was slow going, but hard work nonetheless. I could feel sweat dripping down my spine even though the icy air was burning my face.

I looped around the kitchen wing toward the front entrance.

If they had used the two paths dug in the rear, chances were good that they would also send people in by the front trench. When I brought the front of the building into view, my heart sank. There was a cluster of four big black snowmobiles near the main entrance.

I stumped along the monastery wall, scanning for any activity outside: a sentry or rear guard. But the entrance was deserted, the wide door standing ajar. I got as close to the steps leading into the building as possible, then tore off my snowshoes, wading through the deep snow until I got to the cleared area. From inside I heard voices raised in alarm, then two quick shots. A woman screamed.

I tumbled down a snowdrift and crouched low, moving for the doorway. I was worried about the silhouette I would present as I came through the entrance. Even though the light was still faint, the white backdrop of snow would isolate my silhouette. I hoped Yamashita had it right and all the attackers' energies would be focused inward. I pressed myself against the wall and slowly moved into the building. I ghosted through the dim foyer and then froze.

Twenty feet away and directly across from me, the roshi was sprawled on the floor with a stunned look on his face. Blood flowed across his shaven head and he seemed like a man for whom the world had ceased to make sense. To my left, Yamashita was standing, his face immobile but his eyes glittering with anger. A dark figure in a bulky jumpsuit stood guard beside him, covering him with a pistol. You rarely see my sensei visibly angry. Part of me measured the space between him and the man with the gun, calibrated both the distance and my teacher's fury, and came up with the certainty that once things started, Yamashita would be all over the gunman.

This is what a lifetime of training does to you. However hard the hammering of my heart, the dry acrid feel in my mouth, my brain was calculating options. It's all angle and distance, the math of force, size, and the physics of velocity and impact. I needed to be sure how many targets there were and where they were. A tiny voice way down inside me was keening about impending disaster, but if you listen to the whine of the rational too much, you'd never pick up a sword to begin with. I went back to identifying targets.

With Yamashita: *one*. Just out of the foyer directly in front of me, a bulky form partially obstructed my view—someone facing inward by the door. *Two*. There were four snowmobiles parked outside, so there had to be at least four people—maybe as many as eight. I gripped the shotgun and considered. Five shells. And once things started, there would be no time to reload. The hysterical little voice inside me was screeching that numbers don't lie. But I kept scanning, trying to work out a plan of action, knowing that there was no avoiding it, that whatever situation had knocked the roshi to the floor was going to escalate, that any minute someone was going to sense my presence, that I was going to have to act no matter the odds and then the whole place was going to explode.

To my right, near the staircase to the second floor and the hallway that led to the roshi's office, a man stood with a gun. *Three*. His head was turned away toward the main meditation room and he was calling out to someone just out of my sight. *Four*. But when the man by the stairs turned back my way, I recognized him immediately. *Goro*.

I had a fleeting experience of the fabric of time snagging on an unexpected, jagged surface. I had been anticipating the Koreans. The Miyazaki knew I had Chie and she was out of

Lim's clutches. All they had to do was wait it out. It was the Koreans who were desperate. Or so I had thought.

"Where is she?" Goro demanded. He pointed a pistol at Yamashita, who stood there without saying a word. Now the roshi's condition made some sense: they were interrogating people to find Chie. The presence of the monk as a hostage was the only way I could imagine they would have taken Yamashita without a fight. My master glared at Goro, almost daring him to shoot. A memory stabbed at me: the strange way Yamashita had described the situation. *What a great gift to know when an attack will come … the last opportunity to make amends.* My stomach clenched and the hair on the back of my neck stood up. I thought of the sadness in my teacher's voice earlier in the night. His desire to make up for the lost years with his granddaughter. The crazy Japanese conviction about the bittersweet inevitability of life. Of closure. Sacrifice. *He'll die trying to save her. To save us.* Like the ax fight in the snow, I had the sensation of actions oozing across space, their direction and speed as predictable as that of the planets. And I was afraid.

"I've got her," someone called. A familiar voice, but what it was saying was so incongruous that for a minute I couldn't make the mental connection with a face. Then Chie shuffled into view. Behind her, Sue the kitchen lady pointed the elongated snout of a silenced automatic pistol at the back of Chie's head. Weapons with noise suppressors are heavy and awkward, but the pistol was rock steady in Sue's hand. Must have been the centering effect of all that meditation.

"Where is Burke?" Goro demanded. Sue shrugged and shoved Chie toward Yamashita, who reached out for his granddaughter. "He'll know," she told Goro. "The old Japanese guy." She stood by Goro, as if looking for approval. *Five*, I counted.

Goro called toward the hondo, and a man carrying an assault rifle came into view. Goro looked at him with a silent question and the man shook his head. No. They must have been sweeping the other wing of the building, looking for me. Probably looking for their missing friends too. He was walking right toward me, and if the man directly in front of me shifted even a little, I'd be spotted. The light outside was getting stronger and the darkness in the foyer was disappearing fast. The man across the room gestured with his rifle to Goro. "Come on, let's do these two and then go look for the last one. Simple, no?"

"No!" Goro sounded alarmed. "We agreed. The girl comes with me."

The man with the long gun stopped moving. He looked flatly at Goro. "Your people aren't paying me, man. I mean, we agreed to join forces. But it was supposed to be in and out."

As the man with the rifle moved, my body began to jangle with the sudden certainty that this was not going to end well.

Goro's expression was rock-hard. He was careful not to point his pistol directly at the man, but it wasn't too far from that. "Your friends at the rear of the building?"

The guy shook his head in a negative gesture. He didn't seem too broken up about it. Goro grimaced in satisfaction. "So. You once were four. Now, you are two. I think we have the upper hand." Sue and the man near Yamashita were watching, eyes bright. I had seen the same look in Ito's eyes when he had come to the dojo. It seemed like ages ago. But I couldn't forget the look, and I was seeing it now: the anticipation of a predator. The man in front of me tensed his shoulders and his head swiveled from side to side. *Another one, figuring angles. Weighing options.*

It struck me. The man with the rifle had a Spanish accent. I thought of Alejandro and his wolf pack of hard, quiet men. His comment that knowledge of things hidden can be turned to profit. *Had Alejandro and Osorio figured out where I was? Did they sell me out for a price?*

The Miyazaki had known Yamashita was at the zendo from day one. It was only logical they'd have someone in place to watch out for Chie and me. But they'd need some assistance if they were determined to take Chie away from us. Goro would not have been enough, and I noticed that Ito was nowhere in sight. *Smart man.*

The Koreans may have been penned up in Manhattan, but they obviously had some people on the outside they could count on. Maybe Osorio's hired guns. And the old lizard Miyazaki was a businessman. At the end, he cut a deal: he'd provide some intelligence and limited assistance. He'd promise that Chie would disappear. Osorio would make some money. The Koreans would get the chance to take me out and their concerns would be alleviated. Any other collateral damage was inconsequential.

But then it struck me: *Yamashita was part of the deal as well. Miyazaki would use this opportunity to take his revenge.*

It was still a tangle of possibilities but it really didn't matter. Some of it was clear enough, and time, for all its slow oozing, was running out.

The man with the rifle listened to Goro and narrowed his eyes in thought, doing the calculations. He shrugged in acquiescence, but didn't seem happy about it. "OK. We find the other guy, do him and the old man. But we do it together. Then you can take the woman. And let's make it quick, yes? Otherwise, you and me, we gonna have words."

Despite the bluster, some of the tension among the gunmen seemed to bleed off. This was the type of exchange they were used to, and now the parameters of action were clear. Everyone had been briefly frozen as each person waited to see who would be shooting who, but now, they started moving around, relieved.

It was then that Goro spotted me. I saw the flash of awareness in Yamashita's eyes as well, and there was something like relief flooding through me as I moved in to attack.

I closed in and slugged the guy in front of me, using the shotgun as a club. *Save the ammunition.* It was a shame I hit him so hard, because he collapsed and now everyone could see me. The scene froze for a second: time snagging again, the world catching its breath before a cyclone of noise and violence rushed in.

Too much happening at once. Goro's eyes widening, his pistol floating up toward me. On my left, Yamashita whirled on the periphery of my vision, sweeping Chie off her feet, and then flowing up and around on the attack. There was the report of a pistol, impossibly loud in that snow-muffled world. But now Yamashita somehow had the gun in his possession and drove his fist into his captor's throat. The man's eyes bulged as he collapsed. Sue was on overload as she tried to figure out just who to shoot. Her gun was rising toward Yamashita, but her head was swiveling toward me. I'm not sure she eventually made a conscious decision. The gun simply went off as if on impulse, the slide working, the brass casing arcing up into a ray of morning sunlight. My shotgun erupted, the flash bright in the dim room, and she went down in a mist of blood. My ears rang.

Some of the shotgun pellets must have swept beyond her. I saw Goro flinch from their impact and his pistol jerked slightly off line. The muzzle bloomed and I felt the impact on my hip. Something large and fast and very angry had just plowed into me. I spun around to my right, carried by the kinetic energy, trying to somehow stay on my feet, but it wasn't happening—the floor rushed up at me. As I collapsed, the assault rifle stitched a volley through the air. I heard the bullets snapping above me and then I was down, spasming there on the floor. The guy I had slugged was trying to get to his feet and walked right into the rounds. I thought I heard the wet slap of impact and his yelp as part of his jaw was shot away; then he was down as well.

I was having trouble moving my legs. They swung sluggishly, pushed to earth as if I were under the weight of an immensely heavy blanket. Somehow the shotgun was still in my right hand—no credit on my part, I just think my gloved fingers had gotten twisted in the trigger guard. I pulled the shotgun toward me. My movements were slow and clumsy, the weapon an extension of a distant landscape, a thing slowly dragging itself across the expanse. I tried to sit up and failed. I lay on my side and desperately tried to bring the weapon to bear. Everything I touched was hot and slippery, smelling of copper.

There was blood everywhere. I looked toward my sensei and saw his chest sheeted in red. He staggered slightly, the pistol in his hand. Then he seemed to straighten, his head swiveling from Goro to the man with the rifle, checking his angles, figuring his options. The guy with the rifle dropped a magazine out and rammed home a fresh one. His eyes bore into me and I had no doubt what he was going to do once he reloaded. Goro had started to move toward my teacher, taking aim. Yamashita stood very still and very straight, and in that instant I saw the calculations flash across his face: the imminent threat to himself from Goro, the certainty the man with the assault rifle would finish me off in the next few seconds.

In that moment, the years fell away from my teacher's face. His form swelled with a last flush of vitality. He was the Yamashita I remembered: fully alive, fully aware, a man with no doubts and an iron will. And even in my despair I felt a surge of pride: *This is my teacher.* Then Yamashita blinked once in my direction. I'd like to believe in that last moment he read my thoughts, a last flash of *haragei* between us. His gesture was at least that, I am sure, but also, a final acknowledgment of so much else. His nostrils flared and a great look of calm settled on his face, a still, bright thing in a dim world. Then he aimed carefully and put a round into the rifleman's forehead.

My scream of protest was smothered by the sharp report of Goro's shot. I squirmed in agony as I saw my teacher go down. Goro walked slowly toward him, taking careful aim. "A last message from the Miyazaki family," he said, sneering, preparing for the coup de grace. Then he heard my last grunting attempt to aim the shotgun. He turned my way.

I was belly down in the gore, squinting to keep my target in focus. The barrel wavered and I gulped desperately at the air, feeling the darkness pushing in on me, seeing the light start to bleed from my sight.

Goro took a quick step in my direction, surprised I was still alive. His movements were slow and measured as his pistol swung up at me—I don't think he believed I'd be able to do it. He was still sneering when I pulled the trigger and the world shattered in light and noise.

There was a hushed silence after that, the stunned hum

of air after it's been in violent motion. Voices, cries of alarm that sounded in the distance. Close by, the wet grunting of an animal.

Yamashita was lying not twenty feet away, and Chie was kneeling near him, her mouth frozen open, her already tenuous hold on life close to snapping. I tried desperately to reach him, my elbows digging furrows in the floor, slipping in blood. My body was burning, but I was shivering and whimpering in frustration and pain. My legs were dead weight. The animal I had become kept grunting, kept flailing, but ultimately got nowhere. My visual field was greying out at the edges; my breathing was shallow and desperate.

Someone came to me, tried to calm me down. "Easy, now." A voice floating above me in the mist, trying to be comforting.

I jerked my head in furious protest, maybe the last part of me that seemed to be under my control. "Get me …" I growled. I tried to will myself to his side. "Sensei … Get me …" I couldn't even finish the message.

There were more hands, more voices of concern.

In the end, they dragged me over to my sensei, and set me so my head was close to his.

He was lying on his back, but the guy from the Tenth Mountain Division took one look at the bloody froth around Yamashita's mouth and rolled him up on his side, trying to keep the blood out the lungs. Our faces were very close. I could feel the small, warm flutter of my teacher's breath and smell the blood. His eyes were open but I am not sure what he was really seeing.

People were rushing around, bringing sheets and towels and whatever was on hand. Tenth Mountain was barking commands, his hands moving swiftly and surely across Yamashita's torso. He glanced at me and shouted at the people who had brought me over: "Stop fucking around and somebody get some pressure on that wound!" I could almost have smiled: *not quite ready for the monastery, I guess.*

They had Chie sit by Yamashita's head and help prop him up. Yamashita's sight seemed to sharpen somewhat. He looked at me. "Burke!" he said, the words bubbling with blood. I wasn't sure if he was talking to me or calling me. "The dojo!" he said, his voice panicked and agitated. A spasm hit him and he grimaced, then settled back, his eyes drawn to a distant image only he could see.

His eyes floated over to Chie's tearful face hovering above him. He gazed up at her with a wonder and a joy I had never seen in his face—I swear I heard him whisper—*Himesama*. His head swiveled back to me, his neck muscles cording with the effort it took to focus. Once again he blinked at me. The movement was slow and deliberate.

I reached out and placed my hand on his chest, my head struggling to stay up off the hard, cold floor. He tried again to say something, cleared his airway and with great effort, spoke.

"*Enzan* ..." he said and smiled.

The voice pushed and strained against all that held him down: the past, the present, the tangled bindings he had strapped on in the course of his life. Then, in an instant, he was free. The last sound he uttered swirled and rose, growing fainter, diffusing, up, up through the dark ceiling, into the cold air, where it merged with a morning sky of a deep and infinite blue.

EPILOGUE

Light and cold. My face sticky with blood. There was pain and the taste of vomit in my mouth, jostling and a deep grinding when they moved me. Mercifully I finally blacked out.

Voices and sounds floated around me in the darkness. Some were familiar; others were strange to me. But the one I wanted to hear most was absent.

There were surgeries, they tell me. A doctor came in at one point, his scrubs wrinkled and faintly patterned with blood, a pointillist rendering of his experience. He gave me the rundown. My eyes were open and I nodded when he paused to give him the impression I was taking it all in, but I was still groggy from anesthesia.

"The iliac crest on the right side was pretty well shattered and we did some extensive reconstruction there," he said. I looked it up later. It's the superior border of the wing of ilium, the superolateral margin of the greater pelvis.

"I got shot in the hip," I told him. My voice was thick and I was desperately thirsty.

The doctor gave me a look: *Uh, no kidding.* He continued talking, but also started to fiddle with the machines and lines all around me. "In addition to the blood loss, and you were pretty far down, Mr. Burke, there was significant muscle damage, some potential nerve issues that we'll continue to evaluate …" He flashed a light into my eyes, pulled my lids back, and frowned. I licked my lips and weariness overwhelmed me. His voice faded and I slipped back into darkness.

There was no real day or night for a while—just time spent floating to the beeping cadence of machines. The room was dim and someone had strung small holiday lights around a white-board that had my name and vitals written on it. Eventually, I came back to the world. I spent the week before Christmas in a wheelchair. A series of perky physical therapists rolled me around and introduced me to their diabolical art. They worked me hard. It was a brutal type of care that left me wrung out and aching. But I was determined to be using a walker by New Year's Day.

Mickey was there as often as he could be. He tied a small red felt Christmas stocking to my walker.

"Is there a beer in there?" I asked.

He frowned. "Sorry, bud. They tell me no."

Art was at the foot of the bed, scanning the readouts on the machines above my head. "The PTs tell us you're making progress, Connor." He was using his optimistic good-cop voice.

I snorted. "Half my ass was shot away, Art."

Art shook his head. "Always a glass half empty with you Burkes."

I closed my eyes.

"You gettin' visitor overload?" Mickey asked. "We can leave …"

The holidays plus the eventual clearing of the snow-clogged roads had brought a parade of guests: my mom, frail and some-what confused, my sisters and their worn-out husbands, Ken and a few of the senior students from the dojo. Owen and Ann. They were all so sincere and sympathetic. So intent on being chipper. So deeply annoying.

Art and Mickey were a refreshing change of pace, if only because they refused to treat me like an invalid. Art headed toward the door. "Yeah, Connor. We don't have to hang around here for the abuse. There's no shortage of people waiting to be cranky to us."

I opened my eyes and pushed the button that made the bed support me into sitting straighter. I could feel the pull in my hip but did it anyway.

"God no," I told him. "You're all that stands between me and more physical therapy."

My brother stood, squinting out the window, hands on his hips. "The feds come by?"

I nodded wearily.

"And?" Mickey prompted.

"The usual tight-lipped, smug bullshit. They asked me the same questions I've answered about a million times and gave me no real information."

"They're very conflicted," Art said.

"Yeah," Mickey added. "On the one hand, they are really pissed off at all the screaming and yelling." I started to protest but my brother held up his hand. "The blowing of a federal stakeout on suspected North Korean agents. Not to mention the apparent shooting of the assistant to an elder statesman of the Japanese corporate community."

Art sat down at the foot of the bed and smiled. "On the other hand, they have now broken up a blackmail scheme designed to get access to secret diplomatic information. In the process, they rounded up a bunch of Koreans and turned them into double agents."

"What!"

"Sure," Mickey snickered. "You think any of those guys want to go back to Pyongyang and report failure?"

Art smiled broadly. "Pyongyang, even on a good day, is

nobody's idea of a place to be."

"So we are reliably informed that you are officially off the hook, Connor." My brother shook his head in amused wonder. "Somewhere at an undisclosed location, some functionary has decided that, despite the mess, the pluses outweigh the minuses."

At times the images from that last morning at the zendo flash into my mind, a painful kaleidoscope. I closed my eyes, squeezing them tight against the burning. *A mess ... is that all it was to those people?*

Nobody said anything for a while. Mickey and Art had been cops a long time. They were good at reading people's moods. My machine beeped insistently in the quiet. Then it stopped.

"What happened?" I said.

Art shrugged. "I pushed a button."

"Which one?"

"The one marked 'annoying noises.'"

My hip ached and I motored the bed back so I could stare at the ceiling. I was doing a lot of that lately. My brother left the window and started to speak. Something in the tone of his voice made me look at him. He sounded uncertain, hesitant.

"Look, Connor," he began. "You've lost a lot. We know that."

"And your point?" My voice surprised even me: cranky, vicious, self-pitying.

Mickey glared at me. "He's gone, Connor. There's no changing that. You've gotta figure a way past it."

I swallowed, not sure I could get the words out. My eyes were burning again. I shook my head in frustration. "Not sure that I can, Mick."

Another uncomfortable silence. The bed murmured as Art

got up. He stood shoulder to shoulder with his partner, my brother. They looked at me.

"Not gonna sugarcoat it for you, buddy boy," Mickey said.

"Remember Mr. T in *Rocky III*, when they asked him about the big fight?" Art asked me. "His prediction?"

I smiled despite myself. "Pain," I told them.

"Yeah," Art said. "So it's pretty much like that: pain. But you'll get through it, Connor."

I could feel the tears coming and I shut my eyes tight, not wanting them to see.

"Do you remember much about the first few days in here?" Mickey said.

"Nah," I croaked, the sudden change in topic tricking me into a response despite myself.

"That Miyazaki chick was here almost all the time. Surprised the shit out of all of us, but go figure."

"I asked her why she was here," Art noted conversationally. "Know what she said?"

I just shook my head.

"She said you were one of the most deeply frustrating people she had ever met ..."

"A sentiment widely shared," Mickey added.

"But she couldn't stop thinking about something you told her."

I rolled my head wearily toward him. "What?"

"She said you told her something like, 'The saddest people in the world aren't the ones who don't find themselves; it's the people who stopped looking.'"

I lay there, feeling guilt and resentment and an overpowering weariness. I remained silent. After a time I opened my eyes and Mickey and Art were gone.

*   *   *

"I don't know why we have to go there tonight," I told my brother. A late January evening and the streets were wet with an unexpected thaw. My hip groaned in the damp cold.

"Chie's father has established a foundation in Yamashita's memory," Art explained. "He wants to ensure that the dojo can survive."

"They'll need to find a new sensei," I told them. "Good luck with that." I winced at the asperity in my voice. *Still the cranky invalid, Burke. Get over it.*

"Whatever," Mickey said. "They're doing some insurance underwriting and need someone to go over the place with the agent. Who better than you?"

"I don't want to go," I said.

"Shut up," Mickey told me and eased me into the passenger's seat.

"There are no classes tonight, Connor," Art assured me. They were both proud men and they understood me. I was able to walk with a cane by this point, but I didn't want anyone from the dojo to see me hobble around. They knew I was worried about looking like an invalid.

"I still don't want to go."

"We know you don't," Art assured me. "Shut up."

They double-parked in front of the building. The lights were on inside and I looked at Mickey. He shrugged. "The agent has a key, ya know."

He and Art came around to my side of the car as I levered my creaking form up and out. They stopped me for a minute. "Here," Mickey said, and took the aluminum cane away from me. Art reached into the backseat and took out a bokken, its end rounded to fit in my palm and the tip flattened out. A weapon, now cut down to serve as a crutch. My brother shrugged. "For old times' sake."

I gripped the bokken, moved slowly up to the door, and pushed my way through.

The dojo was brightly lit and filled with people. All the blue-clad members sat in silent rows, facing the front of the dojo. Centered high up on the wall was a framed piece of calligraphy in my dead master's unmistakable hand: *Enzan no Metsuke*. The admonition to perception and attention. The call to see beyond petty distractions.

"You bastard," I whispered to my brother.

They led me to the head of the dojo and I stood there. Etiquette demanded that I kneel, but I couldn't be sure I could reach the floor unaided, and I knew for sure I couldn't get up. In the struggle between pride and manners, pride won out.

The students were all silent, but I saw them looking at me intently, taking the measure of my injuries. They were all experts in movement and could calibrate the extent of my damage just from watching me walk.

But I didn't see pity there, or disappointment. They were expectant. They looked at me with a type of yearning, with hope for something I wasn't sure I could give them.

Is this how it was for you? I had taken to addressing Yamashita in my head. He never answered, but it was good to have him to talk to. *Is this the weight you felt every day that you taught us? Duty, as heavy as a mountain?*

I looked around and gestured at them. Took a breath and opened my mouth to speak, wondering what I could possibly say.

But the dojo captain cut me off. "*Sensei ni rei*," he

283

commanded, the traditional call to bow to the dojo's master. The ranks of swordsmen bowed toward me. I looked to the side where Mickey and Art stood. They nodded encouragingly.

I gave a stiff bow in response. The class straightened up. I felt the weight of their expectation dragging at me. I wasn't sure I could carry the load. I was sure I wasn't worthy. But I knew he would want me to try.

"*Hajime*," I told them.

Begin.

About the Author

John Donohue has been banging around dojo for more than 30 years. He's an expert on the study of the martial arts.

Fascinated with the themes of human action and potential he uncovered in his research, John began thinking about the fictional possibilities inherent in the world of the martial arts. He began working in earnest on *Sensei*, the first Burke/Yamashita thriller, released in 2003. The sequel, *Deshi*, was published in 2005. The third "burkebook," *Tengu*, was published in Fall 2008. The fourth book in the series, *Kage*, was released in 2011.

John has always been fascinated with other cultures and was attracted to the Asian martial disciplines because of their blend of philosophy and action. He began studying Shotokan Karate-do in college. He joined practical training with more formal education, completing a Ph.D. in Anthropology from the State University of New York at Stony Brook. His doctoral dissertation on the cultural aspects of the Japanese martial arts formed the basis for his first book, *The Forge of the Spirit* (1991).

John has worked in the hospitality, advertising, and publishing industries, but for the bulk of his non-writing career he has been a higher education professional, working as both a teacher and senior level manager at a number of colleges—strapped, as he says, to the wheel of administrative karma.

During that time he continued to think about and do martial arts. He wrote *Warrior Dreams: The Martial Arts and the American Imagination* (1994) as a companion piece to *The*

Forge of the Spirit. Always interested in the spiritual dimension of martial training, he wrote *Herding the Ox: The Martial Arts as Moral Metaphor* (1998). Fascinated with the process of learning the modern Way of the Sword (kendo), he wrote *Complete Kendo* (1999). He also edited a book of martial arts readings, *The Overlook Martial Arts Reader*, Vol. 2., published in 2004. John is also the author of many articles on the martial arts. Fusing the way of the pen and the way of the sword, while writing John has trained in the martial disciplines of aikido, iaido, judo, karatedo, kendo, and taiji. He has dan (black belt) ranks in both karatedo and kendo.

MARQUIS

Québec, Canada

RECYCLED
Paper made from
recycled material
FSC® C103567

Printed on Enviro 100% post-consumer EcoLogo certified paper,
processed chlorine free and manufactured using biogas energy.

31901057070593